Shadows of the Truth

LELI TA' ĦAŻ-ŻGĦIR

ĠUŻÉ ELLUL MERCER

A Maltese novel translated by
GODWIN ELLUL

midseaBOOKSLTD

Published by Midsea Books Ltd.
Carmelites Street, Sta Venera HMR 11
tel: 2149 7046 fax: 2149 6904
kkm@vol.net.mt

Copyright Editorial © Midsea Books Ltd, 2003
Copyright Literary © Godwin Ellul, 2003

All rights reserved. No part of this publication may be
produced or transmitted in any form or by any means,
electronical, mechanical, photocopying, recording or
otherwise, or stored in any retrieval system of any nature
without the written permission of the copyright holder,
application for which shall be made to the author of this
translation.

First Edition 2003

ISBN 99932-39-53-4

Produced by Mizzi Design and Graphic Services Ltd.
Printed at Gutenberg Press Ltd, Malta

*To All Those Who Possess
The Power and the Will to Change
in this World of Tradition,
Contradiction and Suffering
This Book is Affectionately
Dedicated*

G.E.

Born in Msida on 22nd March 1897, Ellul Mercer was the son of Salvatore and Jane Ellul Mercer. He was educated at Flores College, the Lyceum and was later employed as chief clerk at Headquarters, Malta Garrison. He served as writer with the Royal Navy during the First World War. On 26th July 1921 he married Marija Tereża Brockdorff who died in 1953.

A member of the *Għaqda tal-Kittieba tal-Malti*, his major works include *Leli ta' Ħaż-Żgħir* and *Taħt in-Nar*.

Ellul Mercer's association with the Malta Labour Party dated back to 1924 when he joined the Party. He was a member of the Executive from 1925 onwards.

In 1945 he formed part of the National Assembly, which was responsible for drafting the 1947 Constitution, and was elected member of the Economic Committee.

He unsuccessfully contested the 1950 election in the interests of the Party but was returned in the elections held in 1951 and again in 1953 and 1955. Ellul Mercer served as Minister for Works and Reconstruction and was Deputy Prime Minister between 1955-1958. He was elected Deputy Leader of the Labour Party in April 1955.

Ellul Mercer was Editor of the Labour Party Journal *Il-Kotra* 1930-1931 and was a frequent contributor to the Press.

Ellul Mercer died on 22nd September 1961.

INTRODUCTION

*L*eli ta' Ħaż-Żgħir is a revolutionary psychological novel that through its protagonist challenges the moral and political basis of Maltese society. This particular feature marked a turning point in Maltese literature.

The novel takes the reader back to Maltese life styles at the dawn of this century. The development of education in Malta, the Language Question, the drive to achieve self-government, emigration and the first religious dispute were aspects that characterized the country's political and social agenda then.

Ellul Mercer challenges these foundations through Leli's inquisitive character. He is a self-educated son of a poor family. If one were to extend this argument two points emerge: the first point is that the protagonist of the novel is the author himself. As one reads *Leli ta' Ħaż-Żgħir* one can constantly feel the presence of Ellul Mercer himself. He speaks with conviction and determination. The novel proceeds from the physical environment to the personal, intimate, psychological and spiritual. The second point is that the author takes advantage of Leli's critical thinking to examine Malta's political and religious scenarios.

The doctrine that Ellul Mercer develops in the course of his work is a socialist one. He emphasizes aspects that were important for successive socialist leaders of the Maltese Labour Movement in later years. The most relevant among those aspects is the idea of work. Work is not only good for the national economy but it also has a therapeutic effect that is beneficial to the person who performs that activity.

Leli's critical character provides a vision to the larger population. This is the goal for a better distribution of wealth and the creation of an improved welfare society.

Leli's vision of truth is unique. Traditional culture alienates the persons surrounding Leli – a resisting force to progress, liberal thinking and modernization. Leli perhaps like Manwel Dimech, Malta's *enfant terrible* is one of the enlightened few to challenge Maltese social customs. *Leli ta' Ħaż-Żgħir* focuses on the poor and the illiterate in Maltese society. It focuses on the disruption of the Maltese family and, on the position of the Church in Malta. All these elements form the anti-thesis of Maltese society. Ellul Mercer's objective was to arouse awareness among the public concerning the need to change and to disrupt the status quo. On this scenario Leli's vision, like Plato's allegory, remains a dream – a fantastic reality.

Like Gandhi, Leli's approach is to defeat Imperialism through a silent revolution. Unlike Dimech, Leli does not offer open resistance. His objective is to change society and the major social institutions through the power of reasoning and constructive criticism. The authors which Ellul Mercer mentions in the course of his work provide an appropriate framework to the philosophy that the author expounds.

The novel refers to two important historical events. The outbreak of the First World War and the 24th International Eucharistic Congress held in Malta in April 1913. These events trace not only the local social relations but also attempt to provide information about the wider international order at that particular time.

The subject realting to faith is a central theme in the novel. Ellul Mercer emphasises the healing power of faith and celebrates the importance of faith in life as he is constantly searching for that higher spiritual power which renders his life meaningful.

Local names and nicknames have been left in the vernacular. The title of the book in its English version *Shadows of the Truth* reflects Plato's allegory which I believe is central for the proper understanding of this novel.

The notes included in this edition provide the reader with additional information about particular points of interest that arise throughout the novel. This translation is based on the 1983 edition.

I would like to thank Simon Torpiano for correcting the script. The Briffa family for giving me permission to reproduce on the front cover of this book *Study of Male Torso* (1930) – a painting by the late Joseph Briffa.[1] I would also like to thank Midsea Books Limited for publishing this work.

My greatest debt is to my wife who took on much more than her share of childcare and left me to my own de(vices).

I am not unaware that in undertaking the work single-handed I have exposed myself to many deficiencies. The usual disclaimer of course holds here: for all shortcomings and mistakes I am solely to blame.

Godwin Ellul
Mellieħa, 18th July 1999

---

[1] Joseph Briffa, one of Malta's leading artist painters of the 20th century was born in B'Kara on 12th May 1901. At a very young age he already showed his ability to draw and design anything that caught his attention. After the normal studies in Malta at the School of Arts, he followed a course at the Regia Accademia di Belle Arti in Rome. Many of his religious works of art adorn Maltese and Gozitan churches. Joseph Briffa was also a famous portrait painter and was also well known for his 'nudo'. Renowned locally and abroad, Briffa took part in exhibitions and his works are found in many private collections. Briffa died on 13th January 1987.

BOOK ONE

DAYS OF HAPPINESS

Several people were in agreement that, Dun[1] Karm a relative of Rużanni, had a hundred and one defects.

His first and greatest defect was that he would get angry and lose his temper over the slightest thing.

If anybody started speaking to him about some changes, even those that were necessary and which appeared to be for the best, it was likely that he would disagree with anything said.

Similarly, if anybody approached him, to greet him, it was likely that he would respond angrily even if one happened to be a very close friend although his attitude would soon change and he would help anybody very willingly.

If his mother removed his prayer book from its usual place, he would immediately grow morose, start grumbling, move from upstairs to downstairs as the case would be, or go to the front door and vent his anger by turning from one corner of his mouth to the other the butt of an extinguished cigar. And woe betide that person who happened to meet him at the front door when he was in such a bad temper and saluted him, because he wouldn't even acknowledge him.

If Toni, the sacristan, failed to bring him coffee in time, that is as soon as Dun Karm would have finished saying mass, he would start complaining and would not cease until Toni went out of his sight.

If he went to hear confessions and found a large number of girls, around his confessional, constantly whispering, like a nest of sparrows, he would tell them to shut up by placing his forefinger of his right hand between his eyes, indicating that as soon as one of them said one more word, he would throw them out of church.

But to appreciate how quickly, at times, Dun Karm lost his temper, listen to when he started complaining to his mother about the behaviour of some women in church.

Dun Karm could barely stand women.

He would strongly oppose those people who, in order to give the impression of being holy, would go to confession three times daily; and he would unhesitatingly scold in a rough manner, some brazen-faced woman who most likely had gone to church for her own intentions rather than to pray.

"What do they expect," he would continue telling his mother, after having got very hot under the collar and after his mother - an old and prudent woman - would have patiently and quietly listened to him; "What do they expect? That I am going to let them make use of God's House without drawing their attention? Of course that is what I'll do! If they intend to take advantage of the occasion to tempt men, they have other places where they can go! What a shame! They should be ashamed of themselves, a lot of dishonourable women!"

But although he used to lose his temper so easily, Dun Karm had other positive aspects in his character and these by far outstripped the aforementioned deficiency.

Notwithstanding that disgruntled and angry look on his face, Dun Karm was a very kind person.

Beneath those sunken eyes shining like burning cinders, Dun Karm's thoughts were as innocent as those of a child.

Very slim by nature as well as by exercising self-discipline, one could notice Dun Karm hurrying from Triq il-Knisja to his mother's house daily. He didn't open his mouth or raise his eyes until he reached home, except to say: "Goodbye" to those who saluted him, or "God bless you, my son" to some boy who approached him to kiss his hand.

Although Dun Karm seemed such a sour-faced man of solitary habits, he would feel overwhelmed by feelings of tenderness when someone visited his house to speak to him in confidence. Very often a tear appeared in his eyes or he immediately surrendered all the money he had in his pocket. Dun Karm would do this unselfishly and unhesitatingly.

After some pitiable person would have left the house and Dun Karm would have done all he could to console him, he would hurry to discuss earnestly with his mother the greatness of mercy.

"Mother! It's amazing, the happiness I feel within when I help others who are in need. Believe me, mother, truly; I cannot understand how some people can be wealthy, insensitive and merciless towards other less fortunate persons.

"In my opinion, being merciful to others is the greatest act a person can perform as long as he doesn't boast about his actions.

"…Alas! Mother, how foolish are those people who constantly seek happiness when it lies so close to them! If they were to ask me where to find happiness and what makes man most happy I would have answered: 'happiness lies in the act of mercy; in always and wherever possible wishing your neighbour well, in honestly and unhesitatingly sharing with others what God has provided, with the intention and belief of making someone else happy.'"

Dun Karm was not a learned person; but his faith in God was strong. His belief was evidenced in his acts of mercy and kindness towards others about which he did not boast but instead put on a disgruntled face and kept as silent as the grave.

When our story starts unfolding, Dun Karm was thirty years old and "during these thirty years," his mother would say whilst pouring her heart out to her neighbour, "I never recall him lying to me, or hurting my feelings, even by a single word."

Dun Karm believed that he did not merit any praise or respect for what he did although people who benefited from his kindness disagreed with his point of view.

II

It was Wednesday,[2] in the early month of May, and in Ħaż-Żgħir's[3] church a religious service was being held in honour of Our Lady.

Until not so long ago no other village outstripped Ħaż-Żgħir in the organization of such religious services. How could it have been otherwise when these activities were entrusted to Dun Karm who would be overwhelmed whenever somebody mentioned Our Lady?

Fifteen girls dressed in white and with a white veil over their heads were kneeling down around an altar which was ablaze with candle light. Further down, there was a large number of boys and girls followed by men and women.

Dun Karm was sitting down and facing the congregation as he preached about the glory and love of God in a strong and solemn voice. From his words one could realize the love this priest had for Our Lady.

At times the congregation watching him and listening to his words would be so immersed in thought that complete silence would reign in church and only Dun Karm's voice could be heard. At times somebody would start coughing and twelve others would follow suit.

At first the children would behave well just like adults, but soon they grow restless and some would yawn, others would get fidgety or tease the person sitting next to them.

However, no other priest besides Dun Karm succeeded in capturing the congregation's attention. The majority of the people of Ħaż-Żgħir never attended school and did not possess any kind of knowledge except for their daily needs. They would listen to Dun Karm with great delight for a long time whenever he preached about Our Lady and Her glory with such enthusiasm even if they didn't understand every word he said.

❖ ❖ ❖ ❖ ❖

Tonin Braġ,[4] his wife Marjann and their three sons Leli, Ninu and Lippu were among the people listening to Dun Karm preaching about Our Lady that day.

Tonin was sitting alone in church. It was very unusual for Tonin to be there that day because he only went to church once in a blue moon. He was a businessman, he used to go to mass every Sunday, receive Holy Communion once a year, and that was it.

Tonin was indifferent to religion because he did not care much about the subject. At that time other people looked after his business and it was likely that it was not doing well. Tonin did not have much good sense. He loved women and he was always thinking about one or the other.

Nobody in the village knew about this except his wife, a few close friends of his and the ladies or young women whom he teased some time or other.

In Ħaż-Żgħir Tonin was generally regarded as a good and friendly family man. The villagers loved him because he did not hesitate to donate money for some cause or other.

This perhaps was true, but as one lady who had severely scolded Tonin was telling another who was praising him: "Simply because a man loves his wife and children when he is in their company and is friendly and generous doesn't mean that he is a gentleman. I am not a man, but I believe that a man who is incapable of controlling himself with women, is no gentleman." The other frivolous woman who was listening to her replied: "I don't know but if men need to have the qualities you describe to be called gentlemen, then I believe there are few such men left in Malta!"

However, although Tonin was frequently thinking about some pretty face, he always kept Lippu his youngest baby son, either in his arms or on his lap in the evening. Lippu's hands at times clung to Tonin's moustache or ear. When Tonin arrived home early he would not hesitate to recite the Rosary together with his family and ensured that the children did not fell asleep while doing so. He would not get a good night's rest until he had blessed his family several times.

It seemed that the children were more attracted to their mother and they longed for her kiss. When sometimes Tonin used to kiss them he would scare the children because his long and beautiful moustache smelled of tobacco.

Tonin was a handsome man. He had a red face, blue eyes and a pretty mouth as pretty as a woman's. On looking at him one would say that he was as strong as a bull. But notwithstanding his strength and beauty, Dr. Tabun after examining him, strongly advised him to look after his health because his heart was not in a very good condition.

❖ ❖ ❖ ❖ ❖

Marjann was Dun Karm's cousin and both resembled each other a lot.

However, Marjann was similar to Dun Karm not so much physiognomically in as much as the way she behaved and in her way of thinking.

She was not a very beautiful woman. She had been skinny since her childhood and that's the way she remained when she grew up. However, her words drew peoples' attention.

Marjann had never been the kind of woman, who would be overwhelmed with feelings of tenderness as soon as she came across a man. Whenever she spoke to a man she would speak to him without too much embarrassment but with lack of enthusiasm as if she was speaking to another woman.

Since she seldom smiled, she would immediately attract attention whenever she did so, just as much as an hour of sunshine in January attracts more people than a hot day in August.

She was a very wise woman and wasn't easily deceived. She dearly loved her husband however, and no one else knew him better than she did. Often, after the children would have gone to bed she would have a *tète-â-tète* with him and scold him until she cried. She would stuff her mouth with a handkerchief so that the children would not hear her weep.

After a lot of caressing, promises and sweet words she would become herself again at least for a short while. However, during the day when she remembered the kind of husband she had to put up with and how much her children had to suffer because of their father's lack of prudence she would eat her heart out and grow mentally weak.

❖ ❖ ❖ ❖ ❖

While Marjann was looking at Dun Karm and listening with great zeal and enthusiasm to what he was saying, she thought: 'How fortunate I would be had my eldest son, Leli become a priest?' Marjann, blushed at this thought and repeated in her heart of hearts: 'How proud I would be if this happened.'

Marjann loved Leli with all her heart; he was very dear to her since every eldest son occupies a special place in his mother's heart.

Leli had given her a great deal of trouble. He was a very naughty boy and although he was fourteen years old and had shown some encouraging signs of maturity, it was not unusual for him to be up to something whenever he felt like it. He used to worry his mother a lot either because he had injured a boy's head, or ran after Lonza's chickens or kicked over a kettle which had been boiling for half an hour on a stove in Sqaq id-Dlam close to the common tenement house known as 'tal-Minsijin'.[5]

When for some reason or another he and his brothers stayed at home, he would tease them and quarrel with them all day long.

However there were times when his mother recognized Leli's good qualities. One of those qualities was that Leli didn't keep secrets from anyone. Whatever he did, good or bad, he did very openly. Whenever he noticed that his mother was sad, he would insist in knowing what was wrong until she told him. When people reported him to his mother for something he had been up to, and he happened to be at home, he blushed, cried and gave vent to his anger by yelling at her. But, when his mother scolded him, he would just quail and remained silent.

Leli was an intelligent person and at school he was generally always first in class. He was an avid reader and he wouldn't come across a Maltese book, which he wouldn't read once or twice. He would ask his mother to explain things to him when he read something, which he failed to understand.

As for the rest, whenever Leli stayed at home he would pester his mother asking her all kinds of questions.

He loved listening to music very much. Once while he was in the window of his mother's house and, hardly eight years old he told his mother: "whenever I listen to the pharmacist's wife playing the piano, I feel a pain right here, in my tummy." Leli's stomach ached for the first time he had heard the pharmacist's wife playing Bach-Gounod's Ave Maria.[6]

On another occasion his father stayed out very late. Leli, seeing his mother worriedly pacing round the house did not fall asleep. At about midnight someone knocked at the door. Leli hurried downstairs like a flash. When he arrived at the door he asked 'who is it?'. His father answered and Leli opened the door. As soon as his father asked Leli: "are you still awake?" The boy started trembling like a frightened dog, threw himself down on a chair, burst out weeping uncontrollably, almost fainted and took some time to recover.

Leli was a handsome boy. When he was thirteen years old people mistook him for a sixteen-year-old. Furthermore, he was friendly, alert and talkative. His mother used to say that he was an impatient boy and was restless even while sleeping. In fact while he would be asleep he could be heard mumbling all the time. When Marjann happened to be awake, she would tell her husband: "Tonin, listen to Leli chattering! He cannot keep quiet not even while sleeping."

III

While Marjann was sitting in the middle of the church daydreaming and imagining her son dressed as a priest like her relative Dun Karm - but more striking than him - preaching with the greatest wisdom and gentleness the Word of God, Leli's thoughts were about a completely different matter.

Leli who was sitting on a wooden bench, surrounded by a large number of boys, all of them younger or shorter than him, was quietly looking at one of the girls who were all dressed in white with a blue sash round their waist and with a white veil on their heads.

At first it was the blue sash round the girl's waist that drew his attention. But when the girl turned her face and looked at him, Leli blushed, turned his face the other way and started telling the other boys sitting near him to be quiet pretending that he was listening to Dun Karm's sermon.

Leli was not paying attention to Dun Karm. He was thinking about that girl who had looked at him. Although he looked in her direction several times later and saw her looking the other way, that girl's look was very significant for Leli.

He had never felt that way before; he was confused but happy and longing for another instance when he would raise his eyes and see that girl with the blue sash looking at him

This was Leli's first love. He was afraid and yet happy more than ever before. However, the difficult life he lived made him forget all about the girl and his delightful experience. Although Ħaż-Żgħir was a very small village, that girl lived on the other side of the area and several years passed until Leli again met that girl with the blue sash.

This girl was Vira Kanwara, daughter of Liża and Master Ġammari Kanwara. They were good people but very poor.

On the evening in question, Leli showed signs that something had happened to him. He appeared less lively than he used to be. As soon as mass ended he went to look for his mother and went straight home with her, whistling all the way back without saying a word.

"What's the matter with you this evening, Lel; you look so strange?" his mother asked him after they had had their supper and were preparing to go to bed.

"Nothing! I'm fine"

"Are you feeling sick?"

"No, Leave me alone!"

❖ ❖ ❖ ❖ ❖

The following day Leli got it into his head to put his dog against the baker's. At that moment Ġanna ta' Frawla[7] was passing by holding two buckets full of water. The dogs got in her way, she fell on the ground with the water and all, and one of the dogs assaulted her and bit her.

Ġanna was beside herself with anger. She started insulting Leli with all her might, chasing him at the same time. But she could never catch up with him! Not Leli!

Ultimately, Leli's mother had to face the music as she received a severe chiding from Ġanna ta' Frawla.

IV

In a small village like Ħaż-Żgħir, the life of the people is like a water wheel: one bucket after another. Village life was very different from town life especially in Ħaż-Żgħir, which at the beginning of our story had just been introduced to kerosene lamp lighting in its streets.

Although the world had made rapid progress, none of the villagers ever bothered with what was going on in the world. The only things that mattered to them were: that the year was trouble-free; the fields yielded a good crop; there was no epidemic and sufficient funds had been collected so that God willing, the village feast, the following year would be better organized than this year's with more fireworks than Ħal-Kbir had.

Notwithstanding the small size of the village, love, hate and jealousy were also present among the villagers. There were good friends and bad ones who incited others by insinuations, cheated, created hostility, made fun of others and stole other peoples' belongings.

There were several others who kept everything secret to avoid being gossiped about by people who gloat over other people's misfortunes.

Anġla, wife of Anġlu known as ta' Kajla[8] couldn't stand Ċetta daughter of Żari known as ta' Laħlaħ[9] because Ċetta loved chatting up with Anġla's husband everytime she met him. People had opened her eyes to the fact, and so they say, there's no smoke without a fire.

That's how Anġla saw the matter.

Pawla known as ta' Seddaq[10] and her husband Wenzu smile bravely when they are in the company of other people. However, they are always sad when they are alone in the upper room of their village house because the field's rent is soon due and they don't have the money to pay it.

Karla better known as ta' Toni ta' Saramni[11] had always been pale and of delicate health eversince she was young. Now that she married and expecting her first child, she has been toing and froing to the doctor. The villagers say: "May it please God that all will be well because she is so physically weak". Karla knows this and besides feeling worried about her impending childbirth she is vexed by peoples' gossip.

Ġużè known as ta' l-Imqarqaċ[12] is a troublesome person and he is always quarrelling with the bearded one. Ġużè insists on his point of view and he is always coming and going to the Law Courts. He has been paying the advocates and is almost broke.

Anni known as ta' l-Indannat[13] is a malignant person; she had been condemned to two days imprisonment but opted for bail instead. A week later she was almost caught giving false evidence and also risked imprisonment. Anni never learns from past experience. She loves quarrelling and gossiping about other people.

There are other instances similar to these. In other words people and events which one comes across in a village. These events have been highlighted for the benefit of the reader to realize that although Ħaż-Żgħir is a small-secluded village it is by no means heaven on earth.

It seemed that life in the Braġ household was similar to the kind of life conducted by the rest of the villagers. In the eyes of the village people everything was fine as long as life went on as usual and as long as Tonin as a result of his recklessness did not get his wife and children into trouble.

Tonin used to accompany his children to school in Valletta every morning. The children were making good progress in their studies because they were clever and their mother insisted with them to study so that they would succeed.

In fact they achieved high marks in the final examinations.

Their mother was delighted to see her children so keen on learning and in her opinion her children were the cleverest of all. Sometimes, she would say in her heart of hearts: "They have more good sense than their father! If I have no fortune in the choice of a husband, I was at least fortunate in having intelligent children"

Their father would be pleased to learn that his children are doing well at school. But his happiness would only last for a short time because he would soon forget. However he would not hesitate to give money to the children when they asked him for a penny. Sometimes he would give them money even when they did not ask for it.

❖ ❖ ❖ ❖ ❖

A few days before, representatives of the small Mission[14] visited Ħaż-Żgħir and thanks to them, Leli dedicated himself completely to the church. One day he told his mother that she should not be surprised if he suddenly left her and his father, because he felt the vocation to become a monk.

You could imagine how happy Marjann was at the news. This happened in the evening before they went to bed. Just before daybreak she hurried to Dun Karm to tell him the whole story.

"I know! Dun Karm! I am not worthy of all this, I don't deserve that God grants me such favour; but how happy I would be if this had to happen; if this had to be, as I think it is, a calling from the Almighty!"

After Marjann finished what she had to say, Dun Karm looked thoughtful for a while and then with pity written all over his face, replied:

"I do not wish to discourage you, Marjann; but something tells me that Leli's vocation is not what both of you imagine it to be. Leli is still young; there is ample time to see whether Leli consolidates his belief and after all nothing would have happened, Marjann, if this did not materialize, do you understand? Priestly life is tough, Marjann! Much tougher than some good women like you imagine it to be. To carry out his duties properly and disseminate Faith, Love and Consolation in peoples' hearts, the priest must overcome himself, and give unselfishly.

"If he doesn't do this," continued Dun Karm in a sad voice, "he wouldn't be doing his duty. If he does his duty he has nothing left except one thing: patience; and with patience the consolation of having served God. For a person to be able to do this, God must give him a vocation for the priesthood; because as long as one forms part of the world, Marjann, the desire to live like the rest is immense; as immense as the passion in every human being towards earthly things!

"The life of a priest is tough, Marjann. After all, for a person to love and serve God, it isn't necessary for him to become a priest. A person can serve God, in many other walks of life.

"Meanwhile, we'll have to wait and see what's going to happen. Then, we'll be in a position to understand things better, Marjann!"

Marjann did not expect this kind of talk from Dun Karm. She knew what a kindly soul he was and considered him the holiest person in the world. She loved him a lot as if he was her brother. However, this time she was angry at him, because she thought that he would have said something different to her.

Poor woman! Who could explain to her that what Dun Karm had just told her was the sum total of his wisdom, kindness and personal bitter experience. However, a mother is not to be blamed for feeling let down. Until not so long ago, the greatest wish of most Maltese mothers – especially those living in the villages – was for one of their sons to become a priest.[15]

V

Have you ever stopped to consider how some terrible, frightful tale is passed down from one generation to the other without it ever having been put down in writing and yet it still remains fresh in people's minds - even after a hundred years?

Listen to this, then:

About eighty-five years before the beginning of our story that is during the last days of February 1820 the authorities hanged[16] six British corsairs from the mast of a ship anchored in the Grand Harbour.

It was the practice in those days to tie the bodies of corsairs on the Ricasoli gallows. Four of the bodies met that fate. The aim of this practice was to serve as a lesson to the rest of the maritime community and as evidence of the harsh laws and customs of our fathers.

A few days after this sad story took place; a similar one happened, in which two persons lost their lives. That event brought in its wake much sorrow to the people who knew those individuals.

❖ ❖ ❖ ❖ ❖

Pietru from Kalkara, a fisherman all his life, was a very courageous person. For him, little did it matter whether he fished in the vicinity of the Grand Harbour or two miles away from the coast. During his fishing life he had met with plenty of trouble. He almost drowned several times and for this reason no one matched his knowledge and experience about fishing and the sea.

Pietru had raised his family from the meagre income of fish he used to catch and which his wife used to sell. When his two sons – Ġorġ, the elder one and Toni – grew up, they started accompanying their father at sea and to share with him the tough life of the poor.

Toni and Ġorġ were very strong persons. They were very healthy and courageous as their father. In a nutshell, they were shining examples of the fame which Maltese people enjoy as seafarers.

❖ ❖ ❖ ❖ ❖

It was a splendid, moonlit winter evening. As usual on such evenings Pietru's boat would be the farthest from land than the rest of the boats.

Pietru and his two sons were fishing in the area overlooking Rikażli. Suddenly, after the three of them had been quiet for some time, Pietru said in a coarse slow voice:

"Don't you think that it would be better to return home?"

"That's what I thought," replied Ġorġ immediately.

"Let's get on with it then, because although the wind is blowing towards the shore, it's getting stronger; and I think the north-east is on its way."

"As far as I am concerned we should have gone back long ago," replied Ġorġ again, while holding on to his cap because a gust of wind almost blew it away.

Toni grasped one of the oars and together with his brother started rowing as much as they possibly could. Their efforts were all in vain as the wind continued getting stronger.

Their father encouraged them not to lose heart: "We will soon get to shore. Have faith in Our Lady[17] and She'll deliver us from every evil."

They were helpless against the fierce waves, which from blue had changed to a green edged with unique white foam of anger.

Pietru prayed to Our Lady whilst encouraging his sons in a weak voice. However, he felt that they were in great danger.

Whilst Pietru was looking in the direction of Rikażli, where the four dead bodies of the English pirates hung from the gallows, a strong breeze made him realize that it would be better for them to return home.

Pietru was the product of his time. The sight of the dead bodies swinging to and fro in the moonlight of that silent night frightened him. He did not convey any of these thoughts to his sons, but deep down he felt sad and that his luck was running out.

❖ ❖ ❖ ❖ ❖

It started drizzling. Thick black clouds immediately covered the moon and soon after it started raining heavily whilst the wind seemed to blow from every corner all at once.

Pietru's sons, although soaking wet and breathing heavily continued rowing. They prayed God to deliver them from drowning.

Pietru sometimes looked at his sons and sometimes at the sea. He was trembling and constantly prayed Our Lady in a loud voice to deliver them safe and sound.

"Our Lady of Mount Carmel save us! Pray my sons! Only She could save us."

The sea that surrounded them was as black as pitch and it got rougher and the waves got bigger as time went by. The rough waves almost capsized Pietru's fragile boat. Ġorġ and Toni although terrified, rowed with all their strength without knowing in which direction they were going.

Time passed quickly; but it seemed at a standstill. One could only hope to save one's life.

❖ ❖ ❖ ❖ ❖

All of a sudden Pietru's sons realized that they were approaching the rocks and they started rowing away from them.

At that exact time, a larger wave than the rest lifted the boat in the air, smashed it against the rocks and capsized it.

A shout of 'Oh dear,' lost amidst the strong winds and the clamour of the sea, nothing more except a broken boat, dashing against the rocks.

Ġorġ's ability, skill and luck, together with his longing for life saved him from certain death. He lay almost unconscious on the ground, very tired but...alive!

VI

The drowning of Pietru the fisherman together with one of his sons had created a stir at that time. People should have forgotten all about it but they never did because Ġorġ kept on narrating the event to his sons and the latter to their sons.

That is why some events although unwritten persist in memory.

❖ ❖ ❖ ❖ ❖

Children grow up in one village and when they are old enough move on to live in another area. This is what happened to Ġorġ's generation.

One of his nephews married a woman from Ħaż-Żgħir and ran a coffee shop in the centre of the village.

He was called Ġorġ after his grandfather. Ġorġ was an agreeable, handsome and happy person. He loved talking as much as women but otherwise he was a man with a very pleasant character, gentle and kind.

He gradually developed his business and started selling anisette and rum for a halfpenny and a penny respectively. His shop soon became the most frequented in the village.

Many people visited Ġorġ's shop including priests, farmers, merchants, coal and cargo workers. Everybody loved his company especially when he started making up stories. He always told his listeners the story of how his grandfather had escaped drowning and, although he tended to exaggerate slightly he kept a serious face whenever he narrated that story. The more he embellished the story the more people listened attentively to what Ġorġ had to say. His listeners would even pay more attention on a cold winter night when the blowing and howling of the wind outside Ġorġ's shop helped to make Ġorġ's story sound more tragic. In this manner his audience longed to hear more of what Ġorġ had to say and they would stay in until closing time.

One day, Ninu the house painter, who took pride in his work, decided to paint the shipwreck of Ġorġ's grandfather. When he finished the painting everybody complimented him and bought him a drink.

The shipwreck of the Kalkara fishermen was the name given to Ninu's painting. The painting hung in the middle of the wall facing a side window in Ġorġ's shop. For a long time it was the delight of children who admired the painting whenever they visited Ġorġ's shop to buy a penny's worth of tobacco or a bottle of wine.

VII

Kelin Miksat who among other people frequented Ġorġ's shop used to be the first one to arrive there.

Kelin was a fifty-year-old man. He was a bachelor and had lived several years abroad. He lived on his past savings. He was knowledgeable about many things and whenever he spoke everybody stopped talking to listen to what he had to say.

Kelin was a huge man with a deep voice. This made his listeners feel in awe to him; he was very careful about what he said. He had a way of chuckling silently to himself. He had a beautiful moustache that he stroked slowly whenever he was in a pensive mood.

Although people believed that Kelin had some money to live on, he was never idle. He used to keep the accounting records of the builders entrusted with the construction of the Breakwater in the Grand Harbour. Several workers in Ħaż-Żgħir had found employment thanks to Kelin.

People in Ħaż-Żgħir used to say that there were few people who knew English and Italian as well as Kelin. Although people tended to exaggerate, it was true that Kelin had a sound educational background. He travelled widely and came across many foreigners. He had to put up with a great deal of hardship and above all he loved reading a means by which he had learnt many things.

Kelin observed his Christian obligations by hearing Mass on Sunday. For this reason he never gave people anything to gossip about.[18] Although he was on good terms with the village priests some said that reading had turned Kelin into an atheist and that his religious practice was only apparent rather than out of conviction.

Nobody knew the reason why some villagers doubted Kelin's religious beliefs. Kelin never gave anyone to understand that he was a non-practicing Catholic. However, those who believed so where correct in their thinking.

Kelin was an atheist. He had lost his Faith some time in the past but being a practical person he realized that it would be better for him to keep this fact a secret. For this reason he never said a word to anyone about his religious beliefs.

One might ask: how did the villagers grow suspicious of Kelin? Who knows how? Sometimes people take after dogs: they smell what they don't see or even hear!

VIII

Work is man's best pastime. Every wise person knows this even if he was born into a very rich family. Indeed health and work are the most important things for a person more important than wealth. While health is everything for the human being a slothful person's health would wither away gradually. These are the words of wise people and nobody can deny them.

Kelin, being a wise man knew that health and work go hand in hand. Kelin worked neither because he was a greedy person nor because he wanted to increase his wealth. He had no relatives who would inherit his money because he lived alone. He used to say: "when I die, everybody dies with me."

Kelin also knew that laziness makes people sick, wears them out, and ages them prematurely.

Hundreds of workers including Kelin became unemployed when construction works on the Breakwater ended. The thought that henceforth he had nothing to do, made him sick and sad.

Kelin had grown accustomed to going to work regularly. He was able to write and hoped to do something with that skill. However, being a fifty-year old man he could never face the competition offered by youths who had just finished school and were full of determination, strength and ability!

Kelin who was single and had some money stowed away in case of an emergency suffered both psychologically and financially. Unemployed artisans with limited financial resources who earned their living for several years at the Breakwater site suffered more.

Hundreds of poor unemployed workers realized that they only had their last week's pay to spend. Several weeks, if not months and years of hunger, misery and unemployment lay ahead of them. Years of unemployment that weaken the human being make him become bitter and render him hopeless.

The years that befell the Island following the completion of the Breakwater were years of mass unemployment and misery. People were looking for work, hoping and waiting; but all in vain!

Nobody knows how unemployed workers and their families lived after the completion of the Breakwater. Only generous people who shared their bread with those poor families are aware how they survived. However, many were those families in those days who simply had nothing to eat and the hunger they endured was no worse than death itself.

"Believe me, mother, I am tired of listening to peoples' just protests!" Dun Karm used to tell his mother then. "Did you know that Karmnu ta' Pina has been unemployed for eighteen months; who knows, what his wife and five kids have been through? I wish I had something to give them every day. Mother, I see all that poverty and misery...They live in a miserable hovel unfit even for animals. They would not be in such a bad state if they had something to eat. The pity of it is that they are starving!

"I visited them about a week ago. It was an incredible sight! Filthy children in tattered clothes. Their ten-year-old eldest daughter is always ill. All of them sleep on some straw like goats do. How terrible, Mother! What a cruel world!" Dun Karm's words regarding Karmnu ta' Pina and his family were applicable to several other families living in Ħaż-Żgħir and in several other Maltese villages.

People used to pester Kelin to write them a recommendation or to speak to someone in authority to find them employment with the Government.[19] Kelin, being a kind person would accede to their request. However, he was still unemployed and living on his small savings.

Sometimes he also donated money out of his pocket to console somebody begging for alms. Otherwise he seemed like a horse tied to a water mill. He went round the village three or four times daily. Kelin, was a generous man but the habit of loitering about appeared to have somewhat changed him.

He visited Ġorġ's shop daily. He spent some time talking or debating but he was no longer the happy person he used to be. He was quick to lose his temper and would send a person packing if one got on his nerves.

IX

One evening, early before sunset, Kelin was sitting at the door of Ġorġ's shop smoking a pipe.

At that moment Leli ta' Braġ was coming down from the direction of the church.

Leli knew Kelin even though the latter did not live in Leli's neighbourhood. At the time Leli was growing up he used to come across Kelin arriving from or leaving for a stroll around the village. Kelin used to smile at Leli as he used to do to most of the villagers.

Kelin loved lively and intelligent children such as Leli and the two of them gradually became friends. They saluted one another heartily and whenever they were alone and came across each other, Leli's face would light up with a smile as he said

'Hello, Sir.' If Kelin happened to be unaccompanied he would reply 'How are you Lel? Where are you off to today?.' Leli would usually answer: 'I am going home, Sir' or 'I am off to church.' Leli would still have had plenty of time left gadding about with his friends before he returned home or gone to church.

Kelin enjoyed talking to Leli because he believed that Leli was a very clever boy for his age.

Leli used to speak almost invariably to Kelin about school and books especially since Leli was growing up and progressing in his studies.

When Leli came closer to Ġorġ's shop, he raised his head, put on his usual happy smile and said: "Hello Sir."

"Hello Leli! Where are you going? You seem in a hurry!"

Leli flushed with excitement and put on an even greater smile: "I am going home, Sir!"

"What's new, Lel? Everybody fine at home? How are you doing at school?"

That evening Kelin seemed in the mood for talking. Leli was a talkative person and once he started talking would never stop.

"This year we started studying British History! History is a marvelous subject, do you agree, Sir? I am also doing well in the other subjects, especially languages. I love Latin and am doing quite well at that. I don't know why my friends hate that subject?" It's Mathematics that I don't like. I simply hate it!"

"The study of languages is beautiful, especially Latin. I used to study the subject in my youth. A wise man once said that whoever does not study Latin and Greek possesses a severely impaired education. On the other hand, Lel, do your best so that you do well in Mathematics. If that wise man was alive today he would say: 'In order to earn a living, study Mathematics.' For this reason, Lel, you would do well to practice that subject because it will be to your advantage in the future."

"I love reading a lot, although my mother worries me. She is constantly on the look out to see whether the kind of books I am reading are suitable for me. As she doesn't understand these things she asks Dun Karm. How can the latter pass judgement unless he reads what I read."

"Listen my son," Kelin told him without answering the boy's question. "Study foreign languages so that you will be able to read in those languages. We have very few Maltese books and we should be ashamed of that! It could be that things would change in the future. The need for such books is great because there are only a few. We lack Maltese books which can be read by those who don't understand foreign languages."

When Kelin stopped speaking Leli asked him:

"Do you have a lot of beautiful books, Sir?"

"Yes, my son. Not that many but enough to learn a bit more before I grow old."

"Will you lend me a suitable book, Sir?"

"Of course I will, Lel! But not now because you will neglect your studies. I will lend you a book when you grow a bit older."

"At the moment I am reading a book in English. It's a very beautiful book. The Doctor's son from Ħal-Kbir lent it to me. He too loves reading as much as I."

"You don't say? And what is the title of this beautiful book you are reading?"

"The French title of the book is *L'homme qui rit*. But as I told you I am reading it in English."

"Well done, Lel! Tell me again? No wonder your mother is always on the look out for the books you read! I believe you are still young to read that kind of book. Do you really understand what you read?"

"Yes, of course I understand what I read. The story is really beautiful. I believe that who wrote the book – Victor Hugo, was not a Christian like us, is that correct? I don't know whether I understood correctly, but I came across certain words which made me understand that he is not a firm believer."

"You're correct, Lel! Watch out because if your uncle comes to know what you are reading he will be quite angry with you. He will have every reason to be. Those books are unsuitable for you, my son. You would do better to follow your studies and disregard that kind of reading."

At that precise moment, two youths a bit older than Leli,

Ġanni ta' Kejla and Ġużè Snien, who loved bird-trapping and shooting[20] came out of Ġorġ's shop.

"Lel!"

"How are you, Ġann?...Any news, Ġuż?"...

"Are you coming with us next Saturday, Lel?"

"Are you going hunting?"

"Yes, God willing," replied Ġużè. "It's a crescent moon, Lel. A few days ago Patist informed us about two heaps of crottels. We went and found them. We are planning to go hunting next Saturday."

"I have to tell my mother about it, Ġuż. I'm sure she won't object. Anyway, we'll meet again before next Saturday?"

"Certainly. Goodbye! Goodbye Kelin!"

"Goodbye, my friends, Goodbye!"

Ġanni and Ġużè left on their way; thinking about rabbits, crottels, fire-arms and bird-catching nets.

"I too ought to be leaving you, Sir."

"Are you going, Lel? Be careful. Take care of yourself, my son; and give my regards to all at home. Goodbye, Lel."

"Goodbye, Sir."

Leli ran back home as fast as a hare, to ask his mother's permission to go rabbit hunting[21] the following Saturday together with Ġużè Snien and Ġanni ta' Kejla.

X

Saturday came; and at exactly 9.00 p.m., Ġużè Snien, Ġanni ta' Kejla and Leli ta' Braġ left for Blat to spend some time hunting rabbits. They used to wait very quietly and motionless behind a rubble wall situated either in an open plain or at the edge of a cliff. They waited patiently for the first rabbit that came their way and if they were lucky they took a shot at it.

Ġanni and Ġużè didn't take any notice of the one hour walk from the village to Blat whenever Leli went out hunting with them.

They liked Leli a lot and they loved listening to him speaking about the books he had read. On the other hand Leli loved listening to them about hunting, bird-trapping, turtledoves and what have you.

Leli listened very carefully to Ġużè's ghost stories. He used to say in his heart of hearts: 'How I wish that some day I too would see a ghost! I know that it will terrify me but at least I would be able to say that once I too saw a ghost, as did most of the villagers.'

❖ ❖ ❖ ❖ ❖

Such splendid evenings are quite common in Malta. Enchanting evenings indeed!

It was one of the last days of September – beginning of autumn – in the evening it started becoming quite chilly but not cold.

As many people are aware deserted streets and paths characterize the distance between Ħaż-Żgħir and Blat. The walk is however very beautiful in the moonlight. Leli adored country walking in the night and he was quite accustomed to roaming about the fields.

When they happened to be walking close to a farmhouse, he could smell the sweet scent of the honeysuckle. Leli would stop talking and tell whoever would be accompanying him: "Can you smell the honeysuckle? A pleasant smell, don't you agree?"

❖ ❖ ❖ ❖ ❖

For those who embrace hunting as their pastime, the silent hours pass as a flash of lightning.

They don't mind if they grow tired of sitting on a stone or a rock, of walking an extra mile or two or that the early morning dew is bad for their health. They are not afraid of the dark, the silence and the open countryside in which they find themselves.

The more they are away from people, noise and home the happier they feel.

Ġużè and Leli would shelter beneath the edge of a rock keeping their eyes open like two snakes waiting patiently for a rabbit to pass by.

Ganni would be squatting down a stone's throw away with the gun in his lap – looking like a woman breastfeeding her baby. He too would be waiting and hoping to mark and kill even a cony.

❖ ❖ ❖ ❖ ❖

A hunter's patience has its limits too! Ġużè and Leli had been watching closely and hardly moving for about two hours lest they scare some rabbit away. Suddenly, Ġużè turned on Leli, handed him the gun and told him: "Here Lel. Hold it and if you see one, fire! Don't be afraid. I need a smoke badly. I am going to roll a cigarette and smoke it beneath that parapet wall."

Ġużè had hardly finished speaking, when they heard the firing of a gun a few yards away from them. It was Ġanni ta' Kejla.

Ġużè and Leli hurried to Ġanni in a state of shock. As they approached him, they heard somebody moaning.

Ġużè immediately asked him: "At what did you fire, Ġann?"

Ġanni who was trembling in a pitiful state, did not utter a sound. He started shaking and stammering. Finally he said: "What the hell do I know! How could I know at this distance? I shot and perhaps hit a pharoah's hound."

"Not perhaps," replied Ġużè; "you certainly hit it. Listen to it moan! Let us return quietly to the village because if the dog belongs to someone, there will be trouble for sure!" Fortunately the dog was unaccompanied. That blessed dog loved hunting so much that it used to go hunting rabbits alone on the cliffs during the night.

The villagers found the dead dog the following morning but nobody had any clue who killed it. The three of them kept silent and Anġlu Buras never came to know who had killed his best dog.

❖ ❖ ❖ ❖ ❖

The clock had just struck two o'clock in the morning when Leli arrived home. He found his mother waiting for him.

"How long did you take to get home, Lel?" She asked him.

"Don't you know that it's a long way from Blat to the village?"

"Come my son, have something to eat before you go to bed."

At that moment Leli heard his father's footsteps coming from the bedroom.

"Is my father still awake?"

"Yes, he is because he arrived home somewhat late!"

Leli said nothing. He took half a loaf from the table, placed it in the palm of his hand and cut a piece of bread with the other hand. He bit at the bread without waiting for his mother to serve him the hot food.

He had just finished eating that piece of bread and was looking at his mother serving food when suddenly he told her:

"Had I known, I wouldn't have gone and left you alone!"

"I wasn't alone my son. Your brothers were here". Marjann's eyes filled with tears at the word 'brothers'.

Leli realized that something must have happened to his mother. She gave him her back and went into the kitchen. Leli stood up and followed her.

"What's the matter, mother? What's wrong?"

"Nothing, Lel, nothing is the matter! My molars have been giving me some trouble!"

Leli was no longer a child and was able to distinguish between pain caused by toothache or by heartache. He also realized that this was his mother's second lie that evening to hide from him his father's folly. He knew that the two of them had had an argument just before he arrived.

He could imagine why his mother and father had quarrelled at that time of night. As on previous instances, his father had arrived home late and Leli realized that it was not because his father had worked overtime.

Leli was feeling different that night. He felt the flame of

manhood burning inside him and while he embraced and kissed his mother he told her: "Don't be afraid, you can rely on me; I love you a lot! I will soon find work and you won't have to worry anymore about why my father arrives home late!"

"Stop it, my son! I know that you love me. I also know that I have your support but always honour your father! Hasn't he cared for you? Go and eat your supper, Lel. I am going to bed. Put out the light after you finish eating. Remember not to make any noise when you come up to bed because otherwise you'll wake up our neighbours."

Marjann had every reason to cry. Her husband had the habit of gambling[22] and on that evening he had gambled and lost a lot of money to the detriment of his family.

XI

"Anni, tell Ċikku that tomorrow morning he is to pick us up at seven thirty to take us to Valletta."

Ċikku was the owner of a horse-driven cab that the villagers utilized as a means of public transport.[23] Anni, Ċikku's wife was squatting next to the stove at the mouth of the shed. She held a fan in her right hand and was blowing at the stove with all her strength.

"Wait, my dear, I can't understand what you're saying because of this confounded firewood! I don't know what's the matter with it; it doesn't seem to burn! Who knows whether those wretched children threw water over it?"

Anni stood up from where she was, flushed of face, untidy and with ruffled hair. She wiped her hands in her apron and approached the boy who stood at the mouth of the shed looking at the stove covered with smoke like a chimney.

"You are Ninu's son, aren't you? At what time did you say you want Ċikku to come for you?"

"Tomorrow, at seven thirty."

"Fine; I will tell him when he arrives!"

Lippu, Ninu's youngest son, returned home to inform his mother what Anni had told him.

The following morning, soon after seven, Ċikku was waiting with his horse-driven cab in front of Ninu's house. From outside he could hear Ninu shouting for this and the other.

After helping the children to dress, Marjann put on one of her best frocks, which she always reserved for some special occasion.

It was a special day for ta' Braġ. They were going to attend their son's school prize day in Valletta. Leli was going to receive two prizes for having finished first in English Language and Religious Knowledge during the final examinations.

They boarded Ċikku's cab after making sure about where they placed the key to the front door, closed all windows and doors of the house and, checking if they remembered to take all necessary items with them. Ċikku cracked the whip in the air and made the horse go fast to show off its beauty.

As Ċikku drove the horse through the streets, the tiny bells attached to the horse's collar tinkled, mingling with the sound produced by the wheels of the cab and the horse's legs. People leaned out of the front door of their houses and shops to look at the horse-driven cab passing by. Those who love horses and are knowledgeable about them would grow envious of Ċikku not only for possessing such a beast and cab but also a horse that gave them such pleasure in driving!

Marjann would feel terrified whenever she boarded a cab and the driver made the horse run faster. It had been such a long time since she had been on a cab. When she did ride a cab, however, she panicked and prayed God to deliver her from every evil. Her sons laughed at her but that's what she was doing still.

"Ċikk, we are in no particular hurry," Ninu told Ċikku. "What matters is that we arrive safe and sound!"

"No, no! don't worry about that! you are in safe hands so don't be afraid Yes, yes, I can see Marjann is! We'll go slower. I thought you were in a hurry!"

As they were entering Strada Rjali in Valletta, the noise produced by the horse's hooves against the flagstones drew the

37

peoples' attention. Cikku behaved as if he was driving the royal carriage. He drove the carriage at a swift pace and looked proudly at the people on both sides of the street, showing off his horse.

It was customary to distribute the prizes to successful students inside the church next to the school. When Marjann entered the church together with her family, she knelt down and prayed. Although her husband and sons also knelt down, it was only Leli who replied to his mother's prayers. Ninu's two youngest children focussed their attention on the surroundings and on the people entering church.

At nine o'clock sharp the Monsignor entered the Church and went to sit on the velvet chair especially prepared for him. It was located at a higher place than the rest of the chairs on which the other dignitaries were to sit. It was only fair once the Monsignor was going to distribute the prizes.

Dun Manwel – a learned man and well-versed in Latin – appeared on the pulpit soon after the Monsignor entered Church. He unrolled the paper he held in his hands and started reading.

The words of the wise man touched everybody's heart. Although it seemed that everyone listened carefully to Dun Manwel there were several people whose mind was on other things. These included the parents of the prize winners. They waited anxiously to hear their son's name being called out to receive the prize from the Monsignor in the presence of that distinguished audience!

Those parents were not to blame for thinking about their sons instead of what Dun Manwel had to say.

Dun Manwel spoke about the importance of education especially in today's world when education flourished among all nations. His words struck all the children listening to him. He told them that besides being useful to them for their future, learning also honours their relatives, friends and their country. Dun Manwel said that that day was sufficient recompense for those children who had done their best during the year and finished first in the examinations.

"Who of you, children," Dun Manwel asked in a loud voice "doesn't wish to form part of the successful group of children who soon shall receive the prize for their hard work?"

As soon as Dun Manwel ended his speech, the children were called one after the other to pick up their prize.

When Marjann heard her son's name being called out she became very excited. She clasped her hands close to her chest and whispered in her husband's ear: "How smart he looks, Nin. There isn't a more beautiful boy than he!"

The audience applauded when Leli went up again to the Monsignor to receive his second prize. Tonin lowered his head, coughed and asked his wife to give him a handkerchief.

This time she didn't hear what he said. She was so happy. Her eyes filled with tears and she had a beautiful smile on her face. At that moment, to her no other boy was smarter, more beautiful and more intelligent than her son Leli!

BOOK TWO

NEW HORIZONS

Whoever entered Master Ġammari Kanwara's little house for the first time, would immediately realize that its owner was an industrious and prudent person. Wherever one moved inside that house one could breathe in the sweet smell of cleanliness. Everything was as neat as a pin and kept in order. There was no luxurious furniture in the house only the bare essentials but it was sufficiently clean to accommodate if necessary the most noble people.

Vira, Ġammari's beautiful daughter looked after the house.

Ġammari was a busy person and his colleagues at the Dockyard admired his skills. He received a good wage[24] and always did his best for the good of his family.

He was an industrious person. He would hear early morning mass and if he had time he would hear a second mass.

He had two daughters from his marriage with Liża Għaxaq. Vira, his elder daughter and Rożi who was two years younger than Vira.

Vira had spent some time with the Sisters of Ħal-Kbir and had received a sound education.

Rożi, his younger daughter was less fortunate. She had caught undulant fever at fifteen and never recovered from that illness.

Once, following a number of questions which Ġammari asked Dr. Pawl Tabun, the village doctor, the latter said, "Listen, Ġammari, we are both practical men! Everything can happen as long as there is life; but your daughter's illness has become critical, and at least as far as I know, there is little hope for your daughter of recovering. Provide her with nourishing food and let her stay in the sun as much as she likes but more than this there is nothing else we can do for her! What can I tell you?"

Ġammari almost cried when he heard these words concerning his daughter.

However, hope is a person's greatest strength.

Time passed with Roży showing no sign of improvement while her parents continued hoping.

Ġammari became a widower two years after Roży's illness.

His wife's death was a severe blow to him. Ġammari loved her with all his heart. Liża had been a strong woman but she used to worry unduly about cleaning the house and that had cost her life. Once she caught a severe feverish cold and died after eight days she took to her bed. She died much before her time calling Roży's name and asking them to take good care of her!

It took Ġammari a long time to recuperate after his wife's death. As they say time is a great healer and gradually Ġammari found his old self again. He continued hoping that his daughter someday would recover from her illness. His hopes would rise on days when Roży's cheeks turned red.

Ġammari loved Vira as much as he loved Roży. He was very proud of Vira and he had every reason to be.

Vira Kanwara was the essence of youth at its best. She was of medium height. She had beautiful breasts and held her head and shoulders straight. She was the kind of girl every man would have liked to court. She had a rosy complexion; happy wide black eyes; full red lips and natural curly black hair. She attracted peoples' attention before she even opened her mouth to speak.

Although she was a beautiful girl, Vira Kanwara was not a conceited person. In fact she was one of the most agreeable persons in the village. At that time Vira was about twenty years old. As she was a very beautiful girl and came from a good family, all the young men of the village had lost their head after her. However, recently Vira had given her heart to Leli ta' Braġ.

Leli who was twenty-one years old was still very unworldly unlike, several other young men who are already mature before they reach that age. Leli was of different stock. His mother's strict upbringing as well as his love for books had preserved him just as pure water keeps a beautiful flower alive after it has been severed from its stem.

Leli had been working for four years. As he had received a sound education he found work that paid well. He was employed with the Buċagħak Brothers who were very rich people. Their well-equipped warehouses supplied goods to most of the local groceries.

At first Leli was engaged by them to assist a person who used to keep their accounting records. After two years that person left his occupation and Leli replaced him. One can imagine how happy Leli was when his wage increased from twelve to eighteen shillings per week even though he performed more than was expected of him.

Tonin, Leli's father had gone bankrupt two years before and to earn some money he started selling goods for some businessmen whenever possible. For this reason, Tonin's family had to live as best they could for a long time.

However, the family gained some respite as Leli started earning full wages and his brother Ninu found employment at the dockyard.

During these last three years Leli had gone out with several girls. He did not date any of those girls steadily.

On Sundays, he would either go to Valletta or play cards at the band club or he would pass his time in Ħal-Kbir. There he would meet Pawlu Sulnata who was Leli's age and totally devoted to books.

During their childhood Leli and Pawlu had been classmates.

Leli left school when he was sixteen. Pawlu continued with his studies and he had only a few years left to become a doctor.

Leli was everybody's friend. However, Pawlu was his special friend and he loved Leli very much.

Leli and Pawlu were intimate friends, something very unusual nowadays!

❖ ❖ ❖ ❖ ❖

It was a public holiday and Leli and Pawlu were returning home from a walk. Leli, all of a sudden changed the subject of their discussion and said "Pawlu, I feel I have lost my head after one of the village girls!"

"You don't say! Who is she?"

"Vira Kanwara, Ġammari's daughter. Isn't she the best girl in the village, Pawl?"

"I believe you would like to marry, Lel? My advice is to take your time. For the time being it's better if you remained single, without any particular worries on your mind than being tied down for the rest of your life to one girl. Furthermore, keep an eye on her father. She is precious to him!"

"If I start dating her, I will continue going steady with her! If I should ever marry, it will be surely her. Not that I am going to marry soon! My mother still needs me. You understand what I am trying to say: If I had to marry, I am sure that I wouldn't find a better girl than Vira!"

"Listen, Lel; have you already started dating her?"

"No, Pawl! Believe me, I'm being honest with you! I have known Vira for quiet some time; but as I told you I never spoke to her since we were never neighbours. Last winter I accompanied the village doctor who called on her sister. Poor girl, her sister has been ill for some time! I stayed outside waiting for the doctor. As I rested my back against the wall near their front door, I heard Vira's voice:

"Please come in and wait for the doctor inside!"

"I thanked her, but to tell you the truth, I was ashamed of entering their house."

"As from that day, we have come across each other several times and we have always saluted each other. That's the whole story, Pawl. However, there's something about this girl. It seems as if she has cast a spell on me. The more time passes the more I think about her; the more I want her; the more I love her!..."

"What can I tell you, Lel," Pawlu replied. "If you feel so strongly about her go ahead and tell her. I feel you have made the right choice. You have set your eyes on the best girl in the village. There's no doubt about that."

Leli was overwhelmed by Pawlu's words.

"Next week I shall write her a letter. I'll make sure that her father is not at home and I'll send it with the girl who runs errands for them."

II

It was the fifth time that Vira read Leli's letter that day. She took out the letter from her bosom, placed the duster on the table and sat down reading it afresh.

"Vir, my dear, if you don't feel attracted to me, if you don't feel anything special for me if you don't love me it doesn't matter! But don't let me know about it, I pray! Let me keep hoping or better still don't answer me. Stay where you can see me, look at me and give me that gentle smile. That will be of comfort to me. But if you feel attracted to me as I do, if you see something special in me; in other words, Vir, if you love me as I love you, tell me without fear: 'Lel, I love you' and in this way you would have made me the happiest person on earth!

"After all what's wrong in declaring one's love? Isn't it true that love is 'Everything'?

"Let me also hope that someday I will meet you some place where nobody can see us or hear us to tell you without fear: 'Vir, I love you! I love you as I have never loved anyone before and as nobody can love you; not even your dear father! I love you more than I love my mother who up to this day has been the dearest person for me! I love you more than anything else in the world! I love you so much that I would rather die than spoil my love for you. In that way I would leave you with a souvenir of my strong and pure love "

Vira blushed every time she read Leli's letter.

She had mentioned Leli's name to her sister. Vira became excited whenever Leli saluted her. She had recently come to realize that when this occurred she would continue thinking of Leli for the rest of the day and this gave her an air of peacefulness and inner comfort.

Once, at that particular time, Vira dreamt about Leli. The following day when she saw him approaching she withdrew from the window and did not salute him. However, when he had passed their house she appeared again at the window and followed him with her eyes until she could see him no more.

Vira had never realized that behind Leli's sweet and quiet smile burnt a flame of love for her. When she read Leli's letter for the first time she thought that she was dreaming and was in a confused state of mind for the next few days.

Her father did not notice this change in his daughter but her sister did not fail to notice that Vira was acting strangely.

"What's the matter with you, Vir, you look strange?"

"Nothing, my dear! Why do you ask?"

"I don't know! It seems as if something has happened to you. You're not yourself! Tell me Vir: what's worrying you?"

This discussion between Vira and her sister took place exactly two days after Vira had received Leli's letter. Vira felt that she could not continue hiding the matter any further from her sister.

"Promise me, Roż, that you won't tell father or anybody else! You keep what I am going to tell you to yourself!"

"Why are you making such a fuss, Vir? Is this the first time that you are disclosing things to me? Did I ever let you down when you entrusted me with a secret?"

"Yes! I know. Forgive me Roż! This time especially, I wish that you keep what I am going to tell you only to yourself! Leli ta' Braġ, wrote to me, Roż!"

"You don't say!"

"Yes! And he asked me to meet him somewhere to speak to him!"[25]

"Show it to me, Vir!"

"I destroyed the letter! Believe me! I was afraid that something might happen and my father would find it!" At this stage Vira was lying. She had put Leli's letter in a crevice in the wall behind a picture.

"What do you say, Roż? Shall I speak to him? He's such a man! He's the best there is in the village what do you say? Shall I tell him: yes?"

Roży's eyes filled with tears. She knew that she only had her sister and her father in the world and that she was totally dependent on them. Her health had deteriorated so much recently that she would cry at every fresh bit of news.

Roży could also notice from her sister's words that Vira was deeply in love with Leli. As time passed, she expected that that love would grow stronger and would distract Vira's attention from her.

Furthermore, the news made her realize her own unfortunate position. Although she was a young woman she had lost every hope that someday she too will find a man to love.

"What's the matter with you! Why are you crying? Stop it, Roż! That's enough! Tell me what's the matter with you?" With these words Vira started kissing her sister Roży.

"How much I would like to be in your position, Vir; strong and, beautiful and having a man who loves me deeply. Forgive me, Vir. I am not being jealous for you. I know how beautiful you are! I know that someday or other you have to leave me. But am I to blame for my sadness when I remember that someday we have to go our different ways?"

"Why do you say this, Roż?" Replied Vira who had started crying as well. "Don't you know how much I love you? Don't you know that as long as I am alive you don't need anyone to look after you? Don't you know that someday you will recover and you will be stronger than I am? You'll find a handsome man who will be mad about you – you deserve all this."

Roży, with tear filled eyes, gave Vira a pained smile.

"I know, Vir, that this is your wish; but there is no hope for me. For me it is only a dream that can never come through. I have only one wish, Vir: that I pass these last few days of my life with you and that I won't lose my father as I have lost my mother.

"Otherwise, Vir, forgive me, for sounding so cruel and selfish. Believe me, Vir : I wish you happiness and may Leli love you as much as I do."

Vira couldn't stand these words and cried bitterly. She caressed her sister's hair and removed it from upon her cheeks.

"And if possible, Vir," continued Roży, "don't do anything you'll regret, until the time you get married and Leli asks father for your hand in marriage. Avoid being the subject of peoples' gossip because that will worry father a lot. I will kill myself with grief should anything happen between father and yourself."

❖ ❖ ❖ ❖ ❖

The two sisters were having this discussion at the door leading to the yard. Vira sitting huddled up on a pail turned upside down and her sister Roży lying down on a specially designed wheel chair, which Ġammari had constructed after his daughter, had become ill. In that way throughout the day when Roży would become tired she would go and rest on it. As time passed Roży could scarcely stand up and walk about the house!

It was in the afternoon and the yard was bathed in sunlight.

Roży was lying on the bed opposite the yard door. She looked pale and drawn with sunken eyes shining with fever. She was in a piteous state!

Vira, partly because of seeing Roży in that grievous state and partly because of the secret she disclosed to her sister, immediately buried her head in her hands and wept bitterly.

Although Vira was twenty years old she didn't know what loving a man meant. However, she was already experiencing the bitterness that love brings in its wake.

"Why did Leli fall in love with me? I need nothing, I am quite comfortable. Wasn't the love of my sister and father enough for me? Why is the devil causing trouble and upsetting my life? After all I am not a child; I am twenty years old. I have grown up and capable to choose what to do with my life. Perhaps continue living as a single woman as I have lived so far!

"May the devils take Leli and all the young men on the Island. Those people make young girls lose their heads over them and forfeit the happiness of their families. If he bothers me again I'll send him away. My responsibility is to stay with my family and I should keep my cool about Leli!"

It seemed that these thoughts somewhat comforted Vira. She stopped crying suddenly, raised her head in anger, removed her hair from over her cheeks and with a determined look on her tear-stained face told her sister:

"No, no Roż, it cannot be. It's better the way we are. After all am I not quite comfortable as I am? I don't want to have anything to do with men God forbid that Leli asks for my hand in marriage because I'll surely rebuff him! I'll snub him and tell my father." Then, Vira stood up angrily from her place. She approached a chair on which there was a pillow as white as snow. She took the pillow in her hands and told her, "Let me put this behind your back, Roż, because the one you have has become quite flat."

Roży was very surprised with the sudden change in Vira's behaviour. At first she couldn't understand how all of a sudden Vira had become such a determined person.

As soon as Vira changed the pillow from behind her sister's back she told her in an angry voice:

"I am going upstairs, Roż; if possible don't call me downstairs unnecessarily. I am only going to change my dress and I shouldn't be long."

As soon as Vira went away, a faint smile appeared on Roży's face and she said in her heart of hearts:

"Poor, Vira; I pity her. I am the cause of all her troubles. As soon as she gets over it, I'll talk to her about Leli once again. I am sure that as soon as I'll speak to her, she'll change her mind!"

That's exactly what happened. Although Roży was only eighteen years old, her illness had made her a more mature person. She was a sensitive person and, whatever she expected to happen, really occurred. Vira changed her mind about Leli just as Roży believed Vira would.

III

By the time Ġammari arrived home, the church bells would have sounded the Avemarija.

Ġammari had the habit of going to church after work to pray. Then, he would visit Fonzu's tobacco shop where he would spend about half an hour speaking to the people in that shop before returning home.

When Ġammari arrived home from work he would stay inside and would not go out for any reason whatsoever. The only exception being when preparations for the village feast would be in hand and he would be responsible for decorating the streets. After supper, he would spend two hours or more working in the warehouse located behind the church. Young band club supporters surrounded him and he would try his hand as a carpenter, painter, and blacksmith in other words at anything that came his way because it was necessary to do so!

It was about that time of year – one evening Ġammari after having had his supper and smoked his pipe rested for a while against the jamb of the door. Afterwards, he entered the house to put on his hat. Then, from the entrance he called out his daughter Vira, who was at the well filling a pail of water.

"Vir, I am going to the warehouse. I'll be back at about nine!"

"Alright, father;" replied Vira from the yard, and she continued saying: "Take your time."

Ġammari had hardly distanced himself a few feet from the front door that Vira didn't hurry to Roży. She closed the door to the yard behind her and, lit two lamps. She left one of the lamps burning slowly in the kitchen and took the other lamp with her. Vira excitedly approached Roży who was almost half-asleep. Vira wiped Roży's face with the handkerchief Roży had on her lap and then replaced the handkerchief where it was.

As soon as Roży felt Vira's presence she half-opened her eyes and then, suddenly opened them wide.

"Have I been sleeping long, Vir?"

"No, my dear. I wiped your face because you were all of a sweat."

Then, she whispered: "Roż, I am leaving I shall not be long!...Good Lord! I am so excited and afraid! "

"Don't be long, Vir, my dear" Roży told her in a pitiful voice; "Talk to him, and come back."

"No, Roż, I shall soon be back. I am going not to leave him waiting in vain "

"Go, Vir."

"Should my father return home to get something he forgot to take with him, tell him that I am at Randi's; and that I'll soon be back"

❖ ❖ ❖ ❖ ❖

Vira ushered herself out of the front door on tiptoes and looked around to ensure that no one was watching her.

The street was empty except for a dog barking at a cat, and two children playing on the doorstep a short distance away from their house.

Vira left the front door ajar, and went out. She was very excited and was feeling as cold as ice. She went down the street and turned into the alley situated behind their house.

Sqaq id-Dlam was different from the area they lived in. It was a noisy place where women stayed on the doorstep day and night.

Fortunately that evening the alley was all quiet and there was no one outside.

However, Vira decided that she would never pass through the alley again because the people there loved gossiping and prying into people's affairs. If any one of the inhabitants suspected anything, then all the villagers would immediately come to know that Vira ta' Kanwara had set her eyes on Leli ta' Braġ and that both were meeting secretly.

Leli was waiting anxiously for Vira at the entrance of the alley located on the left-hand side of Triq Hal-Kbir, a road close to Sqaq d-Dlam.

As soon as he saw Vira approaching, he coughed and moved away from where he was.

Vira recognized him and approached him with excessive timidity.

"At last, Vir? I am sorry, Vir, that I had to bring you here!"

"Don't worry, Lel!"

"Did anybody see you coming!"

"Fortunately no! because the alley is usually very crowded! and some of them are really shady characters!"

"That's what my mother says; she's amazed by the kind of people that live here!"

"Uhh! You can't even imagine! Those people quarrel day and night and when they are not fighting they indulge in gossiping about other people."

Vira refrained from looking into Leli's eyes on that first encounter. She kept her face half turned in reply to every question he asked her.

"Vir, is your father at home?"

"No. He went to the warehouse."

At that moment, Leli and Vira seemed like two friends rather than lovers. However, when Leli had no other question to ask Vira and the latter had nothing else to say to Leli, he plucked up courage and whilst taking Vira's hand in his hands he told her: "Vir, forgive me! I couldn't refrain from writing to you and ask you to come and speak to me! I love you so much, Vir, to remain silent."

At these words Vira lowered her head, did not utter a sound and shivered like a reed.

"Aren't you going to speak to me, Vir?"

"What can I tell you Lel?"

"Are you sorry for meeting me?"

"No. I only fear my father."

"Don't be afraid, Vir. I shall soon inform my mother about everything and I would be able to visit your house."

"No, Lel! Don't say anything to anybody for the time being. We should find another place where we can meet. Write to me, is that alright with you? As soon as I'll find suitable time to meet you, I will let you know."

"Alright, Vir! Your hand is so cold?"

"Lel, it would be better if I go now, because usually my father arrives home at this hour; and I prefer if he doesn't notice my absence."

"Are you leaving already, Vir? When shall I meet you again?"

"I'm not sure when; I cannot tell you but I will write to you and let you know. Goodbye Lel."

"Goodbye, Vir. Remember me and don't forget to write to me."

"No..."

Vira hurried back home.

This was the first encounter between Leli and Vira. They had so many things to tell each other but they had failed to say anything really important. However, their hearts had spoken and they both felt an inner peace.

IV

How sweet and special are the first days of love! Why do those days have to pass so quickly, that we only remember moments of that particular time? They are the shortest but surely the sweetest days that will linger longest in our lives.

Although lovers can sometimes sound frivolous in what they tell each other – those words are more important and meaningful to them than anything else in the world. In this way they forget the bitterness that will ensue and the fact that they live in a world full of hatred, deceit, tears of sorrow, pain and death.

Moments of love are the sweetest moments in life; especially between two young people who fall in love for the first time. At that moment they belong to a different mystical world far from reality. They forget what is ugly and bad and remember only what is beautiful and good. Love makes them dream the sweetest dream that a person could ever dream in his life.

We come across such blissful moments once in our lifetime. What remains afterwards are fairy-like memories that gradually fade away as time goes by. Those memories vanish when the true significance of love turns into one of lust.

❖ ❖ ❖ ❖ ❖

"Vir, it has been such a long time since we've met! In two months we have only met four times? I am not saying that it doesn't help writing to you; but each day seems so long hoping that you'll send word for us to meet and then nothing ever happens."

Vira looked at Leli, pressed his hand and smiled.

"Am I not with you this evening, Lel?"

"Vir."

"Tell me, Lel."

"Why do I love you so much? Believe me, Vir, there comes a time when I start thinking about you, and I feel I want to cry not because I am sorry for something I did or because I am sad. Anyway that's how it is. I don't know why. I feel faint. At night I imagine your face before me, I smile at you, I raise my hands as if to call you and whisper several times: 'Vir, I love you!'" With the words 'I love you', Leli placed his left arm around Vira's neck, drew her face close to his face and kissed her on the lips.

This was the first time Leli kissed Vira. When he realized what he did, he withdrew, as if he had done something wrong. Leli remained with his hand resting on her shoulder and the other hand resting against the rubble wall.

He felt confused and ashamed, but what struck him most was Vira's face, which at that moment had turned crimson. Leli expected Vira to scold him after what had happened but Vira didn't utter a word. She couldn't explain her feelings. She realized that she had never experienced anything like that before in her life. She felt frightened although it was a beautiful experience. She would have liked to reproach Leli not to repeat what he did. Her behaviour resembled that of a drunkard who although being aware that if he persisted in drinking, he would end up as drunk as a lord, he just couldn't help himself.

Then Leli asked her what was wrong and why she was so quiet.

"Everything is alright Lel! I am very happy and I want to enjoy this moment by remaining silent. I fear that if I speak I will lose this blissful moment Lel."

"Tell me, my dear."

"Do you think we shall enjoy this kind of happiness for a long time? Perhaps some kind of trouble will disrupt our happiness? Believe me, Lel I feel so happy; and for this reason I very much fear that I shall pay for the happiness I am experiencing at this moment in time. It took me such a long time to love somebody in my life. I never loved anyone else before you...Nobody ever told me 'I love you' neither did I ever say those words to anyone. However, now that I have met you, Lel, I don't want to hide anything from you. I am mad about you. I only want to think of you. I am unwillingly failing in my responsibilities towards God and my family, because of you!

"Lel! Don't forget that I am not a child anymore; that I am not one of those girls you meet in town Don't let me continue losing my head after you and then leave me when you've had enough of me...

"Leli, promise me that you will never deceive me and that you shall always love me, that you shall never leave me."

"I promise you, Vir. I promise you anything you want; seriously. Don't you feel and can't you see Vir that I cannot live without you? Don't you feel that I will stand by you whatever happens?"

While Leli was telling Vira how much he loved her, she withdrew her hand from his grip, placed her arms round Leli's neck and kissed him on the lips.

Vira's behaviour surprised Leli. He was glad that they had grown so fond of each other but he never expected her to be that crazy about him. Leli was still inexperienced as to how a woman reacts when she's in love.

He had succeeded in making Vira feel crazy about him. At that moment Vira had spontaneously shown Leli how much he meant to her.

Leli had never loved any other woman before. Furthermore, he was a man of good character since his upbringing had been excellent. He immediately realized that only death could take Vira away from him and that nothing would stop him from taking Vira as his wife.

V

Sqaq id-Dlam was situated behind the street in which Ġammari Kanwara lived. The poorest village people inhabited the alley.

It would have been more suitable to refer to the houses located in that alley as styies rather than anything else. Each stone dated back to the arrival of the British in Malta.

Whoever took the trouble to study the way people lived in that alley immediately concluded that three aspects characterized the area namely: poverty, dirt and sin.

Poverty in Sqaq id-Dlam was something that grieved hearts. It seemed that the unemployed, the sick, and the indolent of the village were concentrated in that alley.

It sufficed to walk slowly down the alley and look around the households to realize the kind of poverty people lived in.

Five year olds and younger children ran almost naked in the alley. During winter the children would put on a soldier's old jacket that their father would have managed to acquire.

The lodging generally consisted of one small room furnished with an old table, two chairs or four boxes, and a paraffin lamp with a broken and sooty glass tube. Heaps of straw would lie in two corners of the room – there would be some empty brown sacks of sugar together with a stove made of stone and, a shelf containing empty bottles of milk. A rope running from one side of the room to the other would be used for dirty clothes to dry on. At times a baby's cradle, also made out of empty sacks of sugar would hang from two hooks driven in two opposite walls of the room.

Most families living in the alley used an empty bucket of lard as their toilet. In that way the landowner didn't have to worry about cleaning the cesspool. Neither was it necessary for the landowner to install sewers to prevent the smell of urine from contaminating the air and becoming a health hazard for those people living in the area.

During the period under consideration the health inspectors did not seem to bother a lot about the well being of the inhabitants in that area. It's amazing how the authorities forgot all about those wretched souls living in that alley.

Dirt in Sqaq id-Dlam was a problem as much as poverty and from hunger and dirt, sin originates.

Sqaq id-Dlam was crawling with children.

Lonza, Pawlu ta' Waħħaxni's[26] mistress had seven children; Tona her neighbour had six; Randi tal-Bukketti, had several children. Every year she gave birth to twins. "Thanks God," her mother used say, "sometimes one of them dies! How could she cope otherwise?"[27] This was common practice among the families in Sqaq id-Dlam.

Most families lived and ate in the same room, slept, prayed or swore, hungered and made love, quarrelled, groaned and died all in the same room.

The children living in that alley as well as the dogs that roamed about the place were always hungry and most of them as thin as a rake. However they grew up quickly and became wicked before other well-fed and well-bred children living in other quarters. This could not have been otherwise. Children, mimic whatever they see and hear, just as monkeys do.

The children of Sqaq id-Dlam swore and used bad language as their parents did; they smoked cigarette butts, which they found on the ground. Woe betides the person who attempted to reprimand them.

Some of the children learnt how to beg. Some begged on their own, others begged together with their parents. Four or more children out of ten, although not yet sixteen years old, had already been sentenced to prison.[28]

❖ ❖ ❖ ❖ ❖

As Kelin Miksat walked slowly through Sqaq id-Dlam he glanced this way and the other. When he saw two or three women sitting on the ground or on the doorstep of their front door chatting away and breastfeeding, he smiled, moved his head or laughed like mad. "Good heavens," he would later exclaim to the doctor or to some other close friend.

"After all, monkeys, rabbits and mice are not capable of reasoning however, their life style is much better than that of these people. The place where those animals live is cleaner. Isn't that correct, doctor?"

The doctor was a good friend of Kelin's however the latter could not stand the doctor contradicting him especially if Kelin happened to be absolutely sure that he was in the right. For this reason the doctor sought to agree with whatever Kelin had to say.

"Kelin, what you're saying is correct but it's useless explaining to them. They were born in poverty and dirt, they live like animals and they shall die as they have lived. It's a waste of time telling them. They cannot compare their way of life with the way we live. They cannot understand how important cleanliness is for our health and how better off they would be if they had to change their life style."

"Listen, doctor, do you know what I believe: it is the responsibility of those who lead them to teach them and provide them with a better life. The only time those in authority call on them are to bring them to Justice. In reality these poor people are not to blame because they don't know how to behave any better. The persons who are responsible for this state of affairs are precisely those persons who should have taken the initiative to provide the local poor with better means of education."

❖ ❖ ❖ ❖ ❖

Dun Karm frequently complained with the parish priest about the difficult life of those people.

"It is a disgrace for our village, Father. It doesn't befit our times for human beings to live in such poverty.

"Each one of us must render an account of his actions to God, unless we don't do something quickly for them!

"God has created everything, to be good and beautiful. Man being greedy and selfish, ruins all the good God has created to the extent that he reduces his own race to a pitiable state so long as he lives in comfort.

"How terrible! What a shame! We, the educated, who live in comfort and aware of what it takes to live a decent life will have to render an account of our actions to God. However, we are inert as if nothing has happened. We allow what is harmful to grow and flourish, hunger to increase and sin committed whilst what these poor souls need is education and plenty of pity!"

"Listen, Dun Karm," the parish priest would gently reply after hearing him complaining for a long time, getting hot under the collar and repeating what he would have just said, "It's not easy to teach the great majority of the people as easily as you think. To educate the majority of the population one needs time and a lot of money. It's not easy to provide work for the people. How can one employ all the poor in Malta? With what will you pay them – mercy perhaps? There are plenty of kind people around, who are willing to help the poor but after all charity begins at home That's the way of the world, and it's difficult to change it."

Hardly would the parish priest finish speaking that Dun Karm wouldn't answer roughly:

"Although that's the way of the world, it shouldn't be so; isn't that right? God did not create man to live in hunger and poverty.

"Is this right? Should this be?"

The parish priest wouldn't say anything. He would disregard him as soon as he realized that Dun Karm had completely lost his temper. When the latter noticed that the parish priest was not paying attention he would say:

"I cannot understand! When I look at these people, I feel sorry for them. To repeat, I still feel that we are failing in our responsibilities towards these people, as we're doing nothing to improve their condition.

"Recently I heard my mother complaining about Kalanġ ta' Ħatba's[29] behaviour with his wife. Not even animals behave the way he behaves! Mercilessly beating his pregnant wife. He behaves even worse with his children. This is no news. When he is drunk he hits them for no particular reason. Tell me: how would you react to such things? What kind of citizens will those children, raised in such an aggressive and oppressing environment grow up to be?"

When Dun Karm realized that the parish priest remained silent, he would continue complaining all by himself, and praying to God for those poor souls.

"O Lord, grant peace to all those who need it, render kindness to the hard at heart and have pity on the poor."

VI

Word that Leli ta' Braġ had set eyes on Vira ta' Kanwara soon spread like wild fire throughout the village. How could it have been otherwise since that indiscreet person of Mariroż who lives at the end of Sqaq id-Dlam had seen them together?

"Who would have expected such behaviour from Ġammari's daughter with all her piety? She behaves exactly like modern young girls do. Did you know that yesterday soon after sunset, I caught her talking to ta' Braġ's eldest son, near tas-Snaj's farm?"

Mariroż, said these words to some of her neighbours. A few minutes later these succeeded in spreading the news throughout the village.

Two days later, Kunċett ta' Venuża went to sell eggs and milk to Marjann. As Kunċett approached the Braġ's household, she stuck out her head from under the faldetta, rolled her eyes and knocked on the door. When Marjann opened the door slightly, Kunċett greeted her and asked her how many eggs she wanted to buy. Kunċett instead of putting her hand inside the wicker basket to get the eggs, drew the veil close to her face. She rolled her eyes again and told her: "Marjann, I regret I have to tell you something, which may not please you. However, I cannot keep it from you. God forbid should anything happen and I would have failed to warn you beforehand."

When Marjann heard these words she became very anxious. Her heart stopped beating. Perhaps her husband had done some stupid thing? She plucked up courage and asked Kunċett what had happened.

"Your eldest son has set eyes on Ġammari's daughter!"

When Kunċett said what she had to say, Marjann at first smiled and moved her lips as if she was about to say something. However, she remained silent and took in the bad news just like a person who swallows a spoonful of cod liver oil.

"Who told you this, Kunċett?"

"Whoever told me knows well, Marjann. If I weren't sure of what I' m telling you I wouldn't have opened my mouth. You know how much I hate gossip, Marjann? The trouble is, and this is why I came to tell you, they are meeting frequently late in the evening, some distance away from Snaj's farm!

"They still have no experience of life, Marjann. Furthermore, she is very beautiful and in the prime of life. I believe she must be twenty-one years old if not older than your son. You will agree with me that, it's a bit dangerous for two young people to meet and pass some time together in the dark. People gossip! You don't want for the world that something might happen. A woman must defend her reputation. I bet that if her father comes to know, she'll regret it."

Marjann gave Kunċett a pensive look and remained silent.

Kunċett repeated that she was sorry for giving her the bad news but she felt that it was her duty as a Christian to inform her about what was happening before it was too late. She continued on her way leaving Marjann astounded with the milk bowl in her hand and looking fixedly at the ground.

"I never expected that he was leaving me for the time being," she said in her heart of hearts. "Did it have to be that woman?" At that moment Marjann felt what every mother feels when she realizes that another woman is separating her from her son!

Had Leli found another girl – whoever she may be - Marjann would have just the same exclaimed: "Did it have to be that person!". She would have likewise criticized her, considering her unsuitable for her son.

VII

Marjann spent the day trying to decide what she was going to do. How was she going to greet Leli when he returned home from work? She believed that she should speak to him courteously rather than antagonizing him thus risking an unpleasant outcome.

Besides these thoughts, another nagging thought entered her head on that day.

Marjann was a practicing Catholic not only in name or when it suited her most. Neither was she one of those Catholics who loved their neighbours because of the possibility of gaining some personal advantage from such a relationship.

One must be aware that there are many such Catholics around. One could hear them declare that they love people whom they have never met such as British, Chinese, Italians or even Maltese. However, they cannot stand their neighbour, or relatives, who meddle in what does not concern them.

That's the way most of us know how to love.

Although Marjann was not that kind of person, she was angered by the news that another woman was going to separate her from her son.

When Leli returned home in the evening, he had hardly entered the house that his mother didn't lose her head. If at that moment someone had told her that Vira ta' Kanwara died, the news couldn't have made her happier.

Man is what he is. Who can blame him?

He is more likely to do evil than good. The worst mistake remains for a person not to remedy the wrong he has committed.

❖ ❖ ❖ ❖ ❖

"Mother! I'm home. Mother! Where are you?"

Leli went upstairs as he usually did whenever he didn't find his mother waiting for him downstairs.

His mother replied from downstairs in a low voice:

"I'm here, Lel in the courtyard."

Amazingly, a person immediately realizes from the tone of the voice the mood of the person addressing him!

Furthermore, as the proverb goes "once bitten, twice shy." Leli had long been expecting that some trouble would crop up and what he feared would occur, happened. He realized from his mother's voice that something was wrong.

He went downstairs to the dining room.

"Today I bought an interesting book."

"Is that so?" Replied his mother in a weak and cool voice as before.

The relationship between Leli and his mother was a close one indeed. Leli was twenty-one years old and it was the first time in his life he had lost his head after a girl. Leli loved his mother deeply and for this reason he couldn't stand her speaking to him in such a cool voice!

He stood up and went out into the courtyard. He came back to the dining room, went twice round the table and sat down again.

"Where have my brothers gone?"

"I don't know where the youngest is; he hasn't arrived yet. Your brother Ninu arrived from work and went to visit his aunt in Ħal-Kbir if that's true!"

Leli became nervous and apprehensive. He couldn't fail noticing that something had displeased his mother.

He grew impatient, stood up, and approached her. He was twice her size – he raised her head and kissed her on the forehead. Then he asked her: "What happened? What's the matter with you?"

Although Leli was not that shrewd, he immediately realized that his mother was aware of everything.

"Stop it, mother, for God's sake."

"I never expected you to remain silent on the subject especially since you always asked for my opinion. To add insult to injury I came to know about the matter from third persons rather than from you directly. That hurt a lot."

Leli sat down, rested his hands on his knees, lowered his head and remained silent.

His mother persisted in scolding him without much ado but with words that touched him to the quick.

"I never told you to remain single and I am not going to tell you so now. When the moment comes for you to leave this house you shall have my blessing but I believe I had a right to know what you had in mind. After all I would have provided you with some good advice before you decided to act on your whim."

Leli moved a bit, but soon resumed his original posture.

"I have nothing to say about the girl. Although I don't know her and I was never friends with any of her relatives, I never heard anything wrong said about her. It's unfortunate that she's an orphan and had lost her mother when she needed her most. However, it appears that nowadays it has become customary for every young woman to do her utmost to get married. Perhaps even at the expense of going out daily in the dark to meet a young man in some unusual alley and be the subject of much gossip among the villagers."

Leli stood up in anger: "That's not true, mother. People have wicked tongues. I have been courting Vira for over two months and during this time I only spoke to her three times at a place some distance away from Sqaq id-Dlam."

Leli's words hurt his mother because she confirmed what she had heard.

"Mother, listen to me. I know what my responsibilities are. I also know that you need me at home. However, even if you didn't need me here, I was not going to leave home for the time being. After all, I am twenty-one years old and you should not blame me for fancying a girl with the intention of marrying her in the future."

"Who is blaming you, my son? Who told you not to marry?

Who told you to remain with your parents? No, no, my son. Go, leave your parents, if you feel that now is the right time! However, don't run away with the idea that once you marry you will be better off! I cannot prevent you from marrying. My duty is to let you decide what you want to do with your life. Your father agrees with me on this subject. However if I cannot influence your decision it is my duty to inform you that married life is far more difficult than a bachelor's. You must be a mature person to enter marriage and you also need a good salary to provide your family with a decent life "

Leli again opened his mouth but remained silent, listening to what his mother had to say.

"I am telling you this my son, because I have passed through that experience. As for the rest don't bother yourself about us. When you decide to leave this house, go and God be with you."

VIII

The village band club stands some distance away from the parish priest's house in the main Village Square, exactly opposite the church. Ħaż-Żgħir's was not a popular band. It used to perform just twice a year. One of those two occasions was obviously on the eve of the village feast. To perform the band march the club had to hire several musicians from Ħal-Kbir's band club.

Notwithstanding this, Ħaż-Żgħir could boast of its band just like the rest of the Maltese villages. Several men always visited the band club on Sundays and Public Holidays. Furthermore it was common practice for band club supporters to argue about the street decorations and lights or about the fireworks for the eve of the village feast or on the feast day of the patron saint.

At that particular time, more people visited the band club daily. They wanted to learn about the local preparations for the Twenty-Fourth International Eucharistic Congress, which was going to be held in Valletta.[30]

Although Malta is a small barren Island in the middle of the Mediterranean Sea, it can boast of a rich history richer than that of larger nations. Its name is associated with important historical figures and events. However, since the time Napoleon left the Island and the arrival of the British in Malta, there had been no greater event than the Twenty-Fourth International Eucharistic Congress, which took place in April 1913.

During those beautiful Spring days, Malta welcomed a considerable number of prominent people including Cardinal Ferrata who was sent to Malta by the Pope to participate at the Congress and lead the festivities.

Due to this sacred event, Malta became known throughout the Christian world as the smallest Island strongest in Catholic Faith.

That's why many villagers visited Ħaż-Żgħir's band club throughout the week preceding the festivities. Similarly one can imagine the large number of questions asked every evening to anybody who knew how to read or was aware of what was going to happen.

One person who had to answer these kinds of questions was Leli ta' Braġ. First, Leli was one of the band club directors. Furthermore everybody knew how much Leli loved reading. For this reason anybody who visited the band club asked him what was going to happen and what the Congress was all about.

Leli simply adored answering questions and trying to cope with everybody.

"Lel, is it true that many prominent people are arriving in Malta daily?"

"Yes. It's true. The Duke of Norfolk arrived yesterday on board an English vessel. He is a popular man in England and a devout Catholic. He came to Malta to participate at the Congress."

"Lel, today I was down at the harbour in Valletta and I heard that the British are putting a warship at the disposal of the Cardinal's who is going to conduct the festivities."

"That's correct. It is an appropriate thing to do and the British should be praised for such a thing."

"How come?" asked Majsi tal-Mitħna.[31]

"How is it that the British have decided to undertake such a mission? Aren't the British Freemasons?"

"Stop it! Shut up, Majs, and stop interrupting," replied some of those people listening to what Leli had to say. Ċikku ta' Wenza who was next to Majsi pushed the latter and told him: "How stupid can you be, Majs? Shut up and listen like the rest of us. Just keep quiet because it would be better for you to do so."

"You think you know but you don't!"

One word led to another and Majsi and Ċikku almost came to blows. When both stopped arguing Leli continued telling them what was going to happen. He informed them that an important meeting was going to take place in Mosta church. Prominent theologians were expected to attend that meeting. A procession the like of which the Maltese had never experienced was going to take place in Valletta whilst, a *tribuna* was to be erected on the outskirts of Putirjal for benediction. Maltese personalities, including the Maltese clergy, local band clubs and associations were to participate in the procession besides priests, canons and bishops who arrived in Malta especially for the celebrations.

❖ ❖ ❖ ❖ ❖

Two days before the opening of the Congress, whilst Leli was in the middle of such discussions, he heard somebody calling him. It was Ġanni ta' Kejla.

"Hello Ġanni! How are you?"

"Can I have a word with you in private?"

"Of course, Ġann. After you" and they entered a room used for storing odds and ends.

"How are you, Ġann? It's been some time since I've seen you!"

"I'm so busy, Leli Didn't you know that I'm going to get married soon?"

"Are you serious?"

"Of course I am"

"You don't say!"

"God willing some two or three Sundays after the feast of St. George!"

"Will you be marrying Ċetta ta' Żari, Ġann? You have been going out together for some time."

"Nobody can avoid what's in God's will! What's important is that one isn't unemployed!"

"You are employed, aren't you Ġann?"

"Yes, Leli Thank God. I have never been unemployed. Presently I'm working in the construction industry. Listen, Lel! I want to talk to you about a particular matter. Make sure that you come to the wedding. Tell your mother and father too! I'll be expecting all of you. Make it a point to come to the wedding otherwise I'll take it personally."

"Ġann, don't worry about us. I'm just as pleased and so will be my parents when I tell them that you're about to marry."

"No, Lel. I will not allow any excuses especially if you fail to turn up! Your presence is important for us. If you don't come to the wedding, I'll come to get you. There's nothing to be shy of. All the guests are family namely relatives, neighbours and some persons related to Ċetta."

"I'm not sure, Ġanni I'll think about it. You know that I really feel out of place at such occasions. I would have been more pleased had you invited me to go rabbit hunting"

"Don't worry there will be time for rabbit hunting. Promise me that you'll come to the wedding feast the day I marry. Listen, Lel, I hope that she isn't restraining you from coming to the wedding.?"

"Who?" Leli's face flushed with excitement.

"What do you mean? Who? Aren't you dating Vira ta' Kanwara? There's nothing to be upset about. Ċetta told me so and she told me also that you'll soon be engaged!"

Leli smiled and answered:

"No, no, Ġann! I am not going to feel upset over such a thing. Why should I? What are friends for?"

"I have to leave now. Then it's agreed. Two Sundays following St. George's feast. If you don't wish to attend Mass, don't bother! However, at noon I want you present at the reception. You may bring along anyone you like. Whoever comes along is welcome."

"All right Ġann I'll come to your wedding and thank you for inviting me."

"Don't mention it. Let's go and have a drink."

"No Ġann thank you just the same. I don't drink at this time of day."

"Good bye Leli and make sure you'll be there."

"I'll be there, Ġann."

IX

"Auntie, it doesn't matter if you cannot give a helping hand."

"My son, it's not that I cannot help you but I don't want your mother blaming me for being the cause of your misfortune...What's gotten into you, Nin? You want to emigrate from your homeland leaving behind your dearest ones to find work elsewhere. Aren't you getting along fine in Malta? Won't you get a rise in your wages in the future? Listen my son you know what the proverb says: A bird in hand is worth two in the bush."

"Auntie. I don't think you understand. You are not aware of the many opportunities that exist in Australia especially for tradesmen like me. Recently people were speaking about Wiġi tal-Landier.[32] He is sending home considerable amounts of money. Furthermore there are some five or six other village farmers who, when they lived in Malta suffered from starvation but since they emigrated to Australia they have become rich."

"Do not take things too much for granted, Nin. Don't believe everything you hear. Not everything that people say is true. Young people like yourself believe that everything that glitters is gold. Anyway, I have never denied you anything and I am not going to do so now. I shall give you all that you need. However, before doing so I want to know what your parents have to say about this. I shall visit your house at the first opportunity to speak to them. This is incredible. You are still young. You are hardly eighteen years old."

"You're wrong! What strange ideas are those? That's not the case. I had my nineteenth birthday on All Saints Day."

"Sure! So you're nineteen, big deal, do you have the courage to abandon me and your parents for ever."

"It's easy to say that, auntie! You are unaware of the economic situation at the Drydocks! How do I know what's going to happen within a year or two! For this reason it's better to do what I have to do without shilly-shallying!"

"O God! Children are the source of much grief and anxiety. Thank God I have remained a spinster. Who would comfort me had I to have a son who decides to emigrate?" At these words Dolor ta' Braġ stood up, removed a handkerchief from her hip, wiped her eyes and nose, entered the kitchen, removed the hot coffee pot from the stove and poured out two cups of coffee, one for Ninu and another one for herself.

Dolor ta' Braġ loved her nephews a lot. However, she loved Ninu more given that when he was still a child he used to spend weeks at her house. In this respect there had always been a close relationship between them. Furthermore, he used to go out of his way to please her and his aunt always bent over backwards to satisfy Ninu's request even before he bothered to ask for what he needed.

However, this time Ninu's demand was unusual. He asked his aunt to lend him a substantial sum of money to emigrate to Australia.

Dolor could not care less about the money. She certainly wasn't trying to persuade Ninu to stay because of that, but because she was going to lose forever the person she loved most.

Dolor ta' Braġ had enough money of her own to live a decent life. She had inherited a good sum of money from her father. Her brother Ninu had also inherited a similar sum but he had squandered the money as has been pointed out earlier.

Dolor lived in one of the best houses in Ħal-Kbir.

She had a good relationship with her brother Ninu who was two or three years younger than her. She never saw eye to eye with Marjanna and though they never quarrelled, they contrasted sharply in the way they liked doing things.

In her youth Dolor had been an accomplished girl. She was beautiful and jovial. Dolor wore beautiful clothes and went to every village feast with her friends. It had never crossed anybody's mind that Dolor was going to remain a spinster. However, nobody knew why she never married. She was a close friend of Nina, the daughter of Dolfu tal-Għaġin.[33] They remained friends until Nina got engaged to Bertu, the son of Ganni ta' l-Iskejjen.[34]

After Nina and Bertu married, Dolor continued visiting Nina as she had always done in the past. Then there were people who believed that it was improper for Nina and her spouse to take Dolor with them wherever they went.

Nina's husband died after a year of their marriage. Her husband had always been somewhat weak. He contracted a severe cold and died soon after. Dolor missed Bertu as much as Nina. They remained friends until Nina left the village and went to live with some of her relatives somewhere in Valletta.

Dolor kept Bertu's picture in a drawer where she also kept her valuables. She preserved that picture until she died. That picture brought her memories of the only time she took something that did not belong to her. For Dolor that picture was a souvenir of her unequited love but she was guilty just the same.

❖ ❖ ❖ ❖ ❖

Time changes everything and with time Dolor too changed. That doesn't mean that she became ugly or changed her way of life. She didn't have any life to change, as she never was a bad person! However, as she grew older she turned into a person prone to complaining about anything. Furthermore each year she became fatter and gradually she became one of those women with a beautiful face but who looked as if she had been through some traumatic experience.

Her obesity was her greatest enemy. She would lose breath if she went up a hill or upstairs. She always complained and was always expecting some calamity to befall her.

One also had to consider the fact that she didn't have any children to worry about.

Since she had become so prone to complaining about anything one can imagine how she reacted when her nephew left and she found herself alone.

"I pity them! I surely pity them! My brother's wife is a good woman but she is very strict with her sons! One shouldn't be so strict with children! One needs to be kind and loving! Otherwise they'll flee the nest! eventually the three of them shall emigrate!" This was Dolor's opinion about her brother's wife! However one can rest assured that if Dolor had had children of her own she would have spoilt them to such a degree that by the time they were twelve they would have dominated her completely.

X

The weeklong activities that took place in April 1913 in connection with the International Eucharisitc Congress were an unforgettable experience for the Maltese.
The great procession from St. John's Co-Cathedral to the *tribuna* set up at the entrance of the Capital City deserves to be mentioned together with the greatest events ever to take place on our Islands.

On that day the vast majority of the Maltese went to Valletta in the afternoon.

As the people knew that the Cardinal was going to give his blessing from the *tribuna* a large crowd gathered outside City Gate.

Leli Braġ formed part of that huge crowd. He stood somewhere near the trees surrounding the suburb known as 'il-glasis' down to Sa Maison. He wore his finest clothes for the occasion and was speaking to Ġammari Kanwara.

Vira and Ġuża stood in front of them. Each wearing a big hat. Ġuża was from Ħal-Kbir and she was an old friend of Vira's.

Leli had been engaged to Vira for three days and this was the first time he had gone out with her family and friend.

Ġammari was feeling very happy on that day and he had every reason to feel that way. His children meant everything to him and he was always thinking about them. Previously he used to spend a long time thinking about Vira's future and wondering who could be her future spouse. For this reason, he could now set his mind at rest given that Vira was engaged to an excellent young man from the same village.

"If your mother was still alive she would be so happy!" Ġammari was saying in his heart of hearts. Then, Leli spoke to him and his daughter whispered some sweet words to her lover.

Leli was no less happy than Ġammari. He constantly looked at Vira and spoke to her sweetly. Although, people surrounded Vira and Leli, both smiled at each other every time their eyes met.

The *tribuna* stood opposite them. It was an impressive piece of work. Four beautiful angels stood in each of its corners each of them holding red velvet cloth. These rose gradually to the top until they reached a beautiful golden coloured crown.

A small altar with a snow-white sash spread on top of it stood on the *tribuna*. When the organizers lit the many lamps that surrounded the *tribuna*, the gold, velvet and the other trappings seemed to belong to the world of fantasy.

The Cardinal, accompanied by the Heads of the Church all dressed in gold, moved amidst the sound of trumpets to give his blessing to the humble multitude. Kelin Miksat resting on his cane looked on from a distance at what was happening. He took a deep breath and said in his heart of hearts: "I'm an atheist and nothing will lure me back the Faith, which I have lost forever! However, Religion is great and a person who loses his Faith would have lost a lot!"

While Leli and Vira thought about the beautiful life that lay ahead of them they knelt down beside each other holding hands and prayed for the Lord's blessing.

When most of the people were still kneeling down, Leli stood up and looked around. It was an unforgettable sight. At that moment Leli said in his heart of hearts: "Where are those people who do not believe in God? They should be here to experience the strength of Christian Faith."

These thoughts crossed Leli's mind because they contrasted sharply with the works he had been reading. However, the Christian principles he received when young preserved his Catholic Faith.

❖ ❖ ❖ ❖ ❖

"I felt sorry for you when I remembered that you weren't present! You would have witnessed an unforgettable experience. You would have noticed how the Maltese have preserved the Faith they inherited from Saint Paul!" Dun Karm told his mother at the end of the Congress festivities.

Dun Karm hadn't missed one of the magnificent activities that took place in Malta during the Eucharistic Congress. The meeting in Mosta Church amazed him. He couldn't forget the words he heard from the most learned speakers of the Church nor could he erase from his mind the things he saw. However, the event that evening was the greatest of all the events that had taken place. It was an event that enchanted and strengthened him morally. It filled him with courage to pursue his work in the Church of Christ with greater vigor.

"Don't bother my son! I am just as happy when I realize how pleased you were by what you saw," she replied sweetly.

"You're saying so, mother, because you don't know what you missed. You can't imagine the devotion manifested by all those who participated in the Congress. At least it served as a lesson on how we should behave with respect to religious matters.

"I saw wealthy foreign women wearing beautiful black dresses participating in the procession, their heads covered with expensive black lace. I also saw wealthy men of every race but of the same creed who came to Malta to give praise to the Lord.

"How fortunate for this tiny Island to have been selected from amongst larger nations to hold this International Congress. This event shall be for long remembered by all the participants!"

"You're right my son. We are really lucky that such an event took place in our times and people like you who have lived the experience should be considered even more fortunate. Listen, Karm, how come you didn't take part in today's procession?"

"I don't feel I am so important and I don't merit participating at such important events however, mother, believe me, I feel better when I pass unnoticed and do you know why? Because I am unlike the rest. I am unholy unlike them. I don't know how to suppress my ego. I would have felt so proud and that's bad. For this reason it's better this way: unimportant and unknown. Isn't that so? I'm going to sleep because tomorrow I have to say the first mass. Bless me"

"God bless you, my son and good night."

XI

"Do you want some more rum, Kelin?"

"Ġorġ, I told you many times already. Occasionally you ought to buy some good rum. This rum tastes like water!"

" Kelin, you should know that that is good quality rum! I bought that rum from Maxxata! It has a high alcoholic content!"

"Don't be silly, Ġorġ. What do you know about alcoholic content? Whom do you think you're speaking to? Money is the only language you understand. Alcoholic content, my foot!"

Ġorġ smiled and returned behind the counter. He realized that Kelin was in an unhappy mood besides saying foolish things as usual. He knew that when Kelin happened to be in a foul mood it would be better to steer clear of him or else he wouldn't let anybody get away with it.

After finishing his drink, Kelin stood up and left without further ado.

"Kelin is in a bad mood!" Ġorġ said to Sidor ta' Bċieċen[35] who had just entered the shop noting Kelin's ill-humour.

Both Ġorġ and Sidor started laughing as both of them stood at the front door of the shop looking at Kelin walking at a very slow pace.

"He's a nice man, poor fellow!" Sidor told Ġorġ after Kelin disappeared.

"Sure!" drawled out Ġorġ. "There's no better person in the whole village! I don't know why people gossip about such a man. Between us, Sidor, some people say that Kelin is an atheist. I personally don't believe that. Presumably it must be some made up story from someone who hates him. I know Kelin extremely well. He's a very nice man except when he is angry and starts swearing! If only we had a few other men like him. Furthermore, he's an intelligent man. He's knowledgeable about many things and he never speaks about other people unlike other disgusting people who indulge in gossiping. I know what I'm talking about Sidor, because people speak about many things in this shop. Do you understand?"

"Of course; you're correct. You know who those people are? You know better than I do? Precisely those people who would do well to have a look at themselves in the mirror. Shall I tell you how much this is so?"

"Listen, don't tell me. I know exactly what you mean and God forbid if I had to start telling you a few things from what I hear inside this shop because I would never stop! I have always been a discreet person. If I wasn't that kind of person I would have to become one since I earn my living from my clients."

"Wait a second Ġorġ because you don't know what I'm going to tell you Did you know that Ġanni ta' Kejla is marrying Ċetta, daughter of Żari ta' Laħlaħ?"

"I knew that a long time ago! He had hardly set eyes on her that people didn't inform me!"

"Last Sunday I was at the band club. Next to me there was Ġużé l-Imqarqaċ accompanied by tal-Bukketti!"[36]

"What do you expect? You know very well whom you're talking about!"

"Bear with me for a moment. It so happened that at that moment, Ċetta passed by. As soon as Ġużè saw her he turned on tal-Bukketti and told us: 'Ta' Kejla will have little cause to boast about! He had better be careful about her! The daughter of a mother who spends time gadding about. Just look at how she moves her hips! Poor man! Ġanni just looked at the physical side of it! He'll be sorry for that! ' His friend tal-Bukketti – what a rascal! Continued to add fuel to the flame. Can you imagine Ġorġ what would happen if Ġanni comes to know about this sort of thing? Tell me who is to blame if their marriage does not succeed?"

Ġorġ looked at Sidor and at first didn't tell him anything. However, when Ġorġ realized that Sidor had remained silent as if waiting for an answer, he spat on the ground and told him: "Listen Sidor; let us go back over what we said. Now I'm going to tell you something but you must promise me to keep the information to yourself. If I were a bachelor I would never marry a girl like that. Do you understand? The girl is rather lively and everybody in the village talks about her!"

"What do you mean, Ġorġ?" Asked Sidor in a surprised voice.

"What do you expect people to talk about! Are you unaware of what's going on? Didn't you know about the severe scolding she received from Anġla wife of Anġlu ta' Kejla, a relative of Ġanni? She called her all kinds of names. Anġla even told Ċetta that the latter goes mad over men. That day, Anġla would have killed Ċetta if some people hadn't prevented her from doing so because she was so angry at her!"

"Listen, Ġorġ: this is not the first time that Anġla has acted that way. She is jealous of her husband! He can't even visit his relatives. Any woman who looks at Anġlu or salutes him will regret it because she will either attack her physically or spread malicious gossip about her.

"So?! Take my advice, Ġorġ, Ċetta is a good girl! I am speaking of her this way not because they are my neighbours but because it's the truth! Ċetta certainly has a lively character but she doesn't merit such treatment simply because Anġla says so! Believe me you shouldn't take any notice of Anġla. She is a jealous person, end of story. One should simply ignore her."

Sidor's words confused Ġorġ who replied as if he wanted to take back what he had said earlier:

"I'm not sure about that. I simply repeat what people say in my shop. After all as I told you earlier on, Sidor, nothing annoys me more then gossiping. You do understand me, don't you? Don't run away with the idea that I participate in that kind of activity! First of all I try to keep away from such people, secondly I don't believe most of what they say. It goes in through one ear and out the other. I know how wicked people can get. I hope you understand what I'm trying to say, Sidor?"

Although Sidor's family nickname was ta' Bċieċen, he was no inexperienced person as his family nickname seemed to suggest. He perfectly understood what Ġorġ meant.

Ġorġ was a kind person but he loved gossiping! However, being shrewd he would react according to circumstances. Since he happened to be in Sidor's company he expressed contempt against persons who engaged in idle talk and boasted that he always kept his mouth shut.

However, many people were aware of Ġorġ's character and Sidor happened to be one of them. He knew that the source of most village rumors started in his shop and that Ġorġ was instrumental in spreading them!

XII

When Kelin came to leave Triq il-Knisja and enter the street in which he lived, he heard a lot of noise that sounded like children shouting and laughing their heart out.

He saw a group of children aged between ten and fifteen and an old man at times walking slowly and at times stopping. He held a cane in his hand and wore filthy and tattered clothes.

The children were teasing the poor man and calling him names. The old man would suddenly turn round and after a while, pretended to run after them, grumbled, swore and continued on his way.

"You frustrated man! You dirty fellow! You ugly person! You hungry man!"

All of a sudden one of the children ran past the old man and snatched the cane from his hand. Another boy passed from the other side of the old man, threw cattle dung at him and hit him on his left eye.

The old man wiped his face with his arm, rested against the wall and cried.

Some of the boys took pity on the man and refrained from teasing him any more. The rest flared up when they saw how confused the old man was. However, Kelin's thick voice surpassed the children's shouting:

"You damned children! Is this what your parents have taught you to do? Is this the reason why your wretched fathers brought you into this world? Is this the Christian way to behave with poor and sick old man!

"Get lost, you cruel boys! Get lost before I break this cane on one of your backs!"

The village children were afraid of Kelin. They felt shy and terrified of him. The boys gradually fled starting with the cowards followed by the bullies of the group. Only two little boys stayed behind. Both of them looked at Kelin unable to understand what he was saying.

After all the children had gone away, Kelin approached poor Toni. Kelin put his hand in his pocket and gave him a halfpenny. He then told him:

"How stupid can you get, tell me? Why don't you use your cane and bash the head of one of them?"

"I'm so weak, Sir! I feel I am going to fall with every step I make! Furthermore, nobody takes pity on me as if I'm the source of all evil!

"A month ago those boys did me a worse turn than today! They hit me with a stone and broke my temple; they almost killed me! Nazju, the village policeman saw me waving my cane and heard me swearing. He reported me and I got six days imprisonment. Not that prison isn't a better place for me than roaming about the street! Better and how! At least in prison I receive a decent meal. Who can control these damned children, Sir? I'm a sick man. I'm weak! For a long time I have been asking the doctor to send me to hospital or to an Old Peoples' Home. However, he hardly listens to me!"

"Go, Ton, go. I will speak to the doctor myself at the first opportunity. Go in peace."

"Thank you Sir. May God grant you strength and all that you desire."

"Go Toni Good bye!"

"Good bye Sir. May God shower His blessings on you."

At that exact moment, Kelin heard someone calling him. It was Leli ta' Braġ and Pawlu Sulnata.

"Hello Leli! How are you Pawl? Everything alright?"

"How are you Sir?" Leli asked, "has anything happened to you? You look worried!"

"I've just had an argument with those wretched children! Can you see that beggar to whom I was speaking? Toni, that's the man. Those boys attacked him. What a shame! They certainly aren't the kind of persons we should be proud of! They don't reflect true Christian values!"

"It's really a disgrace!" Replied Pawlu Sulnata.

"Are you going anywhere special?"

"Nowhere in particular," replied Pawlu; "we were just going for a walk!"

"Now, that we have met, you're welcome to join me at home. There are very few remaining people like you around with whom one can discuss certain subjects!"

"Not this evening, Sir" interrupted Leli, "It isn't the appropriate time."

"Listen, Lel: It seems that she has already confused you! You will have time to go and visit her, don't worry! Ha, ha, ha, ha!"

"No, no! That's not the reason, Sir!"

"Then what is it, Lel? Don't you know that for me any time is good enough?" While he said so, Kelin turned the key in the lock and opened the door.

"Come in! Welcome to my house. Don't take any notice of the confusion. Don't forget that I'm a bachelor and men generally don't bother too much about house-work."

Although Kelin lived alone his house was clean and orderly. He had inherited the furniture from his parents and some broken chairs stood here and there.

Kelin used to sweep the floor, dust the furniture daily and wash any dirty plates himself. Vitor, the washerwoman used to wash his underclothes, linen and some other clothes fortnightly.

However, what impressed Leli and Pawlu as soon as they entered Kelin's house was the glass-fronted cupboard in which he kept his books.

"Well done, Sir!" Pawlu said, "you possess some fine books!" and immediately he came closer to look at them from behind the glass.

Although it had been some time since Leli left school he still loved books and reading as much as his friend Pawlu. Leli approached together with his friend to examine the books contained in the glass-fronted cupboard, which took more than half the space on the wall opposite the sitting room.

"As you know books are my great delight. Although I am old, I have always wanted to learn more and I love reading. Books make me happy. At times I wish I were still a young man like you having good eyesight so that I could spend days reading. However today I am no longer young, my eyesight fails me and even these spectacles don't help my reading much. Sometimes I grow tired and have to stop reading."

At that moment Kelin opened one of the two doors of the cupboard. He moved aside and with one hand resting on the open door delighted himself looking at the books together with Pawlu and Leli. Kelin seemed as pleased as a mother when somebody praises her daughter!

"It seems that you really love reading and you're quite selective too!"

Kelin smiled. "Why do you say so Pawl? I bet you're looking at Plato's *Republic*?"

"Exactly! That book contains so much knowledge! Is that correct, Sir?"

"That's correct, Pawl. Although I disagree with some of Plato's arguments contained in that book, every time I open it I find fresh ideas that make me realize how wise the author of that work must have been."

❖ ❖ ❖ ❖ ❖

While Pawlu and Kelin discussed the wisdom of the Greek philosopher Plato, Leli remained silent because he hadn't read the book yet. He listened to them discussing the usefulness of the book. He knew who Plato was. He also knew that he was one of the greatest philosophers who lived about four hundred years before Christ. He had read some of his writings but he didn't know much more. When Kelin and Pawlu finished discussing Plato, Leli turned on Kelin and asked him in a timid voice:

"Sir, with your permission I would like to ask you whether you will lend me Plato's Republic?"

"Why not, my son? Take it and read it. Take care of it. After you have read it, come back bring it with you and borrow another one. If you haven't read a book of its nature yet you will find it a bit hard for you. However, after all you are an intelligent boy and you are quite capable of understanding this interesting book."

"Thank you very much Sir. Don't worry, I'll return it safe and sound. I take good care of the books that people lend me."

"Don't trouble yourself, Lel. Take the book and make use of it as you please."

At this stage Pawlu intervened.

"To tell you the truth, Sir, I have never had the opportunity of reading the whole book, however, the first time I opened that book and while I was examining it I came across the story in which Plato discusses the idea of the good which is held to be the explanation of the physical world. The contents of that story are food for thought, isn't that right Sir?"

"Sure enough. As I have just stated although my intelligence and opinion are nothing compared to Plato's wisdom, there exist aspects in his philosophy with which I disagree. However, it would be impudent of me if I had to state which other arguments that wise man should have brought forward in his thesis or to try and judge his writings. I also believe that that great philosopher merits greater praise than he ever received especially since his writings date back to two thousand four hundred years ago. This notwithstanding, the world still discusses his ideas to this day."

Pawlu looked at Kelin without saying a word.

At that moment, Leli asked Pawlu to tell him the story he was talking about and what it was all about.

"In short, Lel, in that story Plato imagines that all human beings live in a somewhat dark and huge cave. Those people live all their life with their back facing the entrance of the cave looking inwards. The light emanating from a huge bonfire hidden behind a wall outside the cave comes through its entrance.

"When the human beings raise their eyes and look at the cave walls, they only see shadows of all that's happening opposite the cave's entrance. That's all they see.

"If some brave person decides to turn round and look at the light outside, the strength of that light at first dazzles his eyes. However, gradually he gets used to it and lingers on amazed at the beauty surrounding him.

"If he returns to the rest of the human beings inside the cave, he will realize that he has lost his sight, that he can no longer see the shadows on the cave walls. As soon as he starts telling them what he had seen, the people burst out laughing, considering him mad.

"This, in short is Plato's story. You will of course understand it better once you've read it. Isn't that right Sir?"

"Very well, Pawl! Although Plato continues by describing who are those persons that merit leaving the cave to look at the Truth and relating their experience to the blind and to the deceived persons. However, you couldn't have explained such a great story better."

Pawlu smiled, feeling flattered listening to Kelin praising him.

"What are those other books?" Leli asked Kelin indicating a set of seven or eight books all of the same size on the top shelf.

"Those are amongst the books I love best, Lel. I purchased them during my last visit to Naples some fifteen years ago. They represent the biographies and collected writings of the world's greatest thinkers. Although they are expensive I don't regret having bought them. Those books are invaluable.

"In those books, one comes across the writings of the Dutch philosopher Baruch Spinoza who although died at the age of forty five and although he was ill for most of his life succeeded in completing his *Ethica*. An amazing philosophical work for whoever reads it.

"I mentioned Spinoza earlier on. I love that philosopher. However, the writings of Immanuel Kant are no less magnificent. His most important work is the *Critique of Pure Reason*. I read several times that Kant is the greatest philosopher to have lived these last two thousand years."

"Then, Kant's writings must be quite impressive given that people consider him the most important philosopher of modern times?" Interrupted Leli.

"Immense wisdom! Let's make it clear. Don't run away with the idea that I understood all of Kant's writings. However, the little I understood was enough to amaze me and confuse me."

"Once I came across some of Kant's writings," said Pawlu. "Kant argued that Reason makes experience possible by imposing upon the raw data supplied by the senses the forms of understanding. I believe that Kant identified "categories" that were transcendental in as much as they were not derived from experience but were found in pure reason independently of experience."

"To tell you the truth," continued Pawlu, "at first I understood what I was reading. However, as I progressed in my reading I grew confused and failed to understand the message the author was trying to convey. Eventually I had to stop reading because I was unable to follow any further."

"Kant is a great philosopher!" Said Kelin "but unfortunately we lack the necessary training that enables us to understand such philosophical writings."

"What is Kant's nationality?" Asked Leli who at that moment forgot all about Vira and was extremely happy listening to other people speaking about a subject he loved very much.

"Kant came from a very poor family. He lived in the German town of Konigsberg. His ancestors came from Scotland. After the death of his father, he almost died of hunger but gradually thanks to his writings his fame flourished insofar as the Prussians considered him to be another Messiah. Kant however did not make much fuss about his fame and merited praise. He died at the age of eighty respected by the prominent people of his time."

"Sir," interrupted Pawlu "come to think of it most of the greatest thinkers in the world during these last four hundred years were German, is that right?"

"That's right, Pawl," replied Kelin "together with Kant we find several other famous thinkers whose name will never die such as Hegel, Von Goethe, Ficthe, Nietzsche, Haeckel, Marx, Shopenhauer and others."

"You forgot to mention one person, who is still alive and whose name, I believe will be remembered together with the ones you just mentioned."

"Who's that, Pawl?"

"Nordau. Max Simon Nordau. Recently I read an interesting book he wrote since in a way it concerns the medical profession. The title of this book is *Entartung*, which means *Degeneration*. In that work Nordau demonstrates that most works of art including music and literature originate from mental imbalance. Indeed, if one were to examine those works thoroughly one should realize that they were the fruit of mental instablity.

"Nordau in that work criticizes Wagner and refers to him as a dreamer and weak-minded. He goes on to indicate which parts of Wagner's writing and music demonstrate that Wagner was of unsound mind.

"In that category he includes Nietzsche, Zola and other famous authors. He refers to Schopenhauer as a mad monster that deserves to live amongst mad people. Nordau also disagrees with Professor Lombroso who believed that the work of artists is necessary for human progress.

"Believe me, Sir, I have read several books, however I liked Nordau's book very much especially since it analyzes several famous works of literature. From the looks of it Nordau read and evaluated many great books and went on to indicate which in his opinion were the result of either a sound or a sick mind."

"That's quite true, Pawl," interrupted Kelin, "our forefathers used to say 'that is why the old woman does not want to die; because the longer she lives the more she learns'. I'm just like that! Did you know that you have aroused my interest with your discussion on Nordau? As soon as I come across that book I'll buy it and read it. It's amazing when you said that this person criticized people such as Wagner! Schopenhauer! Nietzsche and Zola!"

When Kelin finished speaking Leli said:

"Forgive me! I don't want to interrupt your discussion when I haven't read any of the books you've mentioned. However, about a year ago, I borrowed – I forgot its name – an English book that discusses the trouble most Nations face and that sooner or later there will be a World War. Whoever wrote the book argues that Germany is the cause of all this trouble since its accumulating a lot of armaments. That author agrees with what Pawlu mentioned earlier since he believes that the Kaiser and the German authorities follow Nietzsche's teachings. He argues that Nietzsche's philosophy doesn't lead anywhere since Nietzsche's aim is to change human beings into super humans.

"That author indicates that in fact Nietzsche became mad at the age of forty-four and spent the last twelve years of his life in that state of mind. If I'm not mistaken this is the same philosopher Pawlu mentioned, and which Nordau defined as a person with a sick mind."

"Listen, my sons!" Kelin interrupted with a disgruntled look, "Read as much as you can. You will learn a lot. However, don't believe all that you read. Obviously every book holds some truth but that doesn't mean that every book is infallible in what it says. Furthermore, it's quite easy for an author to criticize the work of another author! However not every person that criticizes another person's work would be able to perform that work any better.

"Please try to understand! I'm not saying this because I prefer Nietzsche's work to that of any other author but only because it's so easy to criticize other peoples' work."

Leli and Pawlu looked at Kelin. They felt that they had touched Kelin to the quick. They grew confused on seeing Kelin getting so excited. However at that moment Kelin went round the room, entered the dining room to fetch a bottle of rum and three small glasses.

"Here it is! This is the kind of rum that should resuscitate a dead person."

Leli and Pawlu laughed their heart out whilst thanking Kelin and pretending to refuse Kelin's offer to have a drink! "No, no Sir, that isn't necessary. Don't trouble yourself."

"Come on! I can see that you're dying to have a drink Ha, ha, ha."

"Then we'll drink to your health, Sir."

"To your health, my friends. I hope that we will meet again soon and spend another evening like this. Believe me I have enjoyed this evening's discussion very much. Drink up!"

❖ ❖ ❖ ❖ ❖

Kelin's wish came through.

After that evening, Pawlu and Leli visited Kelinu several times. From these visits Leli's love for books increased. As he wanted to learn more he not only borrowed books from Kelin but he also purchased others.

However, at this particular period of time Leli was still unsure what to do with his life. Leli was engaged and these were the most beautiful years of his life. Although he was an intelligent person he was still inexperienced. This couldn't have been otherwise. He still needed time to mature for his readings to have an impact on his life.

Furthermore, Leli did not reflect enough on most of the books he bought. He purchased some books just beacause he had heard either Kelin or Pawlu mentioning them. If he found those books hard for him to follow he stopped reading them and simply abandoned them.

However, for Leli this was the beginning. It was the seed that would gradually grow and bear fruit.

The taste of that fruit was as bitter as much as he had believed it would be sweet.

Even if Leli was as wise as Solomon, he was insufficiently trained to understand the kind of books he was reading. Those books made him sad, disturbed his peace of mind, made him feel bitter and could possibly be the end of him before his time.

XIII

When Dun Karm learnt that his nephew Ninu was going to emigrate to Australia, he decided to visit the Braġ family, to gain first hand information about this case.

"Listen Marjann: there's no need to take this matter so seriously. Other people have already emigrated to that country and many others will do so seeking their fortune there. Furthermore, let's be realistic: he's lucky that his aunt is going to give him all that he requires!

"I don't blame him, my dear. To tell you the truth I'm not sure whether I will follow suit if my superiors give me permission to emigrate and if someone pays my travelling expenses. However, I won't emigrate to make a fortune but to win over some souls to Christianity and help those who need comfort. In this way I will be providing better service to the Lord. After all we must understand that we cannot lead a decent life on such a small Island!"

"That's true, Dun Karm," replied Marjann with tear-filled eyes "but my son didn't have to do this. Poor boy, he's so young! Moreover, he has a job and there was no one trying to put spokes in his wheel!"

"I don't even try to influence his little brother Lippu, although he is growing up and frequently grumbles that he cannot find work, let alone Ninu who has been working since he was a boy!

"This is what we needed. We were doing so well, alas! However, the devil always tries to create trouble. Believe me, Dun Karm, I cannot imagine Ninu leaving this house, forever! I get so worried just thinking of that moment!" And with these words Marjann started sobbing.

"Listen Marjann. That's not the way. As Christians we shouldn't worry unnecessarily.

"It is true that you are his mother and it's only natural that you will miss him. However, don't forget that many a time we fail to understand the hidden ways of the Lord. When some trouble befalls us or when we experience some trouble we immediately tend to lose our patience and faith. Indeed, we seem to forget that there are more unfortunate persons than ourselves in this troublesome world and that we could be worse off."

After Dun Karm finished warning Marjann, the latter gave Dun Karm a pitiful look, moved her head and said:

"You speak this way, because you don't know what this means to me. All that you told me is true. I know that I do wrong when I grumble about my troubles but I cannot do otherwise. Ninu's eventual absence from home worries me a lot and I don't know how I'm going to manage when he's no longer here. Who knows what kind of trouble he will have to face far away from his mother's house? I used to look after all his needs. He likes whatever I do. Who knows how much he will suffer far away from those who love him!"

Her husband's voice could be heard at the entrance at that particular moment.

"Hello, Mena! How are you?"

"Not bad! All things considered!"

"Don't worry, Mena! Anyway I wish you good luck! God bless you, but you look as fit as a fiddle.!"

Mena laughed her heart out while Marjann's husband complimented her: "if only I were to marry someone like you! Or if only today's young women had your features! You're such a handsome woman with such a ruddy face!"

Marjann realized that her husband's discussion with Mena was going to take long and thought that it would be better to call him.

"Nin, come in, Dun Karm is here!"

"Coming, Marjann! Would you like to come in, Mena?"

"I really cannot but I thank you just the same. Give my best regards to your wife. Goodbye Nin!"

"Goodbye my dear, goodbye."

Ninu went straight into the side-room near his wife and Dun Karm. His hat was thrown back, his face as red as blood and as always he had a perspiring forehead.

"Look who's here, Dun Karm! *Benedixte*, Dun Karm! What's new?"

"Nothing new, Nin. Thank God that we aren't worse off."

"What's your opinion about our son's decision to emigrate? I still cannot believe it?"

"That's exactly what we're discussing. Let us put our trust in Christ! After all as I was telling his mother: where he's going is a land of prosperity; there are many Maltese there. Ninu is a good boy and he'll be well off. Most Maltese who emigrated to Australia became rich and we hope that Ninu makes a fortune too."

"Yes, Dun Karm, Ninu is a fine boy," replied Marjanna's husband "after all if he stayed in Malta he wouldn't have much of a future for himself or his family just like his eldest brother. He would live in poverty and raise several children. Isn't that so?"

"Only God knows that, Nin. However, if he had to do so he wouldn't be doing any harm. The only thing you have to look out for your children is that they don't become lazy because laziness breeds sin. As for the rest when children grow up, as your children have done you can only provide them with some sound advice. You can hardly interfere in their decisions more so when they take a decision in the right spirit. The last thing I would like to tell you before I leave, especially to you Nin: you should try to find some kind of work for Lippu. It doesn't matter where as long as he finds employment and stops roaming about the village."[37]

"Ask his mother, Dun Karm! Tell him, Marjann how many people I have contacted to secure some kind of employment for him! God knows!"

Dun Karm fairly raised his hand and lowered it, as if he wanted to tell Ninu: "Let me continue because I haven't quite finished yet."

" I' m sorry for interrupting you Dun Karm but that boy has given me a lot of trouble trying to find him work so that he would start contributing his share to the family finances."

"Not only that Nin. It's good that your son starts working to help his family financially but its necessary for him to decide what he wants to do with his life. Lippu has grown up and it doesn't befit him to lead a lazy life while all the young village people of his age have found employment.

"Another thing I wanted to tell you, lest I forget, since we're speaking about Lippu. Try to keep him away from Lonzu's tailoring shop where he can only learn how to play the guitar and how to swear. The last time I passed by Lonzu's shop they seemed to be having the time of their lives laughing and using foul language.

"As for the rest you know as much as I do that the friendship of a young man with a group of scatter-brains cannot do much good especially for an idle person like Lippu."

"You see Marjann. Dun Karm agrees with me! I have been telling her so for a long time, Dun Karm! I know what's going on and they also told me that Lippu has made Lonzu's shop his second home. He goes there frequently! I'll fix Lonzu for good. One of these days I'll turn up at his shop unexpectedly, give him and his wife a piece of my mind and slap Lippu in front of everybody."

"That's not the way, Nin. Don't shout," Marjann told him. "Don't get excited and instruct the children properly!" Then she turned on Dun Karm and told him: "Ninu believes everything people tell him. It's not true that Lippu visits Lonzu's house frequently. The truth is, that opposite Lonzu lives Ġanni ta' Warrabni[38] and since they don't see eye to eye, Ġanni is determined to ruin Lonzu. It was Ġanni who told Ninu that Lippu is frequently visiting Lonzu's house. Such a man is untrustworthy because he exaggerates things."

Ninu gave his wife an angry look but remained silent.

"Anyway," said Dun Karm while preparing to leave, "do your best to find him work. God created work and it's always better than laziness. Laziness is terrible because it leads to sin, I have to go."

"Are you leaving, Dun Karm? I hope that we meet again soon," said Ninu while he too stood up.

"Sure, Nin," replied Dun Karm and then he told him with half a smile: "Don't start quarrelling as soon as I leave! Goodbye and God bless you!"

"Goodbye, Dun Karm. Pray for us!" Marjann told him.

"We'll pray for each other," replied Dun Karm from the entrance.

XIV

It was a beautiful Maltese evening with a full moon.

The time was about nine o'clock and the moonlight flooded Ġammari Kanwara's yard which faced north.

On that quiet evening, the leaves in the flowerpots on the wall that gave on to the garden glittered under the moonlight. The carnations, which Vira had planted in the cracked large kneading pan, blossomed and filled the air with cloying sweetness.

Under that fine cloudless sky one could very well smell the scent emanating from the stacks of hay lying in the field rented from Nardu tal-Wardija. The field borders the alley lying behind Ġammari's house. That scent together with Vira's carnations and the orange blossoms in Wiġi l-Għawdxi's garden was more powerful than the finest scent that money could buy.

The door of the little room that gave on to the yard was wide open. Vira and Leli were sitting on the door step holding hands.

Rożi rested inside the room on a small low-lying bed located opposite the yard door. One hand rested behind her head on the pillow and the other hand hung loosely almost touching the floor.

Rożi looked thin and pale in the moonlight. It seemed that that face belonged to a dead person rather than to a young woman in the prime of life.

Ġammari's voice could be heard downstairs. He was at the front door speaking to one of his neighbours.

"Poor Roży, is so quiet, Lel. She must have fallen asleep. Nowadays that's what she does. One minute she's speaking to you, the next she falls asleep. At times she doesn't worry me at all!"

Vira stopped talking gazed at her sister for a while and then continued: "Why is it Lel that there are people like Roży who are born to spend the best part of their lives feeling miserable and then die young?"

"Who knows why, Vir? Who can understand life? For some it seems full of fun and happiness, for others full of sorrow and sadness. However, we fail to appreciate that, healthy people like us who have all that we desire often perceive other peoples' misfortunes as being even greater than what those poor souls can cope with. We believe that if we had to be in their place we would simply go mad. However when we find ourselves in trouble we adjust our lives accordingly."

At that moment Leli realized that Vira was looking sweetly at him completely fascinated by his words.

"You're such an intelligent person, Lel! I never grow tired listening to what you have to say! You're as knowledgeable as much as I'm ignorant. Tell me, Lel: what would I do if you had to fall ill or die? What a terrible thing!". Vira pressed Leli's arm and kissed it as she said those words.

Leli looked at Roży's bed and when he saw that she was still asleep, kissed Vira on the lips and caressed her hair.

"Do you think, Lel, that there are lovers who love one another more than us? Are there lovers like us who constantly think about one another? Believe me, Lel every night I think of you. I wake up and imagine your face before my eyes.

"Sometimes I long for you so much and feel so attracted to you that I feel sad. When this happens I say to myself: No, this isn't right, I love him so much that I don't deserve him. But then I ask myself: Why don't I deserve him? Am I to blame for being so attracted to him? Do you think Lel, that it is possible to love a person so deeply and share the rest of your life with him?"

Leli replied by kissing Vira passionately.

At that moment Roży took a long deep breath as she turned on the other side of the bed.

"Stop it Lel lest Roży wakes up or father comes upstairs." Vira immediately stood up, silently approached her sister's bed and whispered her name.

"What do you want, Vir?"

"Are you awake, Roż, my dear?"

"Yes,"

"Can I get you anything, Roż? Perhaps some tea or some barley water with milk?"

"Thank you, Vir. Get me anything you like as long as it is something to drink. I'm dying of thirst."

"Very well, Roż. I'll soon be back."

Vira left the room quickly and ran downstairs. Leli stood up and approached Roży's bed.

"Roż!"

"Yes, Lel. Are you still here?"

"Yes, Roż. Shall I get a candle from the staircase?"

"No, Lel, it's alright. The moonlight comforts me more. What a beautiful evening, Lel?"

"It cannot be more beautiful, Roż! It's really beautiful in the yard."

"It seems like an evening we read about in some novel. Isn't that so Lel?"

"I think so too."

Leli sat down at the end of the bed, near Roży's legs and both of them remained silent for some time.

After a while Roży said:

"Lel, I would like to read a beautiful novel. Some time ago Vira borrowed a novel entitled *Driegħ il-Mejta*[39] and we read it together. It was translated from Italian to Maltese. Whoever wrote it is a very good writer.

"I will get you a beautiful Maltese novel. More beautiful than the one you mentioned."

"Really, Lel?"

"Yes, Roż. And after you've read it I will fetch you an even more beautiful one."

"Thank you Lel. At times I grow tired wasting my time. Each day seems so long especially now that summer is approaching. What are the titles of the two books you are going to lend me.?"

"One of them is entitled *Is-Saħħar Falzun*[40] written by Levanzin and the other one called *Nazju Ellul* written by Muscat Azzopardi. Both of these books are written in very good Maltese, with a very good plot and set in a historical setting. These two novels rank amongst the best Maltese novels. They are different from the kind of novel you mentioned. Those kinds of novels are badly translated into Maltese."

"The novel which Vira and myself read is not of that type. You can ask Vira."

At that moment Vira entered the room.

"Sorry for taking so long, Roż"

"It doesn't matter, Vir. Isn't it true, Vir? I was just telling Leli how much we enjoyed reading *Driegħ il-Mejta*. Leli has promised to lend me two beautiful Maltese novels. One of them called *Is-Saħħar Falzun*, the other, what is it called Lel?"

"*Nazju Ellul*."

"Well done, Roż! If Leli told you they are beautiful to read, they must be so because Leli is well versed on the subject. I believe the English and Italian books you have must be very heavy going?"

"Not that heavy, Vir. I think you are quite capable of carrying six of them or more in one hand," said Leli with a smile.

Rożi laughed and Vira smiled too. Vira then told him:

"Did you know, Lel that at times I am jealous of your books especially when I realize your insatiable hunger for them? At other times I say to myself: It's a pity that Leli didn't pursue his studies! Just think Lel if you had to continue studying as Pawlu Sulnata did! If that were so you would be graduating as a doctor soon. Imagine me, Lel! Mrs. Vira, the doctor's wife, my, my! " With these words Vira placed her hands on her waist and walked up and down the room giving herself airs as proud women usually do. She then burst out laughing. Leli and Rożi laughed too.

"But how foolish can we get, Lel? As if, if you had to become a doctor you would marry Ġammari Kanwara's daughter! Obviously! You would certainly marry some rich and famous woman instead!"

"There is no sense in speaking or thinking in terms of "ifs" Vir. I am sorry for not pursuing my studies because I love studying and the time I spent at school was insufficient to learn new things. I certainly would not have continued my studies because of personal pride or find a better woman than you. For me you are the best."

"Don't be foolish, Lel! God forbid you had to learn more otherwise you would have gone mad because of those blessed books!"

"You know that you are saying something stupid, Vir. I should go crazy because I didn't continue my studies"

"If only I knew half the things you know!" interrupted Vira.

"I beg to differ Vir. I don't know anything compared to learned persons. I know that, even though I made much progress."

At that moment one could hear the front door closing.

"My father is closing the front door, my dear!"

"Sorry for staying so long, Vir"

"It's all right Lel! Let's go down before my father comes upstairs!"

"Goodbye Roż and good night."

"Goodbye, Lel! And don't forget the books you promised me."

XV

The wedding day of Ġanni ta' Kejla and Ċetta daughter of Ġari ta' Laħlaħ arrived.

It was the first Sunday after the feast of St. Philip. Relatives and friends arrived at Ġanni's and Ġari's house since early morning. Others went to Church.

All the guests attended the wedding mass especially since they wanted to hear Ċetta and Ġanni saying 'I do'.

Ġanni arrived at Church together with his father Franġisk il-Burdnar and his mother Lieni. Ġużè Snien who was to be his witness at the wedding accompanied him too, together with Anġlu ta' Kejla, husband of Anġla l-Għajjura.[41]

Anġla who was jealous of the bride was in a bad mood and almost quarrelled with her husband before they left the house.

She strutted into church like a turkey. She wore a faldetta over her head and kept her chin up like some Judge.

Her husband Anġlu winked at Ġanni and whispered to him: "Imagine if she were the groom's mother!" Ġanni forced a smile and looked the other way.

Ġanni seemed confused and on his way to church almost fell two or three times. Every time he blamed the new pair of shoes he was wearing.

The bride arrived in church together with her mother and relatives including her grandfather Karmnu ta' Nurat, some time after the groom.

The people who accompanied the bride and the bridegroom to church on their wedding day included Wenzu and Pawla ta' Seddaq, Karla and Toni ta' Saramni, Tona wife of Ġorġ tal-Ħanut, Fonz tat-Tabakk with his wife and son, Ċikku tal-Karozzin with his wife Anni and their children. About forty people in all.

Mid-day lunch was to be served at the groom's residence. The bride's mother made it clear that she did not have the money to pay for an elaborate wedding feast. Ġanni, on the other hand wanted to host a large wedding and invite as many guests as he could.

For this reason it was decided that the wedding feast would be the groom's responsibility. After all there was no harm in that especially since Ġanni was going to marry a girl whose father had died some time before. Furthermore the groom's parents were quite well off. In his days, the groom's father, Franġisk il-Burdnar, had made some money and owned the house he lived in. Hence it was only fair that he contributed financially to his son's wedding considering that the latter was going to marry a poor girl. That's what Ċetta and her mother believed.

"However, do you know why? Because the groom and his family happen to be good people." Anġla ta' Kejla told Mariroż il-Pećluqa.[42] "Speaking for myself, I wouldn't have pleased them and made life easy for them for taking away my son. Of course not!"

Although Ġanni was a sturdy young man and feared nothing he could hardly stand on his feet when the parish priest approached him and Ċetta to marry them. Ġanni was very excited and his knees knocked.

Unlike Ċetta. She was so calm. May God prevent her from the evil eye. Her face is crimson red and she presents a striking appearance. Just like her mother Żari. She kept her eyes fixed lovingly on Ġanni and the parish priest throughout the wedding ceremony.

Everybody congratulated the couple after the ceremony.

Several of them kissed Ċetta, including Lonza, Pawlu ta' Waħħaxni's girlfriend, who also whispered a joke in Ċetta's ear. Ċetta smiled and immediately turned her face the other way to thank others who were congratulating her.

Ċetta and Ġanni then left for home accompanied by their relatives and friends.

Ċetta looked ravishing. Her bosom, hands and fingers were covered in gold which however was no match to her alert black shining eyes and the smile on her face.

Ġanni looked shy although he was doing his best to hide his state of confusion.

When they arrived home, Ġanni was more at ease and immediately opened the bottles of rosolio. The guests clinked their glasses and drank to the couple's health. The children indulged themselves eating biscuits.

Then, the women changed into something more comfortable and started preparing lunch. No sooner said than done, three stoves were burning away and three large earthenware pots were placed on top of them. Each pot contained a beautiful chicken which Ġanni's mother had killed and plucked the day before to expedite cooking on the wedding day.

Everybody was very busy during that morning except for Ġużè Snien, who was Ġanni's friend who together with some other happy-go-lucky fellows played the guitar and invited some of the girls to sing.

It was great fun. The children shouted around Ġużè begging him to play *Sarafina* for them.

At around eleven Ġanni put on his jacket and went to the parish priest to find out why he was not present. The parish priest thanked him, but informed him that he was very busy and had to miss lunch.

Ġanni then went to ta' Braġ's house to fetch Leli. Both returned home after half an hour.

Leli at first was feeling shy but soon got used to the people and, after a couple of drinks, started talking volubly.

Ta' Kejla's house had a large yard. For this reason a table was set up in the middle of that yard. How was it possible to cater for all those people? It is true that half of the forty guests were children, however cooking for twenty adults was not a simple task.

At noon everybody sat at table and the food was served.

"Well done, Lien. This is excellent chicken broth." Ċikku tal-Karrozzin told Ġanni's mother.

Ġanni's mother didn't hear what Ċikku said, but Toni ta' Saramni who was sitting next to Ċikku replied:

"It is very good indeed! You should know that it took three chickens to produce such broth."

The bride's grandfather, Karmnu ta' Nurat, would spill the broth over his clothes every time he filled his spoon and put it in his mouth. Ġużè Snien who sat next to him laughed his heart out together with others surrounding Karmnu.

"Look at his moustache what a mess!"

"Ha, ha, ha!"

Ġużè ta' l-Imqarqaċ who was sitting next to Wenza, wife of Nikol l-Imfattar,[43] slapped his hand on Wenza's knee every time he spoke to her.

"If you do that to me one more time I shall tell my husband. What a disgusting person! Behave yourself!"

"I'm sure you're not that kind of person! Have you turned soft or what? Can't you take a joke?

❖ ❖ ❖ ❖ ❖

Ġanni wanted Leli to sit next to him at table. He did not take his eyes off Leli and, paid so much attention to what Leli was saying that he almost forgot all about the bride.

However, after wine was served the guests forgot all their troubles and made merry. When the sound of the guitar became louder, Ġanni gradually left Leli's side and stayed with the other guests drinking successive glasses of wine.

"Come on, my friends! Be happy! Forget all your troubles because tomorrow we might not be around. Then, let's drink to the newly weds!" Shouted Fonz tat-Tabakk, while standing up and raising his over-flowing glass of wine.

All the guests immediately stood up and did likewise. Somebody said: "Drink up Pepp, drink up Ġużepp, Mikiel, gulp down that wine because this is a wonderful evening."

"Of course I'll drink up, certainly," shouted Ġużè Snien. "If you're referring to me, just watch me gulping it down."

Although there was so much happiness and fun, Leli was out of his element. Everything he saw, heard, smelled, tasted or sensed made him sad and he was on tenterhooks to leave.

"Come on Anġ! Don't be shy and sing us a song!" Ġużè Snien told Anġla ta' Kejla. "What's the matter with you? Everybody happy and you're sad? Come near me and let us hear you sing."

"Certainly, Ġuż. Here I am. Did you think I was asleep? You were wrong if you thought so...I'll soon show you how alive I am."

Ġużè winked at Anġla's husband and told her:

"Anġ, these remarks are uncalled for! Is it possible that it's the wine that speaking?"

At this point everybody howled with laughter. Anġla pulled Ġużè's long hair and the latter took hold of his guitar and started playing. After a while he winked at Anġla and she started singing:

> "I planted a rose in a flower-pot,
> It was nibbled by a bird,
> Sometimes a wink or smile is sought,
> But that's the way love fared."

There was a lot of shouting, laughing and banging on the table until Anġla resumed her singing and everybody fell silent.

> *"My love has gone and left me,*
> *What shall I do to forget him?*
> *I'll find a man for all to see,*
> *And walk with him in the dim."*

"Very good, Anġ. Well done, Anġ! More, more, Ġuż!"
> *"I visit the seashore frequently,*
> *And there I'll go again,*
> *Because there my love waits patiently,*
> *Waving to me in vain."*

"There must be some truth in all this, Anġ! Ha, ha, ha!"
> *"Red lips inviting kisses,*
> *Sweet words full of devotion,*
> *Amongst all men and worldly bliss,*
> *He remains my love's potion."*

❖ ❖ ❖ ❖ ❖

When Anġla joined in the singing the matter became much more animated. Later, Pawla ta' Seddaq and Karla ta' Saramni joined the singing too. To make matters worse, Anni, wife of Ċikku tal-Karrozzin,[44] also wanted to sing. She forgot that it was past her age. For this reason she sang out of tune. Everybody laughed while Ġużè Snien told her:

"Excellent, Ann! You sound like a capon."

Anni felt disappointed and wanted to leave. However they persuaded her to stay.

Leli left quietly soon after. He told Ġanni that he had another appointment, and Ġanni unaware of what he was saying replied with a smile: "Very well, Lel. I hope to see you soon."

❖ ❖ ❖ ❖ ❖

The music and singing continued for some time after Leli left the wedding feast. All of a sudden, Wenza wife of Nikol l-Imfattar, lost her temper and slapped Ġużè l-Imqarqaċ with all her strength. She gave vent to her anger by calling him all kinds of names.

Wenza's husband hurried towards Ġużè and soon both men were rolling on the ground fighting fiercely.

However the men present got hold of them and separated them. The feast resumed after comforting Nikol and showing Ġużè the way out.

Ġużè's and Nikol's fighting spoiled most of the fun at the feast. Some of the guests stayed with Ġanni until it was time for the latter to return home together with his wife. Most of guests left for home tired and drunk. They thanked and wished the newly weds a long life together.

❖ ❖ ❖ ❖ ❖

"Do you realize Lel, that we have known each other for two months and we have never gone for a walk."

"Don't worry Dward, the time will come. However, not this evening."

"What's keeping you, Lel? Tomorrow is Sunday: you don't need to get up early for work. Furthermore, we will not stay out all night long. Until ten, perhaps? Just long enough to forget the silence that reigns in this village. That's what I told my father this week: I'm bored stiff with living in this village. What shall we do, Lel, have you decided to come or not? O, come on Lel! You'll enjoy yourself very much at the place I'll take you to."

"Believe me, Dward, I don't feel like coming. The family is rather upset since next week my brother is going to emigrate. For this reason I wouldn't like leaving my mother alone waiting up for me until very late in the evening."

Dwardu laughed his heart out.

"Forgive me, Lel but I have a different kind of mentality. When as a child I lived in Cairo, my father used to go abroad for a month or more. We wouldn't even notice that he would have left. My mother did the same thing and my uncle was a chip of the old block. Notwithstanding this we never cried or grew sad about such silly things! You Maltese are of different stock."

Leli was at a loss and felt humiliated by such words. However, he wanted to prove to Dwardu that he could make his own decisions. Finally, he accepted Dwardu's invitation to accompany him to Valletta to meet some girls. So, soon after the Ave Marija, Leli and Dwadu took a horse-driven cab to Valletta to spend some good time together.

❖ ❖ ❖ ❖ ❖

Dwardu Buqerq nicknamed 'Tal-Kajr' had been living in Ħaż-Żgħir together with his father for the past two months. He had finally succeeded in convincing Leli to accompany him to Valletta.

Dwardu was the same age as Leli. He was rather short and chubby. One could easily realize from the way he spoke that he had been raised abroad.

Initially when Dwardu and his father - Fredu Buqerq - came to live in Ħaż-Żgħir, the village people started asking questions about them. However, they came to know very little except that soon after Fredu left Cairo he and his children, Dwardu and Klara went to stay in Ħal-Kbir together with Fredu's brother. He lived in that village for two months and then he and his son rented a small house leaving Klara together with her uncle in Ħal-Kbir.

Although Fredu went daily to Valletta nobody knew his occupation and how he and his son managed to make a living.

When Fredu and Dwardu settled in Ħaż-Żgħir, Dwardu started frequenting the band club where he made friends with everyone. He was friendly, talkative and people took him to their hearts the way the Maltese usually do with strangers who come to live amongst them.

Although Dwardu Buqerq was only twenty-two years old he was as cunning as a fox. After some time he had started frequenting the band club, Dwardu realized that everybody esteemed Leli Braġ and therefore he did his best to become Leli's friend.

Leli fell into Dwardu's trap and helped him to find work with the Bućagħak Brothers for a small weekly wage.

Initially, Dwardu's task was to help Leli in book-keeping and to run errands when necessary. At that time Leli's brother started making the final preparations to emigrate and Leli tried to follow his brother's footsteps. However Leli never really made up his mind about the matter and ended by dropping the idea completely.

Dwardu obviously encouraged Leli to emigrate, as his intention was to take over Leli's work if the latter decided to live overseas. Dwardu had tried deceiving Leli even though he had known him for a few weeks.

However, Dwardu failed in this first attempt.

❖ ❖ ❖ ❖ ❖

Leli and Dwardu arrived at the village when the church clock had just struck eleven. Dwardu was as drunk as a lord and so was Leli.

They went their separate ways after hugging each other and shaking hands.

However when he returned home, he realized what he had been through. He pretended to be sober when his mother asked him why he was so late. All of a sudden he became very sad and remembered awful things. He collapsed on a chair, took hold of his mother by the hand, pulled her next to him, rested his head against her waist and wept bitterly.

XVII

Ġammari, as his daughter Vira used to say, was a very busy man. He was a restless person at home too.

He kept some tools at home of which he was particularly fond.

He was very proud of those tools and anyone who removed anything and failed to return it in its proper place would live to regret it.

One evening Ġammari was below the staircase, one leg resting on the floor and the other leg resting against a piece of wood on top of a box. In his right hand he held a big saw. Leli and Vira sat on the first step watching him with a smile on their faces.

"Really, Lel; believe me! I would be very worried if I lose one of my tools! I told Vira many times not to lend any of them. I had three handsaws. This is the only remaining one. I had an excellent handsaw somewhat smaller than this one. But it disappeared as well!"

Leli smiled, nodded and remained silent.

"But, father." said Vira, "what can I do? If a neighbour asks me to borrow one of your tools, what shall I tell him? If I say so he will realize that I'm lying."

"Of course you'll say: no! That's what you should say!" replied her father angrily.

"Make sure that henceforth, you don't lend anything that belongs to me. Whoever wants to borrow something will have to ask me first. Do you understand?"

At that moment Roži could be heard calling from upstairs.

"Coming, Roż." Vira went upstairs near her sister.

"What do you want Roż?"

"Vir, perhaps you can ask Leli whether he would be able to read to me this evening or will he be too tired to do so?"

"Sure, my dear; let me call him."

Leli went upstairs and entered Roži's small room.

"Lel," Vira told him with a smile, "there is some work for you to do."

"Can it be possible?"

"Roži told me to ask you whether you feel like reading to her another piece from *Is-Saħħar Falzun*."

Roži looked at Leli from her bed where she was lying fully clothed and she gave him a smile.

"Who, me tired? Even if I was tired, I am never tired enough to read!"

"I told you that Leli would refuse reading to you!" Vira told her sister with a smile.

"Where is the book, Roż?" asked Leli.

"Here it is, Lel." Roży pulled out the book out from under her pillow and handed it over to him.

"You see, Roż, how much Leli loves you? He loves you more than he loves me! Instead of staying outside for some fresh air, he came upstairs to read to you."

Roży looked at her sister, and smiled at her without saying anything.

Leli started leafing through the book, which he had read some three years before. However, he immediately recognized the passages in that book which he liked best. He now came across a passage which he had enjoyed very much reading.

"Roż! Vir! Listen to this passage; let me read it out to you so that you'll be able to appreciate the beautiful writing contained in this book!"

Leli started reading the following:

"The Mġarr of Gozo is an enchanting harbour! Surrounded with impressive hills, cliffs and valleys that look wonderful especially when the sweet silvery rain sprinkles over them in the moonlight as it did that evening. Kemmuna very quiet and sad looking. Beyond it, Marfa seemed like some impregnable fortress resting after furious fighting. Ras it-tafal on one side, iż-Żewwieqa with its Blata l-Bajda on the other and l-Għolja tan-Nadur and Qabar-il Għarib behind it create a magnificent scene full of love and natural beauty. Its not surprising that Calypso chose to live on this Island! Everything was buried in deep reverie, such heavenly bliss accompanied by the sound of spring running water amidst the rustle of the leaves and the sound of the rushing waves on the sandy shore. It is within nature's embracing arms that one tends to forget the sorrow of life!"

"Beautiful writing, Don't you agree?" said Leli as if speaking to himself.

Vira as usual agreed with Leli while Roży asked him:

" But, Lel, we still haven't reached that stage you just read, no?"

"Of course, Roż. However, as I was going through the pages I came across this passage and since I liked it the first time I read it I felt like sharing it with you. Didn't you like it Roż?"

"Certainly, Lel. However, what I like best in novels are those romantic passages like the ones we have been reading so far. Although I grow sad reading about trouble and difficulties between two lovers, however it's hard for me to explain: it seems as if that same sorrow generates within me a tender feeling "

Leli smiled while Vira's eyes were filled with tears.

"Lel, my dear, if you permit me, I am going downstairs to prepare something to eat for my father. I will take some time, Lel. Do you need anything, Roż?"

"No, Vir; nothing for the time being."

"It's alright, Vir," Leli told her, "you needn't hurry."

Vira went downstairs and Leli sat down on a chair next to Roży's head.

"Lel, I believe you get annoyed reading to me, isn't that true?" asked Roży sweetly.

"Of course not, Roż! I love reading."

And immediately Leli started reading.

After a while Roży stopped him.

"Tell me, Roż?"

"Lel, don't think that I'm an importunate person but do you mind reading again the passage we read last time! You know which one? The first time Ħażan and Kolina met."

Leli laughed. "You liked that passage, didn't you?"

"Won't you read it again to me, Lel?"

"Certainly, Roż and gladly too."

Roży, moved to the edge of the bed to listen to Leli reading her favorite passage. She sat up on the bed, with her elbow touching the wall and her head resting on the palm of her hand. She was so close to Leli that some locks of her hair caressed his arm.

Leli started reading again and she listened to him carefully.

Having listened to him reading for quite a long time, Roży gradually grew tired and hence she rested her head against Leli's shoulder.

At that moment Leli was in the middle of a sweet and exciting passage which Roży referred to as Hażan's and Kolina's first encounter. Leli continued reading the following:

"Lost as he was in these cruel thoughts with his eyes fixed on the first step, Hażan did not realize that Kolina had climbed down the stairs. He glanced furtively. She startled him as she approached him silently.

"Kolina immediately broke the silence. She looked confused but had a sweet smile. Then, in a soft and trembling voice, she told him: "You're still here, Hażan? Where are you going?" She fixed her beautiful eyes on him. Her look helped him to regain his senses. He realized that he was not imagining things. "Believe me I don't know," he replied in a muffled voice. He lowered his eyes and blushed then he said: "I was instigated by my folly and the love I bear for you!"

"Kolina's eyes were filled with tears. She almost fainted as she experienced love for the first time. She caressed his shoulder with her soft hand. Then, she told him: "Don't worry Hażan, you're not suffering alone!". She then hurried upstairs.

" Hażan was an intelligent young man. He was deeply in love, and followed her, when he realized that Kolina was running away from him and that he was unable to share his sorrow with her.

"Kolina was filled with fear. How could she send him away if she had gone to look for him? Shocked and excited her feet became numb. For this reason she rested on an armchair which was on the landing.

" Hażan immediately knelt down, hid his face in his hands which he rested on her lap and wept bitterly. He was unable to express his feelings. Kolina too was stunned. She was excited and pale and was in a pitiful state. She simply caressed his disheveled curly jet-black hair that covered his head and forefront"

When Leli saw that Roży was trembling all over he stopped reading. He immediately raised her head from his shoulder and when he looked at her he noticed that her face was covered with tears.

"Roży. What's the matter with you? If you cry I won't read any further."

"Lel!"

"Yes, Roż."

"Kiss me, Lel!"

Leli was surprised by these words. Roży's unexpected reaction left him speechless.

"Don't go away, Lel! I don't want you to kiss me like Hażan kissed Kolina like you kiss Vira but as if you were my brother. Don't be afraid, Lel! If Vira had to see you, she wouldn't take it against you . You know that I'll soon die! Kiss me, Lel!"

Feeling very confused Leli put his lips against Roży's cheek and kissed her quickly. Roży did not let him move away. She turned her arms around his neck and while she placed her face against his whispered:

"Why wasn't I as lucky as the rest? How happy they are, alas, and they don't know it." After resuming her original position she, continued saying: "Forgive me Lel, if I made you feel uncomfortable! However, I didn't do anything wrong, did I? Lel, how much I would have liked you to be my brother!"

Leli didn't say anything but caressed her hair and sweetly touched her repeatedly on her shoulder. After a while he stood up, removed the book from his hand and the two pillows from behind Roży's head. He turned them over again and put them back in their place. He then laid Roży down like a baby and whispered:

"For today it's better if we stop here, what do you think, Roż? You look tired."

"Yes, Lel. Thank you. Now go downstairs so that you can have a smoke! Lel."

"What do you want my dear?"

"Nothing."

Leli pressed her hand and left her bedside. He stopped in the middle of the small room, looked at her for the last time, drew a deep breath and went straight downstairs.

❖ ❖ ❖ ❖ ❖

That night Leli couldn't sleep. He couldn't forget Roži's shining eyes and couldn't decide whether these sparkled out of love or out of sorrow.

He kept tossing and turning and changing the position of his pillow several times. A fresh thought would assail him and make him shift his position in bed.

Finally he managed to fall asleep. Whilst sleeping he dreamt that he was seeing Roži in a garden full of white flowers. Her clothes were as white as snow. Her face kindled with happiness and her form seemed to belong to a different world.

A handsome young man stood next to her.

Roži looked sweetly at that young man from time to time.

However, Leli seemed to notice that Roži's facial expression changed suddenly. At that moment the young man picked the most beautiful blossom from the rose bush closest to them.

"Lel!" he heard Roži calling him rather angrily. "Why choose that particular blossom? Why did you manage to pick a budding blossom?"

Leli saw the young man raising his head. He gave Roži a sweet and pitiful look whilst replying:

"You don't know the reason why! I alone know why!"

XVIII

Certain types of illness are terminal.

Medical treatment together with the care and love of those who look after these types of patients can help to prolong life but they cannot help them recover for good from such terrible maladies.

Tuberculosis ranks amongst the first on the list of incurable diseases.

It is a deceiving malady. Although the patient and those who love him continue to hope for recovery the damage within the patient is significant and leads to death.

Roži ta' Kanwara was unfortunate to be touched by such a disease.

Her father did his best to help his daughter recover her health. He was even prepared to die for her.

However, it was all in vain, Roży died, after so many years and months hoping that she would live.

It was the last time she had smiled at her father, her sister and Leli. However hers was an unhappy smile. It was the smile of a young person longing for life but who realized that it was time for her to die.

When Roży died she looked happy and peaceful.

❖ ❖ ❖ ❖ ❖

Her father missed her and nothing could comfort him. The loss of his daughter was too much for him, greater than the death of his wife.

Vira missed her too. For Vira, Roży was not only her sister but also her greatest friend. Leli missed Roży as if she was his sister.

The whole village mourned Roży's death. How is it possible not to feel sorry at the death of a young man or woman?

However, there were others, who wondered whether Roży's death had ruined for good Vira's chances of ever getting married.

Those kind of people ensured that Leli's mother came to know about this. On her part Leli's mother replied:

"Such things don't worry me! It wouldn't be fair if I were to encourage Leli to break off his engagement at this stage. God's will be done! Vira is a healthy person and so is her family."

Nobody said a word to Leli. He had learnt a lot on the subject by reading Mantegazza's beautiful and didactic novel *A Day in Madejra*. That work provided him with all the advice he required.

He analyzed the situation and said in his heart of hearts: "Roży had tuberculosis not because she inherited the disease from her parents therefore, I needn't worry."

Leli also discussed the matter with his mother. He could imagine that some villagers would have already spoken to her concerning the subject. However, he didn't want his mother to bring up the subject before he did.

His mother concurred with Leli's line of thought.

"My son! What is done is done! Your responsibility is to marry Vira at the appropriate time."

"No, mother! That's not the way to look at things! My responsibility is to marry her because she's healthy and because I love her. However, notwithstanding how much I love her I would never marry her if I knew that my children would suffer because of her state of health.

"That's the reason why I read books, mother; to learn. This is one of the greatest lessons I learnt from reading books."

XIX

One day towards the end of summer of 1913, Ninu ta' Braġ together with other Maltese emigrants left for Australia via Naples.

On that day all Ninu's friends and relatives arrived to bid him farewell, and wish him luck and a safe journey to Australia.

Ninu had visited his aunt Dolor twice during the last weeks he spent in Malta. However on the day of Ninu's departure to Australia she could not bear staying at home.

For this reason at about nine o'clock she got dressed, hailed a horse-driven cab and went to her brother's house in Ħaż-Żgħir.

As soon as she entered her brother's house and came face to face with Ninu, she started crying and kissing him.

"Why did you have to do it, tell me? Why did you have to bring all this sorrow in your father's house?"

"What are you saying, Aunt? You wouldn't have made all this fuss if I were going to my death or to spend some twenty years in prison! You wait and see what I'm going to send you from Australia!"

"Don't talk nonsense, my son. Make sure of avoiding bad company and everything else that may cause you harm. Furthermore, don't think of marrying unless you are well-off! " After Dolor had finished with her advice to Ninu she turned her face to speak to his mother who up to that moment hadn't uttered a word.

"Marjann would it be pointless if I asked whether you provided him with a holy medal? I brought him this." Dolor immediately took out a small gold chain from her handbag. A small cross of blackish colour was attached to that chain.

"Here, Nin! Be sure to wear this round your neck always! That cross is very dear and will deliver you from every evil."

"Thank you, Aunt."

After several other warnings, it was time for Dolor to leave. She didn't want to stay although Marjann repeatedly invited her to spend the rest of the day with them. "I certainly don't want to see him leave!" said Dolor. "If that happens I will drop dead! No! No! No!"

After she and Ninu kissed each other good bye, Dolor left her brother's house sobbing and excited, her face washed with tears. She spent the rest of the day weeping over the loss of her beloved Ninu.

❖ ❖ ❖ ❖ ❖

The Braġ brothers became more of a family as they grew up. For this reason on the day that Ninu was leaving the Island, Leli and Lippu stayed at home. Their father remained at home too and spent the day pacing up and down the stairs. Although he was sad because he was going to be separated from his son, he was on tenterhooks to see him departing in peace. He said in his heart of hearts: "It would be better if he leaves straightaway before some trouble crops up."

Marjann spent the day busy packing Ninu's clothes and underwear as well as some other things, which Ninu required to take with him. Everytime she found herself alone, her lips would tremble and she would secretly wipe away a tear.

Between packing and running other errands, Marjann had also to find a way to meet those people who came to her house to wish her son a safe journey.

Vira helped in this respect. She knew that Marjann needed

assistance on a day like that and for this reason she stayed at Leli's house.

Vira had started visiting her fiancès house since the time her sister died. The Braġ family respected her as she was a kind and friendly person.

❖ ❖ ❖ ❖ ❖

At noon they sat down to have lunch but they had lost their appetite.

Dun Karm ta' Rużanni and soon after Kelin visited them in the afternoon amongst many others. Both of them stayed until it was time for Ninu to leave.

Ċikku tal-Karozzin arrived immediately after sunset, and as soon as he saw Ninu's father at the door of the side room he told him, "Here I am, Sir. There's no hurry! I'll wait as long as necessary."

Ċikku's arrival was the first blow she received. She realized that it was time to be separated from her son.

Separation from one's dear ones is a terrible thing! Such instances are among the most difficult in life.

A mother's separation from her son, can be the most heart-rending experience of all. That moment is amongst the worst a woman has to pay for becoming a mother and is almost equivalent to when a mother loses one of her children.

"Nin...my son, are you leaving me? Let me kiss you again, Nin, because I' don't know whether I'll see you again as long as I live! O dear! Lord! Deliver this sinner from such a terrible moment! "

The eyes of all those who were present except for Kelin and Dun Karm were filled with tears.

Kelin whilst repeatedly touching Marjann on her shoulder told her with his strong voice:

"Forgive me for intruding. However, that's not the proper way, Marjann! It takes a bit of courage. After all your son is making a difficult decision. He is thinking about his future. God willing, when he becomes a man, you and your husband shall bless the moment your son decided to seek his fortune elsewhere."

Dun Karm too sought to comfort her. He had a determined look on his face yet in a trembling voice he told her:

"Pray, Marjann, and pluck up courage as other mothers who have passed through the same experience have done before you. You, Nin, my son, if you have to go why hang on? Remember that you still have to go to the harbour in Valletta."

"I'm going, Mother! Good bye and pray for me! Bless me, mother!"

"God bless you my son!" And may God give you a safe journey and deliver you from every evil! Keep that holy medal I gave you in remembrance of me!"

"Good bye, father!"

"You're going, Nin? Good bye, my son and God bless you!"

"Bless me, Father!"

"God bless you and may He grant you all that you wish! Good bye Keep close to your Faith! Remember that you're a Christian and you should behave like one every where you are."

"Good bye, Vir. Good bye Sir. Good bye everybody."

"Good bye Nin; we wish you luck and happiness."

"May God grant you a safe journey."

❖ ❖ ❖ ❖ ❖

Some time later, Ninu accompanied by his brothers and Nardu ta' Filumen (a very good friend of Ninu's) was already some distance away from his little village where he was born and bred. However, he still felt at home given that his friend and brothers accompanied him.

It was a different story for his parents, especially for his mother given that mothers are generally more attached to their children than men.

At that instance, although surrounded by relatives and friends all doing their best to comfort them, Ninu's parents were experiencing moments of grief which every parent passes through as a result of their children.

❖ ❖ ❖ ❖ ❖

About two hours after sunset - it was pitch dark - the ship carrying Ninu pulled up its anchors and gradually moved away from the quay until it went out of Grand Harbour. A few minutes later, Leli, Lippu and Nardu who were on a boat in the middle of the harbor could only recognize the flickering lights vanishing gradually.

On board the ship, Ninu together with the other Maltese passengers were looking at Malta for the last time. They could only see some kind of a shadow in the middle of the sea with a few lights twinkling here and there.

As the ship moved further away from those lights the passengers' grief knew no bounds. They knew that they had left their loved ones there, a wife and children, parents, friends in other words they had left their homeland and their memories.

However that's life! And whether one likes it or not, sometimes it is necessary for a person to pluck up courage and do what he has to do and seek a living in a foreign land.

XX

"I haven't found work yet, mother but I hope to find employment soon. After all I haven't been here long? Less than two weeks .

"I am living with a very nice family. They are very friendly! And since I can speak good English they have taken a liking to me.

"How is father? And my brothers?

"I have sent a letter to aunt too telling her mostly what I'm writing to you

"You cannot imagine the size of the town I'm living in! There aren't too many Maltese since the majority of the Maltese coming here are farmers and therefore seek employment outside towns.

"At the moment I cannot explain my feelings. I'm so impressed as if I'm out of my element. How tiny Malta is! We lag behing and cannot imagine the kind of world we're living in until we emigrate to larger countries!

"Pray for me so that I can find work soon and be able to refund the money to my aunt who helped to get here. Secondly to help you financially"

This first letter from her son put Marjann's mind at rest. Everybody was pleased with that letter. First they read it together than individually.

"He'll make a fortune there!" said his father while feeling extremely happy that his son had arrived in Australia safe and sound.

Lippu was struck by Ninu's wishes to Nardu ta' Filumen. "You'll see how happy Nardu will be! He hasn't forgotten him! And Nardu is prepared to join Ninu as soon as he has sufficient money to pay for the voyage."

After Leli read Ninu's letter several times he said: "You see mother, it's just like I always said! And he's been there for only a few days! Later on he will be able to realize how disadvantaged we are!"

"You're not up to something are you?"

Leli looked at his mother, smiled and told her:

"No, mother. I'm not going to leave you for the time being."

BOOK THREE

THE STRUGGLE

SECTION ONE

The year was 1914. The events that took place that year and in subsequent years made it one of the worst years in the history of mankind.

Maltese people, like other people in the rest of the world, little knew what was in store for them. The villagers of Ħaż-Żgħir knew even less.

Ħaż-Żgħir at the beginning of 1914 still enjoyed peace and tranquillity. Aspects which characterized Maltese life prior to the blood bath of 1914.

The villagers of Ħaż-Żgħir in the early part of that year lived and spent their time as their ancestors did. Like their forefathers they believed that better times would prevail because "if the situation persists, we'll starve to death" they would say to one another.

After all this was everybody's wish because unemployment at that time was rampant.

As for the rest nothing much had changed in Ħaż-Żgħir.

Ġorġ the shopkeeper – true to form! – is constantly spreading rumours. At the time the Italians were fighting the Arabs of Tripoli he fabricated the story that there would soon be full employment in Malta. He argued that the Italian Government would offer skilled and unskilled Maltese workers employment in Tripoli. Recently, he also suggested that workers were required in Turkey and that it would be a good idea to emigrate to Constantinople.

Whenever Kelin happened to be in a good mood he would laugh at Ġorġ. On other times he would swear at him.

Dun Karm and Ružanni were always the same. Dun Karm always had a sad face, spoke little, got thinner every day and comforted peoples' hearts wherever he went.

In these last two years his mother's health had deteriorated and she wasn't able to do anything.

There were times when Dun Karm had to look after her as if she was a baby.

However, Dun Karm loved his mother very much and wanted to take care of her single-handed. A person needs to love somebody and Dun Karm besides God and Our Lady had nobody to love except his mother. Recently, Ninu ta' Braġ had sent him a letter from Australia and although he was pleased to learn about Ninu he was somewhat disappointed when he read that Ninu was still unemployed. In his letter Ninu complained that in Australia there is work for farmers rather than for other skilled workers. "*However*," continued Ninu "*there it is rumoured that there will be work towards Spring. God forbid if it wouldn't be so...*" Dun Karm did not say anything about Ninu to Marjann and he did the right thing. At that moment Marjann was concerned about Leli.

Whereas previously he used to be always cheerful nowadays he would become moody as soon as he arrived home.

"What's the matter with you, Lel? Why is it my dear that you're always sad?"

"Who told you that I'm sad? Lately everybody dislikes me. He did the right thing, he made a complete break."

Frequently his mother would just let him talk. What else could she do? Leli had become a man and it would have been silly of her to get angry with her son because he arrives home sad.

However Leli's mother was not deceived. Leli had changed a lot lately but this change was most evident when he was at his girlfriend's or mother's house.

Leli was going through a particular period of time which every young man experiences. It was a time when Leli wanted to be free. However, Leli had grown up within a strict Christian environment and for this reason he learnt to control himself when life tempted him most.

At times the need to act like a man and the temptations of youth find themselves in direct conflict with each other.

The turmoil within him was one of the reasons why Leli had become so moody.

It was impossible for him to marry for the time being. How could he marry if he received a wage of less than one Maltese Lira a week?

It wasn't that Leli gave the Buċagħak Brothers one Maltese Lira worth of work in return. Of course not! The opposite is more likely! His employers were in the habit of receiving more and paying out less.

"Father, for God's sake, it's not Leli's fault. Leli is doing his best to improve his conditions of work," Vira would tell her father whenever the latter asked her whether Leli had made up his mind to marry her. "He works late at night and is furthering his education so that he would be well-qualified when and if the opportunity arises. However Leli, like myself is an unlucky person."

"Alright my dear," her father would reply. "However, you shouldn't be left alone. If your engagement is prolonged any further I will have to ask your aunt Pawla to come and stay with us for some time until you marry.

"And, another thing, Vir; until this situation persists you need to change the habit of staying indoors. It's not right that since your engagement you never went out of the house. Your health has deteriorated, you were such a handsome girl I curse the moment you started thinking about marriage!"

Ġammari was not to blame for complaining. He was a quiet person but he knew what his responsibilities were. However, he would do anything for his daughter Vira and it can be said that he left her at liberty to do whatever she pleased. He also realized that people gossiped about his daughter especially when it was evident that she was engaged and stayed at home alone!

The idea of asking Pawla to come and spend some days with them was Dun Karm's doing.

Dun Karm had told Ġammari that it would have been better if until such time that Vira and Leli got married, he would bring someone to live with them. Ġammari was in total agreement with Dun Karm and thought of asking his wife's sister - a spinster called Pawla - to come and live with them for some time.

Dun Karm didn't speak only to Ġammari but he also spoke to Ninu ta' Braġ and his wife. He was of the opinion that Leli should marry Vira as soon as possible.

Leli's father did not like the idea of encouraging his son to marry quickly. "Why all this hurry," he told his wife after Dun Karm left their house. "They will have time to marry!"

When Marjann spoke to Leli about the matter, he seemed confused as if he didn't understand what she was saying.

After a while he replied: "No, mother! I had no intention of marrying soon."

"You don't understand, my son! Do you know the reason why I'm asking you? Because it's my responsibility to encourage you to marry. Neither you nor Vira are children any longer. You're growing up, time is pressing and you need to decide what you're going to do with your lives! Pray to God so that He may help you decide and assist you in your work. Go and live with the person you love and we shall bless you both."

II

Time passed and Leli remained undecided as to what he should do.

Other events took place, which prolonged Leli's marriage to Vira. Therefore, Ġammari decided to invite Pawla, his wife's sister to go and live with them.

Leli passed most of his time at work and a few hours at his girlfriend's house. Sometimes he would arrive home from work and find his girlfriend there. After speaking to them he would visit the band club. There he would forget all his worries and when he returned home Vira would have left his mother's house a long time before.

In fact the visit to the band club had become a daily habit with Leli.

At that time he seldom met his childhood friend Pawlu Sulnata. Pawlu was about to become a doctor and he had little time to waste. His only interest was his studies.

Dwardu Buqerq had replaced Pawlu as Leli's friend and he accompanied Leli everywhere.

However, there was something in Dwardu's behaviour, which made Leli suspicious of that person.

Leli believed that Dwardu, notwithstanding his compliments, was a dishonest person. In brief, Leli thought that Dwardu would not hesitate to deceive his best friends if it suited him. Dwardu would harm his friends with no qualms of conscience.

Moreover, before Dwardu Buqerq arrived in Ħaż-Żgħir, Leli used to feel at ease when talking to some of his best friends at the band club. Something, which he no longer enjoyed doing.

Dwardu felt uncomfortable, whenever he approached Leli and his friends. In this respect Leli compared himself to a person in a dark room who although unable to see anything could sense that there was someone lurking in that room watching him.

This situation very often confused Leli so that he would generally cut short his discussion as soon as Dwardu approached.

Leli realized that there must be something wrong with him, that something was wrong in his head.

Leli strengthened his belief when at times he reflected on what the villagers referred to as 'Leli's exceeding kindness'. Recently, Leli had come to regard this particular characteristic as some kind of illness.

❖ ❖ ❖ ❖ ❖

It was generally agreed that Leli was a very pleasant man to talk to. He listened to what other people had to say and at times he pre-empted what the other person was about to tell him.

Although Leli always treated other people with the utmost regard he didn't have it in him to confront any person who would be taking him for a ride or deceiving him.

Something told him that success in life was not for cowards like him.

Leli felt that he wasn't as good as the rest. Something restrained him from developing his talents, from speaking up when he was unsure of himself or when he happened to be in the company of other people enjoying better social standing.

However, as our elders used to say, in this life one thing compensates for another and there's some good in everything. Leli regretted being so shy and losing out to other people at work even though he was a learned young man. He felt upset if somebody contradicted him in what he said and blushed if somebody praised him. Notwithstanding this he consoled himself when he remembered that the villagers held him in high esteem rather than despising him for being such a kind and shy person.

However, for Leli this was not enough. Leli knew that to succeed in life he needed more than that. He had to overcome his deficiencies. But, he felt that he did not have the courage to change.

One day, while he was at Kelin's house to return a book he had borrowed they started discussing Leli's career prospects. Kelin asked Leli whether it was in his interest to continue in his present employment for such a small wage.

Leli replied that he was doing his best to find better work however he had not met with much success yet.

At this point Kelin told him: "Lel, to succeed in life you have to fight. You won't succeed if you don't have the courage to fight and wait for luck to smile upon you! You will remain stuck were you are even if you're as wise as Solomon. Quite frankly you are one of the best young men I have ever met. You are a very intelligent person and at times you amaze me seeing you reading and understanding books written by famous authors. However, notwithstanding your intelligence you have one great fault. You're too timid! And besides, you're too nice a person both in your words and in your behaviour with others.

"If this condition reflects your childhood then your parents are to blame.

"My son, you're not a woman and too much tenderness is only good for women!

"You should take a tougher attitude towards life. This is as essential for you as much as reading and learning are, if not more. You won't get far simply by reading books and becoming wiser. You must start thinking about improving your earnings. This is only fair as it would do justice to your widespread knowledge. As I have already told you don't be too nice with everybody. There are several people in this world who certainly don't merit being treated with gloves.

"What I'm trying to tell you is to open your eyes to reality mainly because it's time for you to stand up to your rights unless you want to lag behind the others. Lel, I know you well enough to understand how your mind works. I have also suffered in my life and I know the ways of the world.

"Remember what I told you Lel. Please understand that the tougher you are the better you get on with people and the easier life becomes. Furthermore you'll suffer less by not being too good and too shy.

"Did you get the message, Lel? Don't think that I'm telling you this to ridicule you. I'm telling you this for your own good and because I love you as if you were my son!"

❖ ❖ ❖ ❖ ❖

The kind of books which Leli read since the time he had befriended Kelin also started influencing the way he thought.

Leli also purchased his own books besides the ones he borrowed from Kelin. These included works that tend to confuse peoples' way of thinking unless they possess sufficient knowledge to understand them properly. Leli also loved reading books dealing with history and archaeology.

Leli understood some of those books. Other books were too difficult for him and sometimes he read a passage several times in an attempt to understand it.

Leli never shared the ideas he obtained from those books with his friends and relatives. Furthermore symptoms in his behaviour indicated that he wasn't taking his religious obligations seriously. He only went to church for a short time on Sunday to hear mass.

Leli had not yet lost his Faith completely. However, he was going through a crisis of conscience whether to embrace or abandon the Faith in which he had been brought up. This is the greatest battle a person has to face.

It was in this rather silent but turbulent dilemma that Leli found himself in towards the beginning of summer 1914. His mother noticed that Leli was often sad and pensive.

His behaviour with Vira was likewise but the latter kept her peace and didn't ask him what was the matter with him. She always sought to speak to him sweetly and gently not to scare him away. Through her approach Vira succeeded in making Leli forget all about his sorrow and mental confusion.

III

Towards the end of July 1914 the terrible news regarding the outbreak of war had also reached Malta. What everybody feared would happen was about to become reality.

Some two or three weeks before, Leli took a day's leave from work. Soon after dawn, he drank a cup of coffee, placed in his pocket the newspaper that he had bought the day before and left home to spend some time at Nardu tal-Wardija. There, he lay on some straw in the eye of the sun, happily watching Nardu and his children treshing sheaves of corn.

While he lay on the ground something told him that although a farmer's work is difficult and tough it remains an attractive job. "Who knows" thought Leli, "how many farmers at this very moment throughout the world are working hard like Nardu and his children to provide people with another essential for man's survival?"

Finally he remembered that he had with him the previous

day's newspaper. He took it out of his pocket and when he opened it and was about to start reading he came across an article that captured his attention. The article stated that in the little Serbian town of Sarajevo, a young man named Gabriel Prinkip shot and killed Archduke Frances Ferdinand, heir to the Austrian throne, and his wife.

❖ ❖ ❖ ❖ ❖

Following this, other worrying news about the war reached Malta. Towards the end of July, Britain warned Germany to respect the treaty of 1839, which guaranteed the neutrality of Belgium. If Germany disregarded that treaty than Britain would wage war against it!

News continued reaching the Islands throughout the month of August. Everybody was speculating about what was going to happen next.

Finally on 4th August 1914, Britain declared war on Germany.

Alliances were formed and ultimatums given. Britain and with it the other nations constituting the Great Empire moved into war. Every country prepared for war. One of the worst wars in human history. A struggle that left nine million dead!

❖ ❖ ❖ ❖ ❖

Some people are pleased at a time when distress is wide spread. This may seem strange but it is true. People, similar in character to Leli generally experience that kind of feeling.

It frequently happens that knowledge about some bad news can have a kind of healing effect on that kind of person. This very often takes place in people who have passed through a difficult period in their life. Leli was going through such a phase in his life before the outbreak of the Great War.

To start with, the changes that Malta experienced from day one of the war were sufficient for people to forget their personal worries and direct their thoughts to speculating about what was going to happen next.

Indeed, the unstable political situation abroad gave the confused minds of the local population something to think about. Malta was one of those few fortunate countries that remained unharmed by the atrocities of war. Malta didn't suffer any bombardments neither were its buildings destroyed however many Maltese shed their blood in military campaigns then. At the beginning of the war, the Maltese were in a better position than other countries to analyze how the war progressed.

Moreover, the war brought economic prosperity to these Islands! That's the way life goes. The latin proverb says: *Mors tua vita mea*.*

The Island enjoyed full employment. Unskilled people joined either the army or the navy while some of those young men who the people criticized and considered as cowards demonstrated great courage that amazed the bravest of men. They showed their gallantry on Belgian and French soil, on the rocks of Gallipoli and in the Arabian deserts.

Other men, worthy sons of Maltese mariners renowned throughout the Mediterranean and beyond its shores, died at sea battles such as the notorious Battle of Jutland.

IV

Malta had witnessed the emergence of several extortionists who took advantage of the situation caused by the war since its commencement. They profited out of other peoples' misery to enrich themselves and increase their personal wealth.

The Buċagħak brothers with whom Leli was employed were of that stock.

For the Buċagħak brothers war meant financial prosperity. They enjoyed economic prosperity for four years. Money made at the expense of other peoples' blood!

Buċagħak's warehouses were replete with food provisions then. When the Buċagħak brothers realized the possibility of an

---

**One man's meat is another man's poison.*

outbreak of war they bought whatever they could lay their hands on. Once commodities became scarce they sold their goods with an excellent profit margin.

Notwithstanding the profits they reaped from their sales they failed to increase their employees' wages! They didn't even give a small raise in pay to Leli and Dwardu who were extremely busy due to the workload!

For more than two months after the war started, Leli's and Dwardu's wages remained the same. Both employees knew when they started work in the morning but they had no guarantee about the time they would stop working in the evening.

Dwardu intervened with the eldest of the Bućagħak brothers and asked him for a raise in their wages. Following that Dwardu and Leli received a two-shilling weekly increase.

Dwardu however, was shrewd enough to know how to take good care of himself. Leli wasn't capable of doing such a thing. Dwardu would tell Leli: "They are stealing my work and I rob them just the same. If they catch me I won't allow them to press charges against me. After all you know this as much as I do. God forbid if we had to speak up and tell what these people are doing, the kind of stealing that's going on and the kind of food they are feeding the Maltese poor!"

Leli knew all this. He was amazed at the high prices charged by the Bućagħak brothers for food that wasn't even suitable for animals.

Leli would keep his mouth shut when he heard people asking for products that the Bućagħak brothers had hidden in their warehouse. A few days later they would sell that scarce commodity at a very high price.

Throughout the years that Leli worked with the Bućagħak brothers, he realized that money making and harboring pity don't go together. He noted that when money was at stake one had to be selfish and unscrupulous.

However, he never expected that for a person to enrich himself it was necessary for him to cheat other people. From his desk located in a corner of the warehouse Leli used to listen, observe and think. He wondered why the world was so blind and allowed such people do as they pleased in particular stealing, ruining and killing the poor.

He couldn't find an answer to that question. Neither could he understand why the world is so patient with those cruel people and tough with others who need compassion. It accuses them, separates them from their loved ones and destroys whatever is good and beautiful in the human heart.

"It isn't fair" Leli would say in his heart of hearts. "It's not fair that these people do as they please! Their actions merit imprisonment! If I had to decide, I would strip them and whip them in public! It isn't fair!"

Notwithstanding Leli's thoughts, the Bućagħak brothers persisted in stealing other peoples' money and enriching themselves. They behaved like all other extortionists spread throughout the world who took advantage of the war. They seemed like vultures flying over dead bodies lying in the sandy, lonely Sahara desert.

However, Leli should have realized from his readings that that is the reason behind wars. At least in the past that was always the reason. Until those persons who incite others to war, do not fear that they too stand to lose their lives, wars will persist with the aim of enriching those who trade in peoples' blood.

Greed ruins man and turns this world into a terrible monster or into something even worse given that every animal, fierce as it may be, always cares for its race!

V

"Don't you agree that people are at a loss, Lel?" Gejtu tal-Klarinett asked Leli one evening while they were standing at the band club door discussing the war and what it brought in its wake. "Do you realize, Lel that the band club's position is deteriorating? Look at us standing here all alone! Did you know that this has been the situation for months?"

"True, people don't really know what's happening," replied

Leli in a thoughtful voice "and I don't know what we're going to do if this situation persists!"

"By the way Lel, is it true that your brother Lippu joined the Militia?"

"Yes, Gejt. He signed up about a month ago."

"He did the right thing! After all today whoever is not working at the Drydocks or for the Government has no other alternative but to register either as a soldier or a sailor. However, Lel – say what you like – I would join the Militia as long as I am stationed in Malta. I'm not that mad to join the navy and die overseas as many foolish men from this village have done."

"If everybody shared your opinion, Gejt," replied Leli with a smile "there won't be any wars to fight."

"Wouldn't it be better if there weren't any wars? Alas, how many people would have been spared! And, by the way, Lel," – Gejtu had a habit of saying 'by the way'- "I may be a coward but believe me Lel: I would rather starve to death than join the navy and go overseas."

Leli looked again at Gejtu and smiled. Gejtu tal-Klarinett was forty years old, he was pot-bellied and had the air of a voracious eater. His appearance and look indicated that Gejtu was a strong man but lacking in good sense.

"You cannot say what you would have done, Gejt? Hunger makes you do a lot of things! Do you think that you're alone in fearing war and destruction? Most people hate war as much as you do but a man joins the Militia or the navy either because he is unemployed or because he is forced to do so.

"I thank God, Gejt, that until now enlisting as a soldier or a sailor is still voluntary and conscription of twenty-one year olds and over has not been introduced in Malta. Look what happened to my brother Ninu. When the war started he immediately registered as a soldier. Nobody forced him to do so but he had no alternative since he hadn't earned any money for weeks."

"Is it true, Lel? Is Australia at war too?"

"Australia is not at war but, it forms part of the British Empire and for this reason there are Australians who are joining the Militia and the Navy to fight for the Empire."

" I can imagine what your parents are going through, Lel!"

"You can say that again, Gejt. My brother's issue is no joke. Ninu did not join the Maltese Militia and sooner or later he will have his baptism of fire. May God help him because only He can protect him!"

"What a terrible thing to happen! I wouldn't know what to do, Lel! Imagine Marjann, alas! She loves you so much, Lel!"

"Yes, she really loves us, Gejt. This matter is going to cause her great distress because as I told you, I don't think he has long to live once he leaves Australia. My mother is aware of this. She hasn't stopped crying since she received the news."

"Poor woman! Listen, Lel can't you write to him and encourage him to resign from the Militia and return to Malta? It may be that if you explain to him the trouble he is in and how distraught his mother feels, than perhaps he may change his mind and leave that country. Perhaps, he may even desert and return to Malta."

"Are you out of your mind, Gejt? Don't you know that it isn't that easy to resign from the Militia once a person has enlisted as a soldier? That it will be worse for him if he deserts and is captured? Now everything depends on his luck. But I'm not sure. If it is true what people are saying that the British will invade the Dardenelles by land and that Australian troops will lead the invasion, the survivors may consider themselves lucky."

Gejtu remained silent looking pitifully at Leli. However, when he realized that Leli had nothing more to add, he told him:

"Listen Lel do you mind if we change the subject because I cannot stand hearing people speaking about trouble and destruction. I get goose flesh and feel like crying. Lel, please visit the band club more frequently and make yourself more available. I don't say this to flatter you but most villagers visit the band club because of you... They adore listening to you speaking and respect you a lot. That's what they were saying at the grocery: 'Leli ta' Braġ is a good-natured fellow and without him the band club has much to lose.'"

Leli blushed and his eyes welled with tears. Nothing would have made Leli happier. Not even if Gejtu had to become rich and presented him with a substantial sum of money. The most important thing for Leli was to please people, to be loved by everybody and to make no person his enemy.

"Thank you Gejt. But I don't merit such praise. However, I promise you that I will visit the band club more often. Recently I was making myself scarce because I was working late. You do appreciate that, after all we're in the middle of a war. Goodbye Gejt. Will you stay here longer?"

"Yes, Lel. Goodbye!"

"Goodbye Gejt and Good night."

VI

As time passed, what Leli had predicted, occurred.

Although during the war, the movement of troops from one country to another was kept secret, many people came to know about such manoeuvres even during that time.

This is what happened.

The news that Britain was going to invade the Dardenelles by land spread throughout the world weeks before the struggle started.

When the time was ripe, ships carrying soldiers sailed from every corner of the British Empire. A good number of Australian soldiers left for the War. Ninu Braġ was amongst those soldiers.

The latest news that the Braġ family received from Ninu was that he had left Australia *'for good'* together with other soldiers. However, their destination was unknown He would write them another letter in the future.

Days and weeks passed since the receipt of Ninu's terse letter. Nobody knew what had become of him.

In Malta, the rumour had started spreading that the British were setting up hospitals everywhere to accommodate ill and wounded soldiers arriving from the Dardanelles.

Leli did his best not to disclose the news he had been reading about in the newspapers regarding this particular issue to his mother. He also warned Vira and his father not to mention anything on the subject in her presence.

However, Leli's father couldn't keep a secret and shared with his wife anything that made him sad as it made him feel better.

For this reason, Marjann soon came to know through her husband that her son could be among the many soldiers sent to fight in the Dardanelles.

Marjann didn't know the location of the Dardanelles neither did she know about the weapons nations possessed then to fight the war.

She only felt and knew what every mother senses when her son's life is at risk.

One could imagine therefore with what enthusiasm and ardour she prayed the Lord to protect her son so that he might return to her safe and sound.

"O Lord, I'm not worthy! I'm a sinner. Why should I find favour in Your Eyes when thousands of mothers have already lost their sons? I pray to You with all my heart to protect my son and bring him home safely to me?

"O Lord let me see my son again then, let me die but don't let me suffer this great and cruel fate!"

Marjann was not the only mother to offer this prayer during the First World War.

Hundreds, thousands, millions of mothers offered the same prayer with the same zeal. They failed to realize that politicians were to blame for what was happening. However, before the fighting stopped blood had to run like a river, thousands of young men had to get killed and the hearts of so many mothers had to be broken.

VII

Marjann learnt about her son's death on the day she least expected the news.

It was about ten o'clock in the morning and she had just

returned home after visiting one of her neighbours who had just given birth to a sweet chubby and lively baby.

Marjann didn't speak English so she stared at the officer who handed her a letter concerning her son's death. He uttered some words and left before she opened the letter.

Excitedly she put on her veil and hurried to Rużanni.

"Hello, Marjanna! What brought you here this morning? Have a seat What's wrong Marjann? You look excited."

"I'm confused, aunt. A soldier came to my house and gave me this letter. He uttered some words and left. Something tells me that it's bad news. Where is Dun Karm?"

"He's upstairs. He's just arrived. Karmenu! Karm, come downstairs. Ninu's wife is here."

Dun Karm greeted Marjann and when he saw the paper from the war office immediately realized that something terrible must have occurred.

After reading the letter to himself several times he raised his eyes and looked pitifully at Marjann. That look was enough for Marjann to understand what had happened.

Marjann fainted. Dun Karm together with his mother picked her up, laid her on the bed and took care of her as best they could until she regained consciousness.

Marjann eventually came to and after some time a number of Dun Karm's neighbours accompanied her home and did their best to comfort her.

Vira accompanied her too. When Vira realized what had happened she wept bitterly and stayed at Leli's house to look after his mother.

However, nothing seemed to comfort Marjann for the time being.

She didn't know what was happening to her life, she seemed in a world of her own. Sometimes she moaned and repeated the words: "Alas, poor Ninu, my poor Ninu! "

She didn't shed a single tear. Her husband cried like a baby. She just moaned.

However the following evening she stood up from her chair and walked around the house like some drunkard.

"Mother, why did you get up?" asked Leli. "What do you want? Tell me?"

"Nothing, my dear. I just want to get you a shirt for tomorrow morning because the one you have on is unsuitable."

Being in a confused state of mind she opened the wrong drawer and looked inside it. After a while she took out a pair of trousers and a jacket. They belonged to Ninu.

She gazed sorrowfully at those clothes. She then kissed them and cried over them. A flood of tears followed as she remembered the tragic death of her son in the prime of life.

❖ ❖ ❖ ❖ ❖

Grief effects different persons differently. However, whoever loses a dear person merits sympathy, no matter how the individual behaves, whether at a complete loss for words or bursting into loud lamentations.

Although Leli was quite capable of handling the situation he wished it wasn't him to inform his aunt about his brother's death.

However, it appeared that only he could perform this difficult task.

Fortunately, as he was coming out of the house he met Ġanni ta' Kejla. The latter, after offering his condolences accompanied Leli to Ħal-Kbir and to his aunt Dolor.

Leli could imagine how sorry his aunt would be but he never expected that she loved Ninu so much.

When he uttered the first words, Dolor was beside herself. She started slapping her face and pulling her hair. Soon all the people outside assembled at her house.

Nobody could calm her down and comfort her. Saverja, her servant, quietly hurried to fetch the doctor. He arrived immediately and gave her some medicine to calm her down and regain her senses. He then spoke calmly to her as he was well aware of the influence doctor's words have on patients. She calmed down for a short while.

However, Ninu's death was a terrible blow for Dolor. She

never recovered from the shock entirely because of her weak state of health even though her obesity gave the impression that she was the picture of health.

It is popularly said that nobody dies as a result of grieving over the death of somebody else. This is true most of the time but not always. Sometimes sorrow contributes to the weakening of a person's already fragile health until it destroys him.

That's what happened to Dolor ta' Braġ. Amazingly although Ninu was her nephew, she missed him as if he were her son. The sorrow resulting from Ninu's death intensified her illness. She rapidly lost weight. The doctor indicated that, she would have lived longer if it weren't for the grief caused by the death of her nephew.

VIII

Some women can be very cruel.

Tona ta' Bdielu,[45] wife of Ġorġ tal- Ħanut[46] was one of these.

Tona opened a small grocery in the alley behind the open square soon after the commencement of the war. The grocery was located close to her husband's shop. She furnished the grocery with all the necessities required for daily life. She even had in store salt water which one usually procured from the pharmacist.

People who were jealous of Tona and who wished her ill would say "Some people are really lucky!". "Lucky and they even want more! Besides doing well in her new business, she won't let you have the goods unless you pay ready cash!"

When the war started Tona, like other shop owners of the time planned ahead.

"Leave it to me," she would tell her husband Ġorġ when he tried to interfere and warn her to be careful before the devil tempted her and got them in trouble.

"I told you: don't worry. You're no good at such things! Don't be afraid, we're not the only ones doing such things! Everybody is behaving in the same way as us. Make hay while the sun shines Ġorġ."

Tona had the courage to store as much sugar as she could lay her hands on.

In Malta during the First World War there were times when there was no sugar at all. It was very difficult to buy any. For this reason when Tona believed that sugar was going to be scarce she would sell her stock at a very high price, much higher than the price she actually bought it for. People had no alternative but to buy sugar at Tona's price!

It was common for people with very small children to ask her to give them some more.

Sour-faced Tona would reply: "It's impossible, my dear. Even if I wanted to give you some I don't have any". Meanwhile she would have twelve sacks of sugar stored in the attic besides some other twelve sacks stored in her husband's cellar.

However, as the saying goes: "the devil has come for his share." Here is what happened to Tona because of her covetousness.

One morning, Lonza, Pawlu ta' Waħħaxni's friend entered Tona's grocery holding her baby and asked her for one fourth of a rotolo of sugar.

"Didn't I give you some already, Lonz?"

"Yes, Ton you did. Now I require some more. Won't you give me some?"

"I'm sorry, Lonz I can't because otherwise I won't have enough for other people."

Let's put it this way if there weren't any people in the shop at that time Tona would have given her some.

Tona knew Lonza very well especially her friend Pawlu who had joined the Militia. Everybody feared Pawlu and Lonza.

She would certainly have served her some sugar had she known that there was Pawlu waiting outside the grocery.

Pawlu had heard about Tona's stock of sugar. For this reason he told Lonza to go and ask Tona for some more to test whether Tona would give her any.

By Jove, Tona resisted Lonza's request. She never imagined that Pawlu and Lonza suspected what she had in store.

When Lonza came out of the shop, Pawlu approached and asked her what happened.

"She didn't give me any"

"Come with me and we'll check that out!"

Fortunately at that moment there was Filumen tas-Seksuki.[47] She seemed to realize what was going to happen and took the baby from Lonza's arms. Hadn't Filumen done so something terrible would have occurred.

Pawlu angrily entered the shop. He wore his military cap on one side of his head while his bayonet moved to and fro around his waist. Lonza followed him. Then, at the top of his voice he shouted: "Ton, are you going to give her some more sugar or not?"

Tona's face changed colour and she looked confused. However, since she was a courageous woman she immediately regained her senses and replied courteously:

"Didn't she tell you that I gave her some this morning, Pawl? Don't you know that I cannot sell sugar at will?"

"We don't know anything, Ton. The only thing we're sure of is that you have plenty of sugar in store. You hide that sugar at the expense of poor people like us so that you'll sell it at a higher price in due course. Do you understand me Ton? Anyway, what are you going to do? Are you going to give her some more sugar or not?"

"I'm not going to give her anymore, Pawl! And watch what you're saying otherwise I'll call the police."

"What ?"

Pawlu suddenly jumped over the bench and over Tona's head. He hurried inside the store. Tona ran after him. He climbed up to the attic and threw two sacks of sugar to the ground. He then jumped on one of the two sacks of sugar and, kicked Tona over. Tona was going to throw something at him. He took out his bayonet from its sheath and opened up the two sacks of sugar while shouting: "Come and see where the sugar is hidden! Come! Come!"

All the women outside the shop and everybody else present accompanied Lonza inside. Suddenly a great fight started.

Lonza and Tona rolled on the ground pulling at each other's hair. Pawlu punched Ġorġ while the latter was coming in. All the people present helped themselves to the sugar spread on the ground thanks to Pawlu and Lonza.

The two sacks of sugar had vanished by the time the police arrived and arrested everyone. Furthermore, some people helped themselves to a number of goods from the shop while the fighting was going on.

That's what happened to Tona ta' Bdielu due to her greed. Besides the fact that a number of goods had gone missing from her shop, she and her husband had also received a severe beating.

Notwithstanding the amount of sugar stolen from Tona's grocery, the poor remained poor. Furthermore, who knows how many babies, children and adults died because of the low quality of food the poor bought at a high price. No one really cared what the poor ate.

IX

Dwardu Buqerq happened to be in the village the day the incident took place. He was at the front door of Ġorġ's shop while the fighting was going on.

When he heard the shouting he joined the rest of the people to see what was happening. He returned home after the fighting stopped.

He came face to face with Vira as he was turning into the street where he lived.

Since the time he had been living in Ħaż-Żgħir Dwardu had hardly ever spoken to Vira except for the occasional nod. He first spoke to her at Leli's home and, on another occasion as they were coming out of church after the seven o'clock mass.

Dwardu sometimes told Leli: "Listen Lel, you don't happen to be one of those silly people who are jealous of their girlfriend, are you? I have been living in the village for some time now and I have never met Vira?"

Leli would reply with a smile: "Obviously not! I don't happen to be one of those silly guys. My girlfriend doesn't go out because she doesn't want to. Indeed, she may go wherever she pleases."

However, Leli was not being sincere on this particular issue. He didn't feel comfortable whenever Dwardu spoke to him about Vira and sought to cut the matter short whenever they started discussing the subject.

Leli soon came to realize what Dwardu thought of women.

Buqerq argued that it doesn't pay to buy a cow for a rotolo of meat. According to him women are all the same. They are only good for one thing: to please men for a while and then forget all about them.

Dwardu also happened to be one of those men who boasted that women easily lost their heads over him. In other words, since Dwardu was accustomed to certain type of women, whose job was to please men, he concluded that all women were born for that purpose. Hence, he thought that any woman would lose her head over him just by a word or a look.

This kind of reasoning together with his upbringing and style of life led Dwardu to believe that the idea of woman as the center of love and wisdom was ridiculous. He argued that only foolish men embraced that line of thought. Moreover, Dwardu also believed that men are obsessed about women who on their part immediately fall for men like ripe fruit fall from a tree.

One day while Dwardu was expressing his ideas to Leli and to two other friends, Leli interrupted him:

"Listen, Dward you have to distinguish between different types of people. You cannot measure other people by your own yardstick. You are mistaken to believe that the world is full of men obsessed about women! I am twenty-four years old and I am proud to say that my thoughts and actions don't fit what you describe. Furthermore, I have never taken other men's women or disrupted their happiness and I hope that I'll never do that! I believe I'm not the only person in the world to share such thoughts. I understand there must be others who share my opinion. If this argument is applicable to men it is far more applicable to women. The poet says:

Love is not men's concern,
For women it is their livelihood!

"The theme of this poem not only focuses on physical love but also on another kind of love. A love, which sacrifices itself for others, that even dies for others!

"Furthermore, there is another kind of love. That is the love for the poor who are always with us. Love for the less fortunate ones.

"I have seen women living in poverty. Overworked and with hardly anything to eat. Above all they are slaves to their husband's desires. However, when her husband arrives angry from work because his employer is exploiting him, she forgets all about her difficulties and calms him down.

"She does this not because he's a man and she's a woman but because he's her husband and that no matter what she must stand by him. No one other than him is her companion. He's her livelihood. He's the father of her children!

"Who knows, Dward, how many women have never cheated on their husbands. How many women haven't separated from their husbands, even when the latter were unemployed for months and years – times characterized by poverty, hunger and sometimes punishment too!"

Meanwhile, Dwardu had an ironic smile on his face and burst out laughing when Leli stopped speaking. He bent over double, placed his hand in his pocket and with the other hand removed a lock of hair from over his forehead. Then he said in a frivolous voice:

"You and your poet must be dreaming, Lel. Reality is far different from what you describe!"

However, Leli interrupted him immediately:

"Lives people lead are very different from what we believe. However, Dward, do understand that for many people life does not have such an empty meaning as you understand it. If you wish to disagree with me at least let us split what is right in two that is part of what I said and of what you said is true. That way we'll remain friends. Do you agree, Dward?"

That way thanks to Leli's compromise all ended well.

Some time elapsed before, Leli and Dwardu ever brought up

the subject again. Meanwhile, Dwardu made it a point that he would show Leli how right he was at the appropriate time and that the latter still had a lot to learn about women.

❖ ❖ ❖ ❖ ❖

Most villagers agreed that Dwardu had the gift of the gab. However, he possessed that skill not because he was a wise person but rather because he was as cunning as a fox.

He was a fearless kind of person and was never ashamed of his wrongdoing. These two particular characteristics came to the fore whenever he spoke to a woman.

He greeted Vira that way while his eyes searched hers. He asked her how she was doing, and spoke briefly about the fighting at the grocery. They both laughed. He mentioned the Braġ family and Leli and concluded merrily by saying that he hoped to drink a cup to the newly-weds' health soon.

After Dwardu left Vira's side, she realized what a talkative person he was. She listened to him impatiently as she usually did with anyone who spoke to her. She later explained to Leli that she was upset by the way Dwardu had looked into her eyes.

"That's his job," Leli told her in a somewhat angry voice when Vira that evening, described her meeting with Dwardu. "He says that, to attract women. I don't blame him as long as he finds women who fall for his charms, instead of ignoring him! I suppose you spent a long time conversing?"

"No, not at all!" Replied Vira. "He just said a few words and continued on his way."

"Make sure that next time you ignore him. Don't let me repeat this to you. You will speak to Dwardu only when I'm accompanying you. That's enough!"

❖ ❖ ❖ ❖ ❖

Vira was a pleasant young woman and for this reason most men were naturally attracted to her. She was friendly and not given to airs and graces.

Women generally love to show off, and most men are attracted to such women.

Vira's character left its mark on any man who made her acquaintance.

For this reason, Vira remained in Dwardu's mind and he was fascinated with her. He repeated to himself: "Fancy Leli what a beautiful girl he has! How is it I didn't realize that before? However you have to speak to a woman to get to know her."

Fifteen days after his crucial encounter with Vira, Dwardu was standing at the door of Ġorġ's shop and Vira was crossing the village square. It was necessary for her to pass close to where Dwardu was standing. She was looking at him when Dwardu noticed her. Therefore he made it a point that when she came closer he would nod and if possible speak to her.

However, he didn't get what he wanted. As she walked past the shop she looked straight ahead and ignored Dwardu.

Dwardu remained with his hand half raised. As far as he could remember no woman had ever treated him that way before and said in his heart of hearts:

"This is all Leli's doing! She told him that I spoke to her and he warned her to avoid me. He'll repent it! You just wait and see! You'll soon realize who is Dwardu Buqerq!"

❖ ❖ ❖ ❖ ❖

Leli, at first was pleased when Vira told him what had happened. However, afterwards he felt guilty. It was only proper to greet Dwardu and there would have been no harm had Vira greeted him and continued on her way.

He couldn't get rid of this thought and expected Dwardu to be offended when he met him the following day. Dwardu, however, showed no signs of anxiety and greeted Leli as if nothing had happened.

That morning, Leli felt that the matter preoccupied Dwardu too. The latter, being a shrewd man noticed that Leli was keeping quiet because he was afraid of being accused of his misdeed.

Both remained silent. Days passed and Leli, unlike Dwardu, forgot all about the incident completely.

Dwardu often recalled what happened and every time he would smile and say in his heart of hearts:

"Someday I'll get my revenge too!"

X

It was late in the Spring of 1915.

Ġanni ta' Kejla still enjoyed hunting as much as when he was bachelor. At that particular time of year he would start thinking how he could get his hands on some cartridges and gunpowder. These items were very scarce and expensive during the war and they were difficult to obtain if not through some particular favour.

Ġanni would ask Leli to write a letter to the Inspector living at Ħal-Kbir to procure the licence. That was easy and he received it soon after.

One evening, Ġanni and Leli decided to go hunting the following morning immediately after early morning mass as the hunting season had already started. Perhaps they would catch a golden plover that is a hunter's delight!

"We'll have great fun, Lel if we manage to catch that kind of bird! I have an excellent whistle this year. I'm sure that if we come across such a bird we'll be able to capture it!"

Leli smiled and tapped Ġanni on the shoulder. Ġanni continued:

"At least we'll eat something in peace and your mood will change. Sorry for interfering Lel but recently you have changed a lot. Am I right, Lel?"

"You're right Ġann and that's how I feel."

"Listen, Lel, but …"

"Speak up, Ġann."

"Why don't you get married?" Stammered Ġanni with a smile. When he realized that Leli had smiled too he plucked up courage and said:

"You know as much as I do how much trouble crops up during the time of one's engagement. Why don't you marry then? Take me for instance I am happily married. I earn money for my family and she looks after the house. I can assure you Lel, I'm much better off than when I was a bachelor."

❖ ❖ ❖ ❖ ❖

Vira was extremely happy when Leli told her the news.

She had every right to be so happy! They had been engaged for more than two years and she had been looking forward to such a moment.

The news pleased Ġammari too. When Leli told him that he had not decided earlier because his earnings were meagre, Ġammari replied:

"I never pressed you to marry my daughter. I know that your intentions are good and don't worry if you feel that you should wait for better times. However, since every little helps I want to tell you that if you have nothing to the contrary I am willing to come and live with you.

"Listen to me carefully Lel. I'm not doing this for myself. I can cope very well on my own and my needs are very little. I only want to see you happy and perhaps you'll be better off without me. Do you understand me Lel? If I can be of any help I am ready to stay with you. I'll retire to old peoples' home when I'm no longer good for anything and unable to work any further."

❖ ❖ ❖ ❖ ❖

At this time Leli's head was heavy with thoughts of how best to furnish his house. In a way this served him well because it transported him from the world of books and dreams in which he lived to reality.

However, Leli didn't change much. He still had his books. He simply put in some more effort, prepared himself to adjust to the new way of life and acquired the necessary items to get married.

Leli was born to lead a contemplative life. Every time he changed his life style, this only lasted for a short time. He could never live the kind of life other people pursued. It was not his way of living.

Leli was a daydreamer. That's the kind of life he wanted to lead!

XI

Jealousy is a curse for most people.

Very often it is the cause of much trouble even among relatives.

This is true for most women who cannot stand the sight of their husband talking to another woman whom she detests or of whom she's jealous!

Jealousy was going to be the cause of much trouble at Ħaż-Żgħir too.

As one can imagine, Anġla wife of Anġlu ta' Kejla grew more agressive towards Ċetta daughter of Żari ta' Laħlaħ especially after Ċetta married Ġanni ta' Kejla a relative of her husband's.

Anġla was even more jealous of Ċetta when Anġla heard that Ċetta was pregnant.

Anġla had always been as thin as a rake. However, amazingly enough recently she had changed colour as if she suffered from phthisis. But the reason for this was Ċetta's physical condition since Anġla remained childless.

Ċetta was a beautiful woman and Ġanni was very proud of his wife. The village men except for Dun Karm used to smile and stare at Ċetta whenever she went past.

"Listen to what I have to say," Anġla would tell her husband when she remembered something about Ċetta. "Open your eyes. If I catch you speaking to her I'll blind you and I'll give her a sound beating!"

"Are you out of your mind or what?" Anġlu would reply. "Don't you know that she is my cousin's wife. There's no harm in speaking to her. I'm not cheating on you!...What would happen if people come to know that I'm not speaking to her because of you? Because you don't want me to!"

"I don't care about what people say! They say what they want. Just don't speak to her and that's that."

❖ ❖ ❖ ❖ ❖

One day towards noon, Ċetta ta' Laħlaħ was on her way to the drinking fountain carrying two pails in each hand.

Ċetta was very fat at the time.

Her husband was drinking some wine at ta' Nofs Ras[48] a bar situated exactly opposite the drinking fountain.

As Ċetta approached the fountain she came face to face with Anġlu.

"Ċett!" Anġlu said.

"Anġ!" Replied Ċetta.

"May God be with you! I hope everything ends well for you!"

"I hope so, Anġ. How is your wife?"

"She's fine." At that exact time Ċetta and Anġlu turned their face simultaneously and who should they see walking towards the fountain with a pail in her hand if not Anġla herself.

"I have to go, Ċett," said Anġlu quickly. "I have some work to do."

"Goodbye Anġ," smiled Ċetta and continued on her way towards the fountain.

Anġlu turned into the alley behind the fountain and there he stopped talking to Stejfen ta' Marikarm ta' Sittatlieta.[49] He didn't know what he was telling Stejfen as he was constantly thinking what was to become of him when he arrived home.

Meanwhile Anġla arrived at the fountain. Her face had lost its colour and she was terribly angry.

Ċetta was filling her pail.

Anġla dropped the pail from her hand. As she rested her hands on her hips she asked Ċetta "Listen Ċett, tell me something, don't you have a man of your own?"

"What are you saying, Anġ? Of course I have a man of my

own! Just like everybody else, if not better!"

"Go to the devil! You wicked woman! Listen to me leave my husband alone unless you want to send me to prison. You evil spirit?"

"Stop it, Anġ; there is no need to get so excited take things easy otherwise, the sight of you may scare away your husband more than it already has."

In a fit of rage, Anġla suddenly took hold of one of the empty buckets around the fountain and threw it with all her might in the direction of Ċetta's head. She hit her exactly on the temple. Ċetta immediately fell to the ground.

"Now we'll see whether you are able to call me names, you good for nothing" shouted Anġla in a choked voice when she saw Ċetta lying on the ground.

Immediately many people gathered around. Ġanni, Ċetta's husband approached too. When he saw his wife lying on the ground with her face covered in blood, he ran after Anġla, took hold of her, threw her to the ground and punched her mercilessly. Anġlu heard the shouting. He suspected that his wife was up to something. However, when he saw Ġanni punching his wife, he lost his temper, took out his knife, took hold of Ġanni by the neck and stabbed him repeatedly. The first blow missed him but the second wounded him seriously in the arm. Fortunately some men intervened to calm down the situation otherwise Anġlu would have certainly killed Ġanni.

Due to Anġla's jealous character Ċetta was going to die and lose her child. Ġanni spent a long time in hospital until his wound healed and Anġlu was jailed for one year at Kordin.

BOOK THREE

THE STRUGGLE

SECTION TWO

How blissful are the first months after marriage! The newly weds discover hidden and unexpected happiness. Their hearts beat faster not because they are afraid of the unknown but because they are very happy and stimulated by visions of a wonderful future.

The days, weeks and months pass as quickly as lightning because love is at the center of all things! It is the key to a happy life!

The couple would have known each other for some time before marriage. They would have come to love and respect one another. However, both of them look forward to share those precious moments!

The husband works hard while his wife is busy with her domestic chores. However both of them are eager to meet again and whisper loving words to one another.

Whatever he does or says is good and beautiful. Whatever she cooks is the best!

They eat in a hurry as they look into each other's eyes.

They are everything to one another. Their home is their world – a world of delight, happiness and love!

O love, O love! Nothing is comparable!

II

Leli and Vira lead that kind of life after marriage. It changed both of them radically.

Leli forgot all about his books, the band club, his friends and enemies, the hard work, he forgot everything. He only thought about Vira.

"What a fool I was, Vir" Leli would tell his wife. "Who could ever imagine what kind of happiness I was missing! Believe me, Vir, I just think of you wherever I may be!"

Vira would listen to his words with her head on his shoulder while caressing his hair and telling him:

"You have such beautiful hair! What are these curls? From where did you get those beautiful eyes? Lel, I wish that if we had a son he would look exactly like you — as beautiful as you!"

❖ ❖ ❖ ❖ ❖

The wedding took place a week after Vira's aunt decided to leave Ġammari's house. Ġammari had asked her to stay with them when he realized that Vira's engagement was going to take some time. Ġammari didn't stay much at home after his daughter's marriage.

From the little time he spent there he noticed how much Leli and his daughter loved one another. Seeing them so madly in love gave him great satisfaction as he remembered his youth and his first days of marriage. These thoughts soon vanished as if in a dream and he would say in his heart of hearts:

"The most beautiful time of his life shall soon be over I can still remember Liża and myself – may she rest in peace – we were just like them. Today she's dead and I'm old. There's no place for love in my heart and my daughter Vira is the only memory that remains of my blissful days!"

❖ ❖ ❖ ❖ ❖

A Maltese proverb says that: the January sun encourages young women to get out of their house. However, on a beautiful day in January not only young women go out of their house but married couples too whenever they can.

Who can blame them?

It was a public holiday in January. When Leli and Vira returned home from church, they drank a cup of coffee and went for a walk in the fields.

Leli had resumed the habit of receiving Holy Communion every Sunday and recited the Rosary every evening together with his wife.

He felt at peace with himself by fulfilling his religious obligations and refraining from reading the kind of books he used to read before marriage.

He used to tell Vira that he had never enjoyed such tranquillity before and to this Vira would reply : "That's because you're closer to God."

Vira failed to understand that Leli's health improved because he refrained from reading certain kinds of books and, he had resumed the way he used to live when he was still a child.

In this respect he would cease the opportunity to accompany his wife for a walk in the fields.

❖ ❖ ❖ ❖ ❖

In winter the fields rented to Nardu tal-Wardija[50] looked beautiful. Although Nardu and his sons were not considered rich farmers, they had some excellent fields leased to them. The fields were cultivated from autumn till the beginning of April. One would be amazed at the sight of those colourful fields. In winter the fields would be filled with all hues of green, and the yellow of the cape sorrel. In March there would be patches of deep red a time when the clover would flourish everywhere.

As he used to do on such January mornings, Leli and Vira would go for a walk near Nardu's fields.

While walking along they discussed different subjects and then Vira said:

"Lel, listen to the beautiful song of that bird on the fig tree!"

"That's a linnet, Vir. At this time of year until the end of March the linnets that stay on the Island mate and that's why they sing so beautifully."

" At first I thought it was a sparrow. However, I should have realized that sparrows don't sing that much," replied Vira and after a while she said: "it's amazing how nature generates itself. When the time is ripe, it mates, falls in love, marries and reproduces! Who knows whether we'll have children, Lel? I hope so. It would be a pity if we hadn't any!"

Leli smiled and said: "Of course Vir. But God willing we'll have more children than we would like to have."

Vira remained silent and thoughtful.

Leli noticed that Vira was serious about the subject and therefore changed conversation immediately.

"By the way Vir, did I tell you that Dwardu Buqerq had a fight with the Buċagħak Brothers?"

"No," replied Vira. "What was the reason behind it?"

"You can imagine. As always it was about the money. He asked them for an increase in salary and they quarrelled. The Buċagħak Brothers were going to fire him. However, Dwardu should be more careful because if he's fired he's not going to find employment that easily. Furthermore, now he will have to work harder given that his sister Klara, presently living in Ħal-Kbir will soon be joining him and his father."

Vira looked at Leli, and then asked in a thoughtful voice: "Are you sure?"

"That's what Dwardu said. I believe their uncle is returning to Cairo " Leli suddenly stopped speaking about Dwardu's sister. He looked towards the southwest from which direction the wind was blowing and saw clouds gathering. So, he told Vira: "we'd better hurry up, because there's rain in the air."

Vira concurred and they hurried back home.

It started pouring heavily before they reached the village. Vira and Leli ran and laughed in the rain.

When they arrived home and while they were changing their soaking clothes, Vira asked Leli:

"Did you recognize the person who said "hello" as we turned into our street?"

"It was Dwardu Buqerq. Didn't you notice?"

"No, my dear! I swear I didn't!"

"Don't worry! It serves him right."

III

There come times in a person's life when one feels demotivated. Times in which a person remains passive to his environment.

Leli and Vira were passing through such a phase.

The fascination, which characterized the first few months of their wedding, had waned. However, they were still very much attracted to each other. Obviously they had their occasional quarrel but they cared for one another.

There was a time when Vira would grow very sad. Sometimes she hoped she was pregnant and imagined how proud Leli would be of becoming father. When her hope failed to materialize she would feel very depressed.

Leli teased Vira whenever she was in that frame of mind and almost made her cry. But, when one is still young one quickly forgets and is filled with hope of a better future.

At that time Leli was again busy at the band club. He was appointed president a month after he married. He was very pleased by that and seemed as if he had been running band clubs all his life.

Leli's appointment was accepted by almost everyone and there were only a few who opposed it.

❖ ❖ ❖ ❖ ❖

The Great War was at its height towards the middle of 1916. Whoever is old enough will remember that, together with the difficulties imposed by speculators in terms of essential commodities, discussion about the war had become part and parcel of our daily lives.

Furthermore, what about those families such as ta' Braġ who had lost their dear ones?

Although everybody is sorry and seems to forget such events, mothers are more sensitive to these kind of tragedies.

Leli ta' Braġ missed his late brother a lot. He kept remembering him and whenever he mentioned him he would be filled with sorrow.

Marjann fell into deep silence following her son's death. She stayed for a long time in a corner of the house crying and praying for her son's soul. She fell ill and stayed in bed for about two months soon after Leli married. Vira looked after her and Marjann was very grateful to her.

Lippu, Leli's brother, who had joined the Militia, had grown up to be a fine young man. He was very proud of his two V-shaped stripes sewn on the sleeve of his jacket. Proof that ultimately everyone grows wiser.

Lippu, although carefree like his father and happy-go-lucky, was a very kind person. He was his mother's delight. She would therefore either write him a letter or enquire after his health.

When Lippu would come home for a day on vacation, he would make everybody laugh with the silly things he and his soldier friends used to get up to.

Lippu's sprightly character served as the right antidote that helped his mother recover from her depressive state of health.

Sorrow, more than anything else ages a person prematurely. At times only sin supercedes sorrow in that respect. Marjann seemed to have grown ten years older from the time her son died. Her features seemed to suggest that she must be sixty years old when in fact she hadn't even turned fifty.

The look in her eyes and the sound of her voice betrayed her. Whenever the right opportunity presented itself for her to speak about her son Ninu it became evident that it wasn't time as much as sorrow and trouble that had played havoc with this woman. Marjann was one out of so many battered mothers who in those terrible days had lost their loved ones.

Dun Karm's words were always a comfort to Marjann and she always felt an inner peace whenever he visited her.

At this time Dun Karm was quite busy. His mother had been ill for some time and he had to look after her as if she were a baby.

Dun Karm never complained and, besides taking care of his mother he also had to attend to his priestly duties. Notwithstanding his many difficulties and troubles he always behaved as a Christian priest should. His work, health and money did not belong to him but to those who needed them most. He constantly sought to do some good to others. After finishing his work, he would stay near his mother and attend to her needs.

Kelin Miskat best described the gentle character of this priest.

Although as we said earlier Kelin could not stand priests he sometimes mixed with them simply to avoid peoples' gossip.

Often, after he and Leli had become close friends, Kelin would refer to priests as lazy and selfish people! Aware of what was happening to the clergy in Italy at that time he also argued that such people could only survive in Malta!

However, one day the discussion centred on Dun Karm.

"Listen Lel, I'm going to be straight with you after all you can understand what I'm about to tell you, the people I met in Algeria and in other countries on the African coast made me dislike priests. However, notwithstanding my belief I really admire Dun Karm's dedication to his work. I have known Dun Karm for several years and he has always carried his responsibilities, as a man and as a priest with dignity. Although he may seem an irascible person, I believe there are only a handful of people who are as kind as he is."

IV

When 'tal-Kajr', that is Fredu Buqerq and his son Dwadu settled in Ħaż-Żgħir, the villagers started asking a lot of questions about them such as where they came from and why they had settled in that village.

The villagers became more curious when Fredu's daughter, Klara left her uncle to join her father and her brother in Ħaż-Żgħir. People enquired how she could afford buying expensive dresses for herself, who was going to be her confessor, who was that man dressed in fine clothes who came to visit them after she arrived in the village and other such questions.

Most village people immediately react to anything that they are not accustomed to and the people in Ħaż-Żgħir were no different. They were surprised when they saw Klara for the first time.

She contrasted sharply with the rest of the girls in Ħaż-Żgħir.

Ladies' fashion at that time consisted of a large hat and a narrow skirt. Although most village women did not bother about ladies' fashions, some women did. However, the hats and skirts that Klara wore were larger and narrower than what the villagers had ever seen. They could be compared to those worn respectively by the doctor's wife, the pharmacist's daughter and a few others.

The way she moved made the clothes look more conspicuous. Her figure seemed to defy whoever looked at her.

She was a tall and beautiful lady. However her beauty was artificial. She powdered her face and wore a very strong perfume.

The tone of her voice was the first thing that struck any person who spoke to her.

At first Klara's voice put you off. She also sounded impudent. However, gradually one would feel attracted to her and soon a person would start fancying her. These particular aspects were enhanced by her gentle behaviour.

Klara had been in Ħaż-Żgħir for less than a week and everybody in the village was trying to bend over backwards to make her acquaintance and to please her.

Klara spoke to everyone and laughed when someone addressed her as Miss. or Mrs. She insisted that her name was Klara.

People were attracted to her and everybody spoke about Klara and what a friendly person she was.

One thing which most married women were not pleased about however, was the way Klara looked at their husbands.

She would smile broadly and stare into their eyes as she bid them farewell. Obviously men were infatuated with her.

This really upset the wives and as soon as their husbands returned home they would warn them never to look at her again.

After a few months of her arrival in Ħaż-Żgħir, all was back to normal. Everybody grew accustomed to her with the exception of a few women such as Angla. Indeed most women didn't bother whether their husbands greeted Klara or not.

❖ ❖ ❖ ❖ ❖

Leli Brag had only spoken to Klara a couple of times before she settled in Haż-Żghir together with her family.

The first time he spoke to her was when her brother Dwardu asked Leli to accompany him to Ħal-Kbir and whilst they were there they paid a visit to Dwardu's uncle. Instead they found Klara at home. Leli was somewhat shy and he forgot all about her soon after.

Leli was also accompanying her brother the second time he spoke to her. They met her in Valletta while they were returning from work. Although they were not quite dressed for the occasion and she looked very elegant they stopped to exchange a few words. She spoke to Leli as if she had known him for a very long time rather than for a short period.

When he returned home in the evening he told Vira that he had met Dwardu's sister. She immediately told him:

"Then you must have been very pleased!"

"Not at all, Vir. On the contrary she really gets on my nerves. I just cannot stand that kind of woman."

Vira trusted Leli completely and she wasn't jealous of him. If only all women were like that!

❖ ❖ ❖ ❖ ❖

It happened that Klara had been in Ħaż-Żgħir for only two days when she met Vira. She obviously didn't know that she was Leli's wife.

They were in church and both of them had their veil on. They stood up together to leave.

Vira had a premonition that that woman must have been Dwardu's sister. However since she couldn't recognize her properly she was unsure whether it was Dwardu's sister or not.

As they were leaving church, Vira remembered that she had forgotten something on the chair where she was sitting. She turned her face and on another chair located a few yards away, she noticed a silver rosary. It must have been Klara's.

She picked it up and hurried to reach Klara. She then asked her whether that rosary belonged to her.

It was her's. As a result of that incident, Vira and Klara came to know each other and became friends.

It was then that Klara invited Vira into her house. The latter declined the invitation but promised her that someday she would pay her a visit. Vira reciprocated.

Klara thanked her and told her that one-day she would. In fact that's what she did six days later. She went in the afternoon while Leli was at work and stayed talking to Vira for some time.

When Leli returned home in the evening, Vira told him:

"I always tell you that you like to exaggerate things. Dwardu's sister is quite a pleasant lady. There are certainly people who are more impudent than her."

Leli smiled, shrugged and remained silent.

Vira saw Klara passing by a few days after her visit.

Klara was wearing a hat and a very narrow skirt, which would split in half if she ever, tried squatting.

"By Jove!" said Vira in her heart of hearts. "I'm not surprised that Leli described her as an impudent woman. She ought to be ashamed of herself wearing those clothes and walking that way."

When Klara visited Vira again after some time the latter greeted her sweetly. She didn't tell Klara that she was disappointed with her. Their discussion centered on the beautiful drapes exhibited at the shops in Valletta. Vira completely forgot to keep Klara at a distance and to keep her away from her house.

V

Malta served as a large military hospital until 1917.

Two and a half years before, that is in the beginning of summer 1915, an immense number of wounded and sick soldiers who had fought in the Dardenelles were sent to Malta for their recovery.

Other soldiers arrived from Salonika and the Eastern parts where the fighting went on almost until the end of the war. Many of the soldiers suffered from severe diarrhoea and from the foul air in those lands. They were sent to Malta to recover or to be buried here instead of being buried in the desert outside the city of Salonika.

It is estimated that almost twenty-five thousand soldiers per month arrived in Malta for their recovery between September 1916 and April 1917.

Their numbers decreased in the beginning of summer 1917. However, in the beginning of autumn of that year there were still about twelve thousand patients on the Island.

As can be expected several businessmen at that time made a lot of money by supplying hospital goods.

There is no harm in that as long as a person works hard for his profits. As the saying goes: One man's meat is another man's poison.

However, in those days there were some traders, including the Bućagħak brothers who sold shoddy foodstuffs at a very high profit margin.

Who knows how much money the Bućagħak Brothers made during those two years when Malta was replete with casualties of war?

❖ ❖ ❖ ❖ ❖

One afternoon towards the beginning of Autumn, Manwel the youngest of the Buċagħak Brothers, after having eaten a substantial meal, drank some wine and relaxed for a while on the mattress behind the sacks of sugar, woke up with an irresistible urge to have some fun.

He started teasing Leli and the latter either replied, smiled or remained silent.

Finally Leli could contain himself no longer. He had been working for the Buċagħak Brothers for several years and he was considered as one of the family. Although shy by nature, especially with his employer, there were times when he felt that he had to hold his ground. When he took such a stand he did not mince his words. Indeed he would compensate for the time he remained quiet.

Leli used to keep a book with him so that when there was nothing to do he would spend some time reading.

Manwel used to tease Leli about his love for reading.

"Listen to what I am telling you my son," he would tell him in a mocking voice "don't let those books get the best of you because otherwise you will soon go mad!"

Manwel's comments were getting on Leli's nerves.

"You're quite right Sir. It's foolish of me to spend my time reading when I can spend my time like you and your brother: extorting people, enriching myself and going to church to make people believe that I'm a magnanimous person.! It's true you're quite right Sir! I'm the foolish person, not you."

"There's no need to get so excited Lel!" Then, after laughing it off and twirling his moustache he continued in a mocking voice:

"I bet Leli is angry!"

"Leave me alone, Sir! I have no reason to be angry. It's those businessmen who are making money out of other peoples' blood or those people who enriched themselves by exploiting the poor that ought to be angry. They should be hanged in public, the only things I possess are my health and abilities. I'm not wealthy!"

Although it seemed that Leli's words touched Manwel to the quick, the latter remained silent and resumed laughing.

"You have every reason to be happy," Leli told him. Then he continued saying "those who hunger, the sick or those who go to war to make you richer certainly cannot share your happiness

"When the war started Mr. Macdonald said that businessmen are the reason behind wars. He was jailed for expressing his opinion. If only leaders of other countries had shared his point of view! He shouldn't have been the one to be imprisoned for instigating British workers to resist from going to war. It should have been those who are making money out of peoples' blood that should have been jailed!"

Manwel together with some other men who were listening to Leli speaking with such vigor stared at him after he finished talking as if they wanted to hear more. Manwel quickly regained his composure, approached Leli, tapped him on the shoulder and told him:

"You see how well Leli speaks! Who could ever imagine what had to come out of Ħaż-Żgħir! Not even town people know how to speak like that! Truly, Lel what you said remains among us, because you spoke a lot of nonsense in the spur of the moment such as businessmen are in favour of war and that the British Government acted unwisely when it jailed a person for instigating workers not to fight for their country. You think that's unjust! Listen to what I'm going to tell you and you will not get into trouble. Make sure that you don't repeat what you just said to anybody else or you may find yourself imprisoned. Then you will really have something to complain about!"

While Manwel was speaking to him, Leli didn't move and continued reading.

Manwel sulked. He couldn't stand people ignoring him. He left Leli's side, walked along the warehouse, turned round, took out a cigar from his pocket, lit the cigar and told Leli in an authoritative voice:

"Let's stop talking nonsense because we have wasted enough time already. Furthermore, ensure that tomorrow afternoon you and Dwardu visit the hospital to discuss matters with the police sergeant who came here a few days ago. We may get lucky if he introduces you to the right person. Tell him that if he helps us he will receive an appropriate reward and put in some more effort because these last two months have been rather poor!"

Leli closed the book he had in front of him and moved his head. He took out a cigarette from his pocket, lit it and took a deep breath. He placed the cigarette on the lid of a can which was full of cigarette butts, opened the ledger which was in front of him and with no more ado pretended to be working on that ledger. In that way he got rid of Manwel's pestering.

VI

The police sergeant Manwel had mentioned did more than was expected of him. Since they finished their work early, they went to have a drink together. However, before sunset both Leli and Dwardu were as drunk as a lord.

This was not the first time that both got drunk however, Leli could never forget what happened the first time in Valletta.

At that time Leli and Dwardu were on very good terms and saw eye to eye on several subjects. Dwardu, often quarrelled with the Buċagħak Brothers and Leli did his best to calm him down and intervened on his behalf. Indeed if it hadn't been for Leli, Dwardu wouldn't have retained his employment for more than a month.

However, Dwardu was never sorry for Leli and did not hesitate to make fun of him with others.

Dwardu was a hypocrite and a deceitful person. He misled people by concealing his true intentions regarding Leli.

Nobody realized this and many believed that both were bosom friends.

The reader knows very well what I mean I guess and must have already come across insincere persons like Dwardu Buqerq in their lives.

❖ ❖ ❖ ❖ ❖

Dwardu used to lend some books to Leli too. Buqerq cared little about books. He generally read erotic books usually written by unpopular authors and addressed to the younger generation.

What Spinoza, Kant and Goethe were to Kelin, and St. Thomas, St. Augustine, and Duns Scotus to Dun Karm so where Mariani, Pitigrilli and Notari to Dwardu.

Dwardu obtained the books he lent to Leli possibly from his uncle and from Klara. She had brought them along together with some other things when she left her uncle's house to live in Ħaż-Żgħir.

The books that Leli borrowed from Dwardu were different from those written by the aforementioned authors. Two popular French writers wrote four or five of those books: Voltaire and Anatole France. The former a great satirical writer and the latter a skeptic with a deeply pessimistic view of mankind. Voltaire was one of the greatest pre-Revolutionary writers of 1789 while France is considered as one of the greatest contemporary writers.

When Leli had read Voltaire's *Candide* he revived the thoughts and anti-clerical sentiments he reaped from his earlier readings. France's writings such as, *Les opinions de M. Jerôme Coignard, La Revolte des Anges* and *Les Dieux ont soif* seriously threatened Leli's Faith which at one time had deep roots within him.

While Vira slept, Leli would repeat to himself: "I believe, how can I live without Faith?" At other times especially when he would be reading he would feel very hostile towards Religion. However if someone had to ask him at that time to give a sincere reply to the question whether he still believed in God or not he would say: "No! I used to but I no longer do!"

This was the stage Leli's Faith had reached. That same Leli who was born and bred a Christian and of whom his mother and the villagers were so proud until a few years before he married. It certainly wasn't Vira's fault who did her best to renew his Faith.

However, it was all in vain! The books he read and the ideas he absorbed destroyed his Christian Faith and made him forget all about God.

Although Dwardu never read those books, he failed to realize the moral damage they caused Leli. He had destroyed what provides the greatest comfort to a man's heart.

❖ ❖ ❖ ❖ ❖

Leli and Dwardu had drunk too much beer that evening to bother about the harm those books caused them. They longed to return home and get into bed.

For this reason when the cab stopped in front of Buqerq's house, Leli remained seated to continue with his journey home. Dwardu, however pulled him by the hand and told him: "get down and come inside!". Leli refused to do so. He was keen on returning home to bed.

At that moment Klara opened the front door and said:

"Eh… look who's here this evening .You're celebrating! Come in! No! You have to come in at all costs at least this once. We're honoured to have you."

Leli couldn't offer any further resistance. For this reason he followed Dwardu who was walking unsteadily in front of him.

"Do I need to hold you by the arm Lel? You won't fall will you?" said Klara jokingly. "However, it's better if I stay by you." and she immediately took him by the elbow and led him into a side room.

Leli sat heavily on the sofa. Then, he told her: "thanks Klara, this sofa is very comfortable!"

"You see Lel," Klara replied with a smile "You see! At least your visit has served some purpose! You've found something you liked."

Leli laughed.

Leli used to speak to Klara when the latter visited his wife. However, those conversations only lasted for a short while. Leli hardly ever went to Dwardu's house and only did so whenever Dwardu failed to turn up for work.

So this was really the first evening that Leli and Klara found themselves alone.

"Where is father, Klar?" Dwardu asked in a heavy and tired voice.

Klara took her brother by the arm, and directed him to the opposite chair covered in old velvet. She tapped him repeatedly on the shoulder as if to put him to sleep and stop bothering her.

Dwardu's head soon drooped to his chest and he started snoring. She then went to sit next to Leli.

"So finally you came to visit us, Lel! Although you had to get drunk with my brother to do so! However, it doesn't matter."

"No! Believe me, Klar," Leli told her in a shy voice; "I meant to come over together with Vira a long time ago; however, I was busy with my work."

"I appreciate that Lel! Let's not talk about this now. I was only joking my dear! Listen! Did you realize that you men are very fortunate people! You go out whenever you want and go wherever you like and nobody asks you where you've been or what you've been up to unlike us women. Always kept under lock and key."

Klara placed her hands on her lap, looked at Leli and smiled that particular smile that so fascinated men.

Leli blushed and felt excited. He felt the room warmer than it was. He mumbled some words, laughed, took a handkerchief out of his pocket and wiped his profusely sweating face and neck.

After exchanging some more words Klara continued:

"People like me are the unfortunate ones, Lel. Day and night all by myself and deprived of company." Klara stopped speaking for a while, sighed and said: "Uh, Lel! At times I'm sad. Alone in this village!" She lowered her head and when she raised it up again, her eyes were full of tears.

It's amazing how a woman can feign crying.

Leli, who was sitting close to Klara was full of affection. He failed to understand how in the past there were times when he had resented that young woman. He failed to understand how he never realized how beautiful she was.

He took hold of Klara's hand instinctively and caressed it.

At that moment Dwardu took a deep breath and then continued snoring.

Klara didn't say a word. She didn't withdraw her hand and her eyes showed that she was thankful for understanding and caressing her. Then she told him:

"I would have had a different life in Ħaż-Żgħir if only I had someone like you with whom I could share my feelings instead of being surrounded by such incompetent people. However, how can I turn the clock back?" Klara smiled again and looked Leli in the eye.

There come times when a person forgets all about the past or disregards what the future may hold in store for him. He only cares for the present moment.

Leli was precisely in that state of mind.

At that moment Leli didn't realize what was happening. He forgot all about his responsibilities, he forgot all about his wife, he forgot that a few feet away there was a man whom he had resented in the past. The only thing he cared about was that a beautiful woman was standing before him. Her sparkling jet black eyes approaching him as her lips pressed against his.

At that moment of breaking his marriage vows, Dwardu Buqerq woke up, watched them kiss and closed his eyes again. He smiled and almost laughed. He immediately became sober and whilst keeping his eyes closed said in his heart of hearts:

"Enjoy yourself, Lel! I'm glad for you. This is the beginning of my revenge against you. My objective is to see you separated from that proud wife of yours."

VII

"Believe me, Sir! This is my only wish! Nowadays you know me very well and I trust in you very much. I feel sad when I remember that I have to spend my life on this silly Island where I cannot express myself!"

"You're right," replied Kelin Miksat. Leli had paid him a visit that day and as always they spoke about books and shared their ideas that differed from those held by the rest of society.

"My experience has taught me that I have lived peacefully in Malta because I never sought to upset anybody with my views," continued Kelin. "As you know I will soon be leaving the Island and I shall never return. I don't regret that at all. There is no reason to stay in Malta for people like me. However, please understand what I'm trying to say, Lel. I can see that you have reached my stage.

"However, don't expect to change the world by going abroad or that everyone will agree with what you have to say!

"Foreign countries are similar to Malta in this regard, the majority of the people there are illiterate. Few of them have been lucky enough to receive some kind of education you must understand this. I had to grow old to understand it. Don't ever believe that you are going to be any happier than the rest just because you further your readings! As I told you on other occasions, this doesn't mean that I'm going to dispose of my books. If I experienced it, you will experience it too. At times I feel that perhaps it would have been better if I hadn't read any books and retained the Faith during my younger days.

"The friends I had and the books I read didn't foster any happiness. However, one should not disassociate from friends and ignore reading. How can I maintain that if I made it a point to learn and travel during my lifetime? It seems that those who differ from my views lead a happier life and it therefore appears that what they believe in is nearer to the Truth, than what atheists propose."

Leli remained stunned. It seemed that he was listening to Dun Karm rather than to Kelin who, was speaking from his wealth of experience. Leli was still young and inexperienced to understand such complex issues.

He found it convenient to be an atheist without any particular obligations towards anybody and without the need to answer for his actions. In that way he justified his illicit liaison with Klara Buqerq.

Leli wondered whether Kelin was out of his mind! How can a person forget all that he read and return to his childhood days as if nothing every happened? Leli therefore replied:

"There is much truth in what you say however, once a person becomes aware that alternative views exist there is no way of turning back."

"Indeed, my son. Few people succeed in retrieving the Faith they once enjoyed."

❖ ❖ ❖ ❖ ❖

Before leaving Malta to spend his last days with his distant relatives in Algiers, Kelin gave Leli two more books.

"I am giving you these books so that you will surely remember me," Kelin told him. These are the last two books written by Dostoyevski. One of the best Russian writers ever. *The Devils* is simply the best! *The Brothers Karamazov* is regarded by some as the greatest novel ever written. I don't know whether it's true but I believe it is the best novel I ever read. In that novel, Dostoyevski brings together two great Schools of Thought. That is those who believe in God and those who don't. Ultimately he leaves the reader to decide for himself. What do you think, eh, Lel, what a writer! I would say that Dostoyevski was an atheist but on the whole that book represents story writing at its best."

Leli was not in a position to reply. He not only hadn't read the books, which Kelin mentioned but he hadn't even ever heard that author's name before.

However had he read and understood those books, he would have realized that Dostoyevski, in his work *The Brothers Karamazov* suggests doing what Kelin had just proposed. In reality Dostoyevski never converted to Christianity. That author saves the toughest questions for Ivan, the middle one, who is a non-believer and puts in Alexi's mouth, the youngest one who is a believer, the weakest arguments.

In this way Dostoyevski succeeds in destroying Christian belief. He imitates that young lady who to look prettier seeks the company of uglier women and in that way she looks more beautiful than she actually is.

In time, Leli read both books which he liked a lot. If there was any hope that some day Leli would return to Christianity, the contents of those books eradicated that hope completely.

It was at this time that Leli started expressing himself against the Catholic Faith. It appeared that as long as Kelin was still in Malta, Leli was able to share his opinion with him. When Kelin emigrated and Leli was all alone he was unable to do so and he started sharing his views with others. He also started making fun of people who spoke about spiritual affairs.

Although Leli didn't waste time contradicting what others had to say on the subject and although the villagers had other problems on their minds such as war and starvation these didn't prevent them from gossiping about Leli's attitude towards religion and his relationship with the Buqerq family.

Ġammari, went to live on his own in a small house located on the outskirts of the village. Perhaps he suspected something and had he retaliated the result would have been counterproductive. It may be that he had grown tired of living with his daughter.

Ġammari didn't act wisely on this issue even though he did what he thought was best. However, it would have been better had he continued sharing the same house.

❖ ❖ ❖ ❖ ❖

"Believe me Lel I don't know what I'm going to do," Vira one evening told her husband. She looked worried. "Klara has taken the habit of coming here once or twice daily regardless of the time of day. You know how much the villagers gossip? It is easy to fall prey to their tongues even if they notice someone entering and leaving this house frequently. However, I don't know how I'm going to tell her. Furthermore, you know Klara's character: she's so sweet, kind and she'll do anything to help you."

Leli remained silent since he had a guilty conscience. Moreover, he couldn't care less what people said as long as he didn't break up with Klara.

Vira's words had been instigated by the fact that Leli's mother had pointedly warned her not to allow any girl friends inside her house.

"But, mother, do realize that Leli wouldn't betray me with another woman not even if she happened to be the most beautiful woman in the world," replied Vira. "From the time Klara has started visiting our house Leli, has always behaved like a gentleman."

"Yes, dear, I believe you and I understand what you mean," at that time Marjann recalled her own experience. "I'm not blaming you however, it is always good to keep an eye open because one should never risk placing straw too close to a fire. Even if a husband loves his wife as much as Leli loves you."

Marjann couldn't speak to Vira better than she did. After all Leli was her son and no mother would criticize her son unnecessarily or make his wife suspect that her husband is betraying her.

Although Vira heeded her mother-in-law's advice, she remained confused, as she did not know how to keep Klara away from their house.

Notwithstanding Vira's explanation, Leli couldn't tell her what she had to do to keep her away especially when it was in his interest to keep Klara close to him.

Leli and Vira used to speak about Klara quite often. However, he would start getting angry whenever his wife praised Klara for her help. His wife's innocent look troubled him more than if she had to get to know the truth.

He would have become angrier had he known that Klara was seeing another man who paid all her expenses. He was also unaware of the fact that she had already ruined other men's lives before his.

Leli was unwilling to give up his life style as long as Klara didn't object to their relationship and his wife didn't come to know about his secret love affair.

VIII

In Ħaż-Żgħir, the villagers celebrated the nine days proceeding Christmas with eagerness and enthusiasm.

The church used to be full of people to listen to the sermons that used to start at about sunset.

The preacher the year before the Great War ended was Dun Ġużepp from Ħal-Kbir. The villagers liked the way Dun Ġużepp preached. Most women flocked to church an hour before the sermon started while the men stayed on the parvis exchanging words prior to entering church.

One such evening while Leli was returning home from work he came across his father and Dun Karm near the church. His father recognized him and called him even though it was getting dark. Leli pretended to be in a hurry.

He greeted Dun Karm and exchanged a few words with them. Then, he told them that he had an appointment and had to leave. He wished them good night and continued on his way.

When Leli left, Ninu told Dun Karm:

"Leli has changed. If the right opportunity arises I would like you to have a word with him. The type of books he reads confuse him. He will listen to no one and he is keeping away from church. His mother informed me that sometimes he even failed to go to church on Sunday."

Dun Karm remained silent. He joined his hands behind his back in his usual manner and lowered his head as if he was looking for something on the ground. Then he coughed and whispered:

"Yes, I need to talk to him! Leli is not a bad boy! However, the difficulties a person comes across in our day and age are great. A person needs to struggle with himself to overcome those difficulties! He who goes near the edge falls over."

At that moment Dun Karm was thinking about Buqerq's family and about the rumor that was spreading in the village.

Although Dun Karm knew that Leli loved books he never imagined what kind of books Leli had read. Neither was he aware of their repercussions on Leli's character. Dun Karm thought that this was an unusual case for him to handle.

If Klara was Leli's only problem there could be some hope and Dun Karm's words would have helped. However, the bad influence that those books exerted on Leli required a stronger remedy than the words that this good priest could utter.

❖ ❖ ❖ ❖ ❖

Sometimes it seems that a person picks up a fight without realizing that a solution to a difficult situation is possible through some effort at discussion.

That's what happened to Leli on the day he met his father and Dun Karm.

When Leli arrived home, Vira, as if in agreement with her father-in-law spoke vigorously to her husband about his religious obligations.

"You should be ashamed of yourself," she told him "you haven't been to confession for months! Christmas is close and you should go to church like the rest of the men and make peace with God."

"I have told you many times, Vir, to stay out of my religious responsibilities!"

"What do you mean stay out? Have you forgotten that I'm your wife? Don't you know that if I don't warn you I would be failing in my duties? I repeat, you should be ashamed of yourself! You would go and give thanks to God even if you were a Moslem. You should be ashamed of yourself when you recall the good education your poor mother provided you with and the kind of life you are leading. I am certain that you are the only person in the village behaving in this way!"

Leli stood up, removed the chair angrily and started swearing and blaspheming. He warned Vira that he would throw her out of the house if she didn't shut up.

They had had several fights since the time they married but she never realized that Leli could lose his temper so badly. However, Vira was not afraid of him and she threw the overall, which she had in her hand at his face.

Leli reacted by punching Vira severely on her chest with his right hand. She fell backwards and rested against the wall.

She started crying and sobbing. Vira never realized that Leli would ever hit her. Her father never punished her and although she was physically hurt, the thought of being hit by the person she loved most of all was more painful. She hated him for what he did to her.

Leli looked desperately at his wife crouched on the floor groaning with pain.

He immediately realized that he had committed a big mistake.

He begged her to forgive him and promised her that he would never hit her again no matter what.

They didn't have supper that evening and, she spent most of the night sobbing.

In time Leli forgot the promise he had made but his wife loved him otherwise he would have lost her as he had lost his Faith.

Vira, gradually also realized that a man could disgrace his wife in other ways. That kind of behaviour touched her inner feelings and caused her much psychological pain.

IX

" You simply can't imagine Nen, what those poor people go through, unless you experience it yourself Beasts receive better treatment! Their hearts always throbbing with fear of death. One can see fear, weariness, sorrow and discouragement in their eyes.

"Sometimes some of them go to their death by fighting on purpose in dangerous zones with the hope of being killed in order to escape that terrible way of life.

"Come on Nen! Put everything behind you and join me on the battlefield. Stop saying that you don't know other languages except Maltese and Italian. You can help and comfort a person without speaking to him.

"At this moment this is where we should be. It is our duty to stay in the midst of fighting and death. Our responsibility is to comfort these poor soldiers, to save their souls and to teach them that He is waiting for them to grant them peace!

"Come near me, so that you can comfort some of the many soldiers who are dying daily in the prime of life, butchered and badly wounded, far away from their dear ones!

"Come, Nen! Come so that you too can experience what human beings do when they forget Christ's teachings! When they forget that

mankind is one! When instead of loving and forgiving, they hate and kill each other!"

Dun Karm received this letter from another priest towards the beginning of 1918. That priest had been in Belgium for two years. He was the soldiers' chaplain and he was always close to where the fighting happened to be.

Dun Karm immediately replied to his friend's call.

He forgot his family and friends with whom he lived happily and peacefully and within a month he was ready to leave the Island dressed in uniform. He looked paler and thinner than ever, he was over-excited, and his eyes sparkled. Everybody congratulated him and told him: "You look fine in that uniform." While his mother with tears in her eyes remarked: "Imagine what my son had to go through!"

Ta' Braġ were to look after his mother in his absence. Marjann didn't want him to leave her with anyone else. She would stay with them and Marjann would take care of her until his return – 'unless he meets my son's fate!' Marjann said in her heart of hearts as she started crying.

Some villagers said: "What on earth is he going to do!" Others said: "He did the right thing! He is doing what is expected of him!" Yet others said: "Dun Karm won't stay long abroad His health is weak!" In other words people speculated on this and the other until one morning Dun Karm left the country. He left everything behind to answer his friend's call and share with him tears, pain and death!

His mother was the only person to receive any news of him when he was abroad.

Dun Karm's work abroad involved constant risk in Flanders and on the Belgian fields. He helped the wounded and the dying. He gave them comfort and brought them closer to God.

He constantly expected to meet the same fate of those surrounding him.

He had hardly been a month on the battlefield that he hadn't learnt sufficient English to hear confession and speak the language to help those poor soldiers.

Many of those soldiers respected him a lot. They were very close to him. He was such a holy man.

The rigid life he led in Ħaż-Żgħir served him well during the time he spent on the battlefield amidst the smoke, fire and danger. Soon, all the soldiers in those areas came to know him. They respected him especially. In fact with time they started calling him: the little dark-skinned saint.

X

The English say that the pen is mightier than the sword. There is much truth in that saying.

What made Dun Karm go to war in Belgium? Wasn't it another priest's letter? Imagine the power of the written word!

Now listen to another kind of letter – a cursed letter that is aimed to do harm:

"*Dear Vira,*

Believe me if you want but I can no longer watch you being deceived and dishonoured! Listen to me and open your eyes. That woman comes to your house daily because of your husband and not because of you.

She is mad about your husband. Your husband is betraying you with her! He is not the holy man you imagine him to be! You know this, even though you pretend not to and you vouchsafe for him. He who beats his wife cannot love her and neither can she love him.

Before this woman Leli had another one and rest assured that after this woman you're not going to be the only woman in his life. He'll behave just like any other man in his position.

Listen to me and open your eyes! Pay attention to where he goes and you'll see that he isn't worthy of your love you stupid woman!

A person who wishes you well."

Vira received this anonymous letter one afternoon, about a month after her quarrel with Leli.

Vira was on the doorstep waiting for the milkman when the postman gave her the letter. Meanwhile, she gazed at her neighbour's two small children. One child was about four years old and the other child somewhat younger.

They were really beautiful children. They had golden locks of hair. They were so playful and full of life.

Vira had one disappointment: she wanted to have children. She thought how happy she would be if she had at least one son - who looked like her next door neighbour's children.

She was so lost in this thought that the postman almost startled her when he gave her the letter. He greeted her and left her thinking who could have written to her.

After reading the anonymous letter rapidly and then more slowly she sat down on the steps leading to the garden holding the letter in one hand and resting the other hand on her lap. She wondered who could have written that dreadful letter.

She tried to convince herself that the letter was a lie. However, she still felt very confused. She waited for Leli to tell her that he loved her and that she was the only woman in his life.

When Leli returned from work he refuted the contents of that letter. He swore to Vira that he never loved anybody else except her. He also decided to act before something worse happened.

Vira remained worried for days wondering whether Leli was sleeping with Klara. Finally she concluded that Leli was still faithful to her. However, she made up her mind to tell Klara to keep away from their house to avoid peoples' gossip.

Klara too refused the contents of that letter and swore that she had never encouraged Leli in anyway. Although she stopped visiting Leli's house, both met secretly somewhere else. However, they soon stopped seeing each other not only because Leli wanted to break up the affair but also because Klara suddenly became engaged to the man who originally used to visit their house. They married after two months and went to live in Ħal-Kbir.

❖ ❖ ❖ ❖ ❖

Dwardu was the person who sent the anonymous letter Vira received.

He tried several times to ruin Vira's reputation but she always kept her ground. However, he never lost heart and strived to take his revenge on her.

After his sister's marriage and his failure to separate Vira from Leli, Dwardu sought an alternative strategy to get at this courageous woman.

He started spreading the rumor that not all that glitters is gold. A woman's appearance doesn't make her respectable. She could easily deceive others and her husband.

Since many knew that ta' Buqerq and ta' Braġ families were very close friends, many also believed that Dwardu must have had an affair with Leli's wife some time or other.

Dwardu felt very pleased when he realized that his words instigated people to such conclusions. He felt satisfied and content as if he was saying the truth.

XI

It was the day when the Church commemorates the dead and for those who are old enough to remember, exactly nine days before the Armistice was signed!

Marjann, Leli and Vira visited the Addolorata cemetry in the afternoon.

There were many people. Many seemed to be having a picnic as they laughed their heart out. Leli looked sullen and grumbled. Vira told him to stop it: "I don't care what they do! Everybody minds his own business!"

Marjann and Vira stopped to pray near a grave where there were several other women praying for the soul of whoever was buried there.

Leli distanced himself from the rest and as he was reading the inscription on one of the graves he heard somebody calling him.

It was Klara.

Leli was surprised and he didn't know what to say.

"How are you Lel?" Klara told him "Are you pretending you don't know us?"

"I'm not alone Klar. I'm together with Vira and my mother. Won't you speak to them?"

Vira raised her eyes and noticed that Leli was speaking to Klara.

It had been some time since Vira met Klara. In fact she hadn't met her since her wedding. Vira wasn't pleased to see Klara as the latter was the reason that had isolated her from many friends. She called Leli's mother and together they approached her. They greeted her and asked her what had become of her.

They spent some time in idle talk as most women do when they meet other women with whom they don't want to have anything to do. Then, they said their goodbyes and every body continued on his own way.

However, just before they left Klara shook hands with Leli and Vira noted the way Klara looked at him. Vira didn't say a word and she didn't address Leli at any time until they arrived home.

That evening Leli noted that Vira's eyes were filled with tears.

"What's the matter with you, Vir?"

"Nothing, Lel! I feel lonely tonight."

"Why are you feeling lonely?"

"Lel!"

"Yes!"

"Will you sleep with another woman if you had the opportunity to?"

"Why are you asking me this? Don't you know how much I love you?"

"But if I had children like other women you would love me more, no?"

"Vir, don't be foolish! You know how I feel about these things. You know that I cannot love you more than I do."

"But I would have loved you less, Lel because I would have to share my love with someone else!"

XII

It was Armistice Day. An important date in the history of mankind.

On that day, at eleven o'clock, the war amongst the world's greatest nations stopped for good. The useless, terrible fighting that had been going on for four years in the air, on land and on sea finally ceased. During that period many young people had changed into murderers and thieves. It had changed Europe into a land of atrocities, sickness, starvation, murder and death.

The so-called Great War ended on 11 November 1918. That war killed 9,000,000 men and left many widows and orphans. It left behind the greatest ever havoc in human history and ended after dismantling empires, changing customs and hardening men's hearts to what is true, good and beautiful.

❖ ❖ ❖ ❖ ❖

When the news about the cessation of war reached these islands many Maltese who had lost their dear ones in that war lamented their loss.

Many of those Maltese wondered why it had to be them to lose their sons or their husbands.

However, there were millions of other people who were asking the same question and who remained without an answer.

Marjann was one of those people.

On that day she missed her son more than ever. One thought racked her mind:

"Alas, my poor son! If he had been alive he would be coming home! But who knows where he is? Where is he buried? Poor soul!"

Indeed, where is he buried! Who could tell Marjann that her son wasn't even lucky to have a grave and that his body lay under the scorching Gallipoli sun for several days until the rainfall carried his body somewhere else.

❖ ❖ ❖ ❖ ❖

There was so much agitation in one of the main streets of the Island.

When people excite themselves there is no accounting for their behaviour. Men behave like children and women behave like babies. Everybody does what comes to his head.

That's the way most Maltese who happened to be in Kingsway on 11 November 1918 behaved.

Who could blame them?

Neither did anyone attempt stopping them behaving that way!

The Maltese hugged soldiers and sailors. Everybody was extremely happy. They sang, shouted, kissed, laughed and greeted everybody.

Alas!

At times man is to be pitied!

He does everything to earn a living. He goes to his death without offering resistance, he even kills when programmed to kill as long as he gets paid. Then, when those who rule the world say "that's enough" with the consequence that unemployment and hunger ensue, he rejoices. He fails to realize that one day he could die of hunger just the same as when he was at war. That would be more terrible.

But why bother about tomorrow? Just live for the day.

The most important thing now is that there's nothing to be afraid of. He can work without fear of being killed by the atrocities of war.

❖ ❖ ❖ ❖ ❖

Ta' Bućagħak were pleased given that they had made a lot of money. Who cares? They wouldn't mind if there was another war. It would provide them with another opportunity to fill their coffers with gold!

Leli was also pleased with the news. He was a lively person by nature. Since many people were going to Valletta, Leli asked his employer whether it was possible to take the day off. Ta' Buċagħak approved Leli's request.

Dwardu was fired from work a week before this event occurred. He had a fight with the owners and resigned from his place of work. As from that day the Buċagħak Brothers adopted a positive attitude towards Leli. Perhaps they thought that Leli was going to quit his job too?

Leli was very sorry that Dwardu had lost his employment. Poor Leli! Notwithstanding the many books he read he was still naive! Who knows whether he ever realized how much Dwardu hated him. However, Leli loved even his worst enemies. It seems that knowledge does not make a person hard-hearted.

Initially he would feel very angry but after some time he would forget everything as if nothing had happened.

❖ ❖ ❖ ❖ ❖

That evening Leli and Vira went to Valletta. They had a coffee in a bar located close to the law courts, then they went to the pictures and afterwards listened to the band playing. It was marvelous looking at the lights after a four year black out. They also watched the people enjoying themselves.

As they were leaving Valletta, Leli noticed Klara and her husband walking on the other side of the street.

Vira didn't notice them.

Klara and Leli stole a quick look. He revived the desire he once harbored for Klara and wished that he had not ended his affair so abruptly. The way Klara smiled at him indicated that she was still attracted to him.

That evening Vira was quite herself. Leli and Vira didn't go out so often and as they arrived home she started preparing dinner. She then pulled her husband's hair and told him:

"Lel, this evening we were like two young lovers! Eh, my dear?"

Leli replied: "Isn't that so, Vir?"

XIII

That day was a great day for both Leli and Vira. However, they didn't realize that it was also the eve of one of the worst days in their lives.

It couldn't have been otherwise because on that day Vira came to know that Leli was deceiving her And with whom!

Leli and Vira loved each other since their childhood. Furthermore, both were in the prime of life.

For Vira, Leli was everything.

She was childless. She loved her husband very much. How could she fail thinking about him?

For Leli, Vira was an important person in his life. A woman who deserved to be loved and honoured.

For this reason, every time he met Klara, he could not be at peace with himself especially after having betrayed his wife so many times. However, he would say in his heart of hearts:

"It wasn't my fault. It was Klara's fault! What could I do?"

In other words it was the old story that started in the Garden of Eden. A story that will remain with us as long as women continue tempting men.

However, he would get excited when he remembered that Vira could some day discover that he had been unfaithful to her. In other words he would feel weighed down with guilt.

That's the way Leli felt when he understood that all his efforts had come to nothing. From then on things were going to be different. He was no longer the man who loved her and honoured her, and who deserved her love and honour but, the person who ill-treated her when he got angry and betrayed her with another woman.

❖ ❖ ❖ ❖ ❖

Leli possessed an old mahogany desk. It contained two drawers on either side. In one of the drawers, which could be locked, he kept some things that belonged to Klara together with seven or eight love letters that she had written to him when they were having an affair.

Leli at times left the drawer of his desk unlocked. He knew that Vira was not going to open it and examine its contents.

Indeed, Vira never opened the drawer.

However, once she gave in to temptation. She saw that the drawer was half-open. Instead of leaving it that way, she opened it, looked inside, rummaged through the papers and other things contained in it and there found evidence that her husband was cheating on her.

❖ ❖ ❖ ❖ ❖

When a person finds himself unexpectedly in deep trouble his state of mind cannot be easily described. In other words he can be compared to a person who has lost his mind. He cries, runs about without knowing where he's going, sits and stands up immediately, lies down, puts his head between his hands and imagines that it's all a dream. In particular he's living in some kind of fantasy world. However, he immediately realizes that what he's passing through is real.

That's how Vira reacted when she read the love letters that Klara had written her husband. Vira was deeply hurt by every word contained in those letters.

❖ ❖ ❖ ❖ ❖

Leli remained seated without uttering a word for a long time. He was paralyzed as he listened to his wife crying and scolding him. He remained silent. It seemed as if some weight was pulling him down and he couldn't stand up.

Vira cried as if she had wakened up suddenly in the middle of a beautiful dream. The only thought that passed through Leli's mind was that he had committed a serious mistake. Through his actions he had lost what he cherished most and that his life would never be the same again.

"I'm sorry! I'm sorry" he started saying in his heart of hearts. Then in a lofty voice he begged Vira to forgive him:

"Forgive me, Vir! I know how much I have hurt you! I'm

sorry. However, from now on I'll pay for my mistake! I'll start a new kind of life. I'll respect you as no other man respects his wife! Forgive me Vir! "

XIV

Although the bad days pass just as much as the good ones, those days cast a kind of shadow that takes a long time to disappear. In fact, neither Vira nor Leli forgot the event. Vira looked pale for a long time after the incident occurred. She told inquisitive people who asked after her health that she was sick.

She didn't speak much to her husband. They lived together like strangers for a long time. Speaking to each other when necessary. Leli did his best to make her forget the past and resume their normal married life. However, Vira couldn't forget what she had been through so easily.

Amazingly, as Vira recovered her health, Leli fell into a state of depression. He spent days without uttering a word. He felt that he was the one who suffered most from what had happened rather than his wife.

Vira noticed that Leli was no longer himself and that something must have happened to him. She thought that the friction between them, for some reason or another had effected him more.

She was not mistaken.

❖ ❖ ❖ ❖ ❖

Dun Karm returned to Malta after two months that the war had finished.

The months he had spent among the bloodshed didn't change him much. He was still as thin as a rake as he couldn't get any thinner. He had sunken eyes and an even more shrunken face.

However, his facial expression did change a little.

When Dun Karm returned from the war he greeted and smiled at every person he met.

The villagers welcomed him back with open arms!

They loved Dun Karm!

He always helped those in need, those who needed a word of comfort and those who needed food.

For this reason, as soon as the word spread that Dun Karm was returning home, many people visited Ninu ta' Braġ's house either to congratulate Dun Karm's mother or to welcome him. Dun Karm greeted and thanked everybody. Everyone remarked: ""God bless him!" Who knows what he has been through and yet! He almost looks better now than before. His face has changed, isn't that true? He no longer seems the angry person he used to be."

Others who were totally dedicated to the church, rejoiced and said to one another:

"The village church will be revived! He will celebrate and give Holy Communion before and after early morning mass as he used to do before he went to war!"

Those who turned to Dun Karm for some money hoped that he had saved a substantial sum from the war and that they would soon share part of that money with him.

❖ ❖ ❖ ❖ ❖

Dun Karm returned together with his mother to their home two days after his arrival.

He thanked Ninu and Marjann for looking after his mother in his absence.

They started speaking about Leli as they were together in the room, which Marjann had prepared for Dun Karm's mother.

"Believe me, Dun Karm!" Marjann told him "his father knows how much I pray for him. Much more than I pray for the soul of my dead son."

"That's true," interrupted Ninu. "Sometimes she really gets on my nerves. I start shouting at her and tell her: 'who cares! We gave them a good upbringing; now it's their business if they don't want to lead a good life.'"

"Since when has Leli changed so much?" Dun Karm asked in an unconvincing voice.

"It's been a long time now," replied Marjann. "A long time! Since the time he met Kelin Miksat. I never liked that person and it was he who confused Leli's mind with the kind of books he gave him to read."

"Listen Marjann, there's nothing wrong in reading and learning," replied Dun Karm. Then he continued: "As long as he reads books that are morally sound."

"Certainly, Dun Karm. However, I suspect that the books Leli reads aren't so. He not only fails to go to church but he also criticizes its operations. Moreover, his neighbours say that he scolds and beats his wife! Can you imagine, Dun Karm! I'm such an unlucky person! Didn't I provide him with a good upbringing? Did he have to become such a person?"

"We did sacrifice so much for him!" continued Ninu.

"Listen, both of you. Don't believe every word you hear about Leli. I'm not aware of the books you're mentioning. Before I left I never heard anybody criticize Leli's behaviour - except for his friendship with ta' Buqerq, which I personally disapproved of.

"Since I've been here I can only say this about Leli: while I was speaking to him, in his look, in his eyes I thought I saw something that I didn't like, that worried me a lot."

Marjann and her husband didn't say another word and waited for Dun Karm to continue.

Then, Dun Karm said:

"Leli is not himself. Something must have happened to him and if I'm right you have to make sure that you speak to him gently and tell his wife not to resist him.

"From Leli's look I believe that he should be pitied rather than scolded. For this reason disregard whatever you hear about him. Don't forget that people like to exaggerate things - especially bad news!

"Continue praying God for him and ignore what people say."

❖ ❖ ❖ ❖ ❖

Dun Karm was correct.

Leli was not himself. He hadn't been well for some time but he had hardly noticed his deteriorating physical condition let alone the people surrounding him.

The life that Leli led was effecting his health badly.

Leli was not prepared to meet the challenges offered by the books he had read.

However, he yearned to learn. He didn't mind if he stayed all night reading until he finished the book and got something out of it.

Furthermore, Leli was as good by nature as much as he was intelligent and wise. However, his goodness and his love for the truth contrasted sharply with the ideas he obtained from certain books he had read. Such ideas included the belief that man is not answerable for his actions to anybody; that a man is no better than a stone; that there is no afterlife; that there is no God and the like.

Leli could only discuss these ideas with Kelin as long as the latter lived in Malta or with his friend Sulnata who had now graduated as a Doctor. His inability to share his ideas led to a struggle within. That struggle was harming his health as he was constantly pretending with others to be what he wasn't in reality.

To make matters worse it was at that time that Leli met with his greatest trouble in his life: Klara ta' Buqerq!

There were several other men who betrayed their wives however, these were not Leli's type.

While Leli was physically attracted to Klara he also felt sorry about deceiving his wife who loved him very much. In fact he felt guilty everytime Vira told him how much she loved him. He feared that some day Vira would come to know of his affair with Klara and realize that their married life was not as beautiful as she imagined it to be!

The period of time he spent with Klara was detrimental to his health.

Finally, his wife came up with the evidence and threatened to send the love letters to Klara's husband when he least expected it. Leli was sorry that their marriage was ruined for good. All these aspects had an impact on his health.

Three months after the incident, Leli suddenly noticed that he was sick of mind and that he was behaving very much like a mad person.

XV

Ġużè, the eldest of the Buċagħak brothers was a serious looking person. It goes without saying that people who constantly think about ways and means of making more money scarcely find time to be happy and enjoy life. Most likely he keeps a constant eye on his revenue and on the number of debtors.

However, one day he succeeded in having a good laugh.

His brother Manwel who as we read earlier always teased Leli about books, war and businessmen, started pestering him.

He argued with Manwel about those people who fail to help the poor. Suddenly, Leli's eyes welled with tears, his lips dried up, started confusing words, and looked around him as if he wanted to know what was going on. Finally he was lost for words.

Those who were surrounding Leli and looking at him couldn't help laughing. No one had instigated Leli to lose his temper on the subject neither did anybody hinder him to lose track of what he was saying and stop speaking.

To make matters worse, at that moment Manwel stood up from his place winked at two other workmen who were next to him and told Leli in an ironic voice:

"Lel, I am going to open the windows for some fresh air and send for some medicine to help you recover your senses! "

Leli was not pleased with this. It would have been better for Manwel to pass some other remark.

He started swearing at Manwel, picked up his hat from the top of the box where he used to keep it and left the warehouse, looking as red as a turkey-cock, eyes bulging and grumbling.

As soon as Leli left, Manuel, Ġużè and the rest of the people present in the warehouse, laughed their heart out.

❖ ❖ ❖ ❖ ❖

If, the band club was important to Leli, the latter was more valuable to the band club. In fact, as Gejtu tal-Klarinett observed, when Leli neglected the Club's management, the number of band club members dwindled.

Leli was considered the lifeblood of the band club. Everybody gathered around to discuss matters with him whenever he happened to be there.

His friends would get very excited listening to him telling them news about the war or about events that were taking place overseas.

Ġużeppi ta' Snien, with reference to Leli, would say "Among all the villagers, nobody is better informed than he! Nobody can speak and explain better than he does. Not even the parish priest, the police inspector or the doctor put together!"

For this reason one can imagine, how Leli must have felt when one day while at the band club he was lost for words and the people around him stared at him sarcastically.

The funny thing is that the more he tried to make sense out of what he was saying the more he grew confused, the more his lips dried up, the more he became excited until he had to cut short his conversation and asked them to forgive him. He then left abruptly, saluted them and returned home.

Those present realized that something was wrong with Leli. Someone asked whether he was drunk.

Somebody else replied: "Of course he's not drunk! Who can say what's on a person's mind!".

❖ ❖ ❖ ❖ ❖

When Leli arrived home he felt dizzy and went straight upstairs to lie down on his bed.

Vira heard him going upstairs and called him from the dining room. However, she didn't suspect what had happened to her husband since it wasn't the first time that he had done so and hence remained in the dining room preparing lunch.

However, Leli was obviously not thinking about food. At that moment he was looking at the empty space on the opposite wall. He recalled how people had made fun of him both at work and at the band club.

It was at this time that Leli realized that he was going mad.

When Vira called him to have lunch, instead of answering her or going down to the dining room, he started crying like a baby.

Vira immediately ran up to him and asked him what was wrong.

But Leli continued crying.

A woman who really loves her husband quickly forgives him for the mistakes he committed.

This was the first time that Vira had seen Leli, with all his good sense, crying. At that moment she felt sorry for him and she started crying and, caressing him.

Afterwards, Leli replied:

"I don't know, Vir! But I believe it's time for me to suffer for the harm I caused you. I don't know what I'm feeling in my head. I have become the laughing stock of most people and if I continue behaving this way I shall soon go mad!"

XVI

Those who remember the post war years will remember that those years were characterized by three important events, that is: the rise in the cost of living, the Spanish influenza and the political upheaval that led to the 1919 riots.

However, as far as Leli was concerned it didn't matter much what happened.

At that time Leli was in the middle of a fierce struggle with himself, trying to recover from his illness.

Pawlu Sulnata was among the first to visit him and after examining him spoke to him like a true friend.

"Listen, Lel," said Pawlu, "you are the cause of your own trouble. I am not telling you this to blame you but to help you remember that you are the remedy for your own trouble. You must overcome yourself.

"You are going through a lot of pain because of your illness I know. You needn't tell me. I understand that perfectly. You may come across people who make fun of you however, they will really be making fun of themselves.

"My prescription to you Lel is this and you should never forget what I'm about to tell you: first, you must never fear pain! Secondly you need to socialize, even if every one you meet tries to make fun of you!

"Now is the time to prove yourself, to show your ability and courage!

"To repeat, Lel, if you want to recover you must struggle and win yourself! Do you understand?

"From now on you must forget what happened to you, and look to the future. You should only think what's going to happen next and constantly repeat to yourself 'Tomorrow shall be different from today. Tomorrow will be a better day!' Do you understand, Lel? If you do this you will recover more quickly than if you take the pills that all the doctors in the world can provide you with.

"As for the rest: eat well. You can drink as much milk and vegetables as you like. Avoid piquant food and alcohol!

"Burn all the books you possess, or if you like to keep them, ensure that you disregard them for the time being. Do your best to forget yourself. You know what I mean, no, Lel, with the words: Forgetting yourself? That is: think about anybody and about anything you like as long as you don't think about how sick you are, the pain you're going through, what people are doing to you and that people should pity you.

"Try to forget that you're the center of the world and that when you die everybody else and everything will die too.

Remember that you're one of many other people and that with or without you the world will continue revolving.

"Finally, make sure that you do your best to retain your employment especially as long as your employers are prepared to keep you on their books. Anyway, ensure that you keep yourself busy!"

❖ ❖ ❖ ❖ ❖

Dr. Sulnata couldn't have spoken to Leli any better. He had spoken to him as his friend not as his doctor although, Leli didn't pay much attention to the doctor's warnings during the first days of his illness.

Leli persisted in his employment with great effort. He used to reply to others in a suffocated voice. There were times when he didn't feel like going out to avoid being ridiculed. On other instances he felt so ashamed that he wished the earth could swallow him up to avoid peoples' looks.

Who could blame the mentally sick patient who disregards doctor's warnings? What's the purpose of telling the mentally sick patient: "Forget yourself," if he is the cause of his own sickness?

❖ ❖ ❖ ❖ ❖

Dun Karm together with Vira and Marjann was also sorry for what had happened to Leli. It wasn't the first time that he wept while thinking about Leli or praying for him.

Once, while he was speaking with Marjann and Vira, Dun Karm told them:

"Poor boy! Although he damned his soul and became mentally ill in reality, he is such an understanding and kind-hearted person, always ready to forgive even his greatest enemy!"

"True" replied Vira as a tear ran down Marjann's cheek.

"Believe me, I am prepared to sacrifice myself for him to see him well again! However, I fear that Leli's illness will take some time."

"You think so, Dun Karm!" interrupted Marjann and Vira.

"That's what I think although I am neither a doctor nor a prophet. There is one thing, which gives me a lot of courage about Leli. Although Leli is a quiet person, he is a fighter and does not give up easily. He is not a coward and for this reason I think he can overcome his illness. This is the greatest battle of his life but I'm confident that he will succeed in overcoming this great difficulty!"

❖ ❖ ❖ ❖ ❖

The news that the eldest son of ta' Braġ was mentally ill spread like wild fire in the village.

People said all kinds of things. Some said: "I'm sure he's got nothing serious!" others said: "I'm not sure how he's going to get through this one. He walks through the village square like some drunkard without recognizing anybody. If he continues in this kind of life he'll soon find himself confined to a lunatic asylum!"

Everybody spoke about Leli especially at the band club and at Ġorġ's wine shop.

The way people talked about Leli at the wine shop was quite different from the way they talked about him at the band club. They wished Leli well and referred to him as 'Poor, Leli' or said 'God willing he'll soon recover.'

It wasn't the same at Ġorġ's. Ġorġ did not have any sympathy with the band club members. The band club made him lose customers and he therefore despised all its members including the Club's President.

One day, while Ġorġ was speaking about Leli, Dwardu Buqerq entered the shop and after exchanging some words, Ġorġ shrewdly whispered to Dwardu.

"Listen, Dward, is it true that he lost his mind because of his wife?"

Dwardu smiled and said nothing.

"I am asking you this question because some people are saying that the reason for his illness is due to the fact that he must have had some bee in his bonnet."

Dwardu smiled and said:

"Why are you asking me Ġorġ? Do you think that I know more about peoples' business than you do? I can only say one thing: you shouldn't be surprised by anything in this world. Everything can happen. There are many men who have lost their head because of a woman!"

Some of those who were inside the shop listening to Dwardu speaking, interrupted and said:

"You're quite right. You are indeed a man of character! What you say is true."

Dwardu was quite capable of playing with words.

"Listen my friends! A person who swore that he was telling the truth told me that members from both sides of his parent's families died in a lunatic asylum. If that is so there is no need to be surprised that Leli is in the same situation. Children take after their parents."

"That's very true," replied Lonzu the stevedore. "I have a mole just below my chest. Do you believe, that all of my children, except one, have a mole in some part or other of their body?"

"We belielve you, of course, we believe you," interrupted the others.

"Listen my friends!" said Ġorġ, when he realized that the discussion was changing course and dying out. "I don't know how to say this, but until recently there was no better man than ta' Braġ, but at least from what people say – he has been acting strangely lately. He swears in the presence of others! There are people who say that they saw him in the company of Freemasons. God reaches everybody and one mustn't show off and do as one pleases!"

"That's true," replied two or three persons who were almost asleep due to the wine they had drunk.

"God reaches everybody, Ġorġ" said Dwardu, as he moved his head and raised his cheeks "and one would be committing a mistake not to believe in Him!"

This is how malicious persons discuss things when they meet. Dwardu and Ġorġ were such people. However their venom was deadlier than that of snakes.

❖ ❖ ❖ ❖ ❖

Little did Ġorġ and Dwardu realize that what they were saying applied to them rather than to Leli. However, that's the way they repaid Leli's kindness.

In less than three weeks after this discussion had taken place, Dwardu was brought to justice accused for political incitement. Although he escaped imprisonment he had to leave Malta suddenly for another country.

Ġorġ too had his due. He had indulged in excessive eating and drinking during the Imnarja feast and died two days later.

XVII

Several months passed since Leli had become mentally ill. They were terrible days for Leli.

An old saying goes that time sometimes moves quickly like spring water at other times it moves slowly like oil or tar. This is how Leli's first year of illness passed.

Leli did not lose his mind completely. He didn't go mad. He struggled against his illness and looked after the little health he had left like a mother looks after the health of her baby. He hoped to recover and persisted in going to work although many a time he behaved like a drunkard.

The Buċagħak brothers loved him. As long as he did his work they didn't bother how he lived. If he spoke to them they would answer him, if he didn't they would let him continue with his task. When he got angry with someone over some unimportant matter they simply excused his behaviour.

Leli divided his time between work and home.

He felt that he was still not in a position to socialize with others. He learnt that few people show compassion for the sick and the depressed. People wanted to see smiling happy faces.

Sadness formed part of his life.

"Lel, smile at me!" Vira used to tell him.

He would obey her just to please her. However, Leli's smile

attracted more compassion than happiness. When Vira realized the state of her husband's health she would go away with tears in her eyes.

At other times she would grow impatient especially when Leli started breaking things, swearing and throwing things at her. She would burst out crying and screaming so that the neighbours would hear her. Leli would shut up as he regained his senses. Then he would remain frightened and quiet for days.

When he controlled himself at home he would lose his temper at work. He would grow angry and start swearing even if someone laughed for some reason or other.

He was lucky in this respect because he always found people who felt sorry for him and tried to comfort him. But as soon as he left their side they would say to one another: "Poor man! He's to be pitied He's not himself."

❖ ❖ ❖ ❖ ❖

A mentally sick person is easily irritated if someone laughs in his presence for any reason whatsoever.

This is one of the things that keeps him isolated from other people.

People who suffer from tuberculosis, the blind, and the crippled draw compassion towards themselves. The mentally sick person with his angry look always ready to jump on whoever speaks to him, many a time makes himself an object of laughter instead one of compassion.

It's impossible to imagine a crueler and sadder kind of life in which a person instead of compassion is ridiculed and laughed at.

This is the greatest disrespect a mentally ill person can experience. For this reason he can only live in isolation or with other mentally sick persons.

Leli, as we said, lived in isolation from everything and everybody. He went to work and never went out of the house.

Vira knew that the fact that Leli never went out was causing him a lot of harm. She would put on her veil and tell him, "Come on Lel! Let's go for a walk to Ħal-Kbir." When Leli agreed to accompany her they would only reach half of the way. He would start feeling sick when he saw people coming towards him as he thought that they were going to greet him or that he would have to speak to them.

Although he didn't feel at ease at his parent's house and looked forward to returning home it was different at his father-in-law's house where he stayed without complaining.

Ġammari was one of those few people who allowed Leli to say what he liked. He would let him speak about his illness, and let off steam.

When Leli happened to be at his father-in-law's house and he would have liked to speak about something, Ġammari wouldn't stop from his work and fix him in the eye to listen to what he had to say. He would continue with his work and let Leli speak. Ġammari's behaviour at that moment did Leli a lot of good.

Leli also realized that although Ġammari was a man of few words he knew that he wished him well. For this reason, Leli used to feel a lot better when Ġammari used to tell him: "Don't worry Lel! Rest assured: one day you will recover and resume your normal way of life,"

The positive relationship between her husband and her father increased Vira's confidence and peace of mind.

❖ ❖ ❖ ❖ ❖

Fear is a terrible thing. In a moment of fear a person loses his dignity as a human being and resembles a beast that shivers all over when it identifies its master with a stick in hand.

The fear that such a person experiences every time he finds himself in the company of others remains one of the chief pains that a mentally sick person has to endure. Indeed, this is one of the greatest worries resulting from this terrible illness.

Have you ever seen a sick dog when it curls itself up into a ball beneath a wall? Did you ever notice how it shivers when it sees someone coming near? That's what happens to the mentally sick person when it sees an acquaintance approaching.

I suppose people will ask: 'What is the cause of such fear?' Generally a human being is afraid from someone who is either going to harm him physically, or damage his property or cause him moral damage?

Doctors argue that the fear of the mentally sick person comes about because the roots in a person's body lose the strength that binds them together. Those who do not understand the arguments put forward by the medical profession, agree that the mentally sick person fears others because the patient believes that people are making fun of him. This kind of behaviour hurts a person more than physical abuse. The mentally sick person, who is incapable of defending himself, cannot but stare helplessly at the other person.

❖ ❖ ❖ ❖ ❖

Sometimes, after a good night's rest and while preparing to go to work, Leli would say in his heart of hearts: "How is it that I cannot overcome this problem? Why is it that I'm terrified when I remember that I may come across Sergeant Ċens or 'Arakemm-naf[51] on my way to work? Am I not better than they? They certainly aren't as well-read as I?"

As soon as he left home and found himself alone in the street, Leli would become a different person. When somebody looked at him to greet him, his eyes would turn as red as a cherry. Leli would become very excited, his legs would become weak, his lips would dry up and turn as pale as death. He would hurry to reach the warehouse and stay in that little wooden corner. He would stay there and wouldn't move before it was time to return home.

He would burst out crying whenever he thought about this problem and realized that he couldn't do anything about it. At other times he would lose all hope of ever recovering from his illness. He would then consider whether it would be better if he committed suicide. In that way he would escape the troubles and pains of life.

XVIII

"Lel, I would like to know when we are going for a walk together?"

Instead of smiling Leli made an unhappy face. He muttered some words that Dun Karm failed to understand.

Leli was returning from work as Dun Karm was standing at the door. When he saw Leli he called him to speak to him.

Since the time he had become ill, Leli couldn't stand somebody speaking to him outside, even if it was his father. In this respect he felt ill at ease speaking to Dun Karm. Leli was neither listening nor paying attention to what the priest was saying.

Dun Karm immediately noticed Leli's behaviour and said: "Would you like to come inside Lel? I have just made some coffee, would you like some?"

"Thank you, Dun Karm," Leli suddenly whispered. Then continued saying: "Because I don't feel well."

Leli would feel very disappointed when he had to admit that he was sick. However, sometimes he would feel so confused that he couldn't help doing otherwise especially when he was speaking to a person such as Dun Karm.

He followed Dun Karm inside, sat down, and took out a creased handkerchief from his pocket. Then he started wiping his face, dusting his trousers, inserting and extracting his hands from his pockets and wetting his dry lips with his tongue.

"Can I please have a glass of water, Dun Karm? I am very thirsty."

Dun Karm fetched him a glass of water.

"I have some very good water in the well. Would you like some more, Lel?"

"No. Thank you."

"I have been feeling lonely since my mother died. I am very pleased when somebody like you comes to speak to me Listen, Lel another thing, Vira won't get worried if you returned home half an hour late?"

"No, Dun Karm. Sometimes she herself tells me that if I meet someone I shouldn't hurry back home."

"Very well, very well you're a fortunate man, Lel. Not that Vira isn't fortunate to have you, let me make myself clear but, truly you ought to be very proud of your wife. God willing, your brother's wife ... isn't Lippu marrying soon? will make a good wife too!"

Leli smiled and said nothing. By now he had regained his senses and his mood changed too. Dun Karm noticed the difference but he didn't ask him whether he was feeling any better. He knew that that would not have been of much benefit.

"Sometimes I've seen you passing by together with Dr. Sulnata. Few are those who are friends during their childhood and continue their friendship when they grow up. You should cherish friends like Dr. Sulnata! Good friends have always been scarce and today they are rarer to find."

"Yes, Pawlu is an honest man," replied Leli. Then he continued: "Nowadays you can only find me in the company of a doctor, Dun Karm."

"It isn't such a bad idea to look for their company. You can only learn more from them."

"You didn't understand me, Dun Karm. I'm in their company because I'm sick, I'm unhealthy, I'm mentally sick."

"Don't talk nonsense, Lel. What do you mean you're mentally ill? I'm the one who is in that position and I'll soon go completely out of my mind. Mentally ill people do not argue the way you do! Of course not! You have such a healthy look on your face!"

"It would have been better if I looked pale and weak, Dun Karm!"

"No one can say what's better, my son? What counts is the present moment and what Christ wants us to be. Let me pour you some coffee. It must have cooled down by now. Do you like your coffee with lots of sugar, Lel?"

"No, Dun Karm. Thank you! I won't have any coffee now that I have drunk some water. By drinking coffee I will only suppress the little apetite I have left. If you don't mind I must be going, Dun Karm!"

"Are you leaving Lel? I would have liked you to stay with me for a little while more! However, it doesn't matter. Since it's time for you to go, I won't stop you…"

"Good bye Dun Karm. Good night."

"Before you leave, Lel, when shall we go for a walk together?"

Leli was fed up, he was feeling sick and was in a hurry to return home. For this reason although he was not looking forward to accompanying Dun Karm for a walk, he answered abruptly: "Next Saturday, Dun Karm."

"Very well. Lel. I'll be expecting you next Saturday at around three o'clock. We'll go walking in the fields up to the place known as 'tal-Blat'"

"Good night, Dun Karm."

"Good night to you too, Lel."

Finally the day arrived. Leli went to fetch Dun Karm at about three o'clock.

Leli didn't feel at ease until they had left the village. This was a rare occasion for Leli. Since the time he became sick - he seldom went out for walks except for a few times with his wife Vira and sometimes with Dr. Sulnata.

Although the villagers had grown accustomed to his new life style, Leli's behaviour didn't change much and felt at ease when he would be alone.

Leli was irritated by the fact that people looked at him. He was not paying attention to what Dun Karm was saying but rather at the way people stared at him. He thought that they were wondering in their heart of hearts: "How is it that Dun Karm is in the company of that mad man? Perhaps he is encouraging him to change his life with God's help?"

Leli was right in thinking so. That's how people react: they either praise because it makes them feel better or else they criticize others without justification. That's why it's unadvisable to pay too much attention to what people say and want given that, peoples' expectations of the way others should behave are always impossibly high!

However who could explain to Leli and to people like him

that the more one ignores what people say the better it would be for their health.

Leli felt better as they left the village and took the first path leading to 'tal-Blat'. He started speaking about himself and his illness. No one could stop him once he started speaking about these things.

Dun Karm, at that moment, was saying that everyone has his own cross to bear and there is no one who is totally satisfied with his lot.

"What did you say, Dun Karm? Everybody has a burden to carry? That's not true! He who isn't sick, is happy without being aware of it and he who has never suffered a long sickness doesn't know what trouble is and what it means to be sad.

"God forbids if I had to tell what I've been through and what I'm going through together with the pain I had to endure since my illness! I'm not referring to physical pain but to a different kind of pain, which I cannot describe. Heartache, headache and body pain all at once. Pain accompanied with fear and fatigue. You don't endure this kind of pain, over which you have no control, for a short period of time. No! It seems that you can never get rid of it, as if it has become part of you. Moreover, sad thoughts and images representing past events haunt a person's life.

"No, no, Dun Karm! There is no worst illness than mine! It would have been better for me if I'm completely insane! .Believe me, I'm sick and at times I feel helpless when I remember that its' been eighteen months now - struggling within myself trying to hold my ground. However, after all this time I don't feel any better. There come times when I feel completely lost.

"Believe me, Dun Karm, I'm not exaggerating! At times I feel like screaming, laughing and crying all at once. I feel like swearing and destroying everything I see. I feel like screaming and shouting so that everyone hears me: 'I'm mad! You're right! I'm really mad! Come and take me away because I can no longer hide this illness. I don't have anymore strength left to fight this illness, to struggle against myself, to fight against all of you! Come, you hyenas and take me away among insane people, remove me from your midst because your cold looks, your breath, your words and gossip are killing me. Your laughs ridicule more than if I were living for the rest of my life amongst insane people!'"

At that moment Leli was so engrossed in his talk that Dun Karm did not attempt to stop him. He felt that it would be better to let Leli say what he had to say and that's what he did.

Leli continued speaking breathlessly and had adopted a husky and angry voice.

"You don't understand, Dun Karm, what it means to be gossiped about, to be mentally sick.

"When this happens to you, one stops appreciating the beauty of life.

"You will no longer be able to stand people being happy or laughing. You feel that you have lost all that was once good and beautiful in you! If you happened to be a kind person you'll lose interest in others and become egocentric. You don't care whatever happens as long as it didn't happen to you. You become indifferent to other peoples' happiness or sorrow. No! What am I saying? At times you are pleased at other peoples' distress and their worries seem to comfort you.

"As time passes life only gets worse. One cannot cope with the pain, the laughter, the ridicule and the heartache, and when one looks for comfort, there's no one to give you a helping hand, no one, there's no longer any sense to go on living, one starts cursing life and one would only long for death!"

Leli stopped suddenly and started gasping for breath. He stopped walking and asked Dun Karm if they could rest for a while until he regained his strength.

"Of course Lel," Dun Karm said, "Why not! I am tired too. Let's sit down for a while on that low stone wall."

❖ ❖ ❖ ❖ ❖

Dun Karm was a practical person. He had gathered a lot of experience in the few months he lived in Belgium during the war. However, he had never come across a case similar to Leli's.

Moreover, he never expected to hear what Leli had told him and was surprised at the way he had lost his self-control.

After resting on the stone wall for a while, Leli came to his senses. When he realized that Leli had calmed down, Dun Karm placed his hand on Leli's shoulders and told him:

"I sympathise with you, Lel. I really do sympathise with you! I can appreciate what you're feeling because of your illness. However, don't lose courage and try to control yourself during your fits. Furthermore pray. Lel! Pray!

"Remember Lel that we are weak and that not everyone makes fun of us, forgets all about us and does not sympathize with us. There is One who can comfort us like nobody else. However Lel we must pray to Him. Lel we must not forget Him! Pray, Lel! When you lose hope in human beings, raise up your eyes and tell Him: 'Lord, grant me patience! You who are Almighty, comfort me and help me recover!' If you do this Lel you will acquire patience, peace and comfort!"

Leli gave Dun Karm a sad look and replied:

"I would very much like to do so! I know that it will do me good but, I don't have the courage to do it! I have changed, Dun Karm I have changed totally! I have lost not only my strength but my Faith too! I don't want to lie to you. You're too kind to lie to! I'm an atheist and what I do is all in vain. I cannot return to what I used to be. I cannot! I have strayed away too much from the Truth, to retrieve It!

"I would very much like to do what you're suggesting, but I cannot! For this reason at times I feel sorry when I remember that together with the loss of my health I have also lost my Faith. What's the use of praying, if I don't believe? Tell me, Dun Karm, should people pity me? However, I don't want compassion, I just want to die, only death, which up to now I haven't had the courage to face, can help me find that kind of peace which is lacking in my life! However, I'm a coward! I don't have the guts to do anything!"

At this point Leli couldn't take it anymore. He buried his face in his hands and cried bitterly as he used to do since his illness.

Dun Karm looked around and felt better when he noticed that there was no one near. He didn't want any farmer passing by to see Leli in that state so he let him weep as much as he liked. He knew that weeping helps to comfort a person and as long as a person weeps there is still some hope of recovery.

When Leli stopped crying and came to his senses, Dun Karm asked him whether he felt any better.

"Thank you, Dun Karm. I feel much better. Forgive me Dun Karm. However lately, I have been feeling a kind of emptiness in my heart. I cannot do otherwise but cry as children and women usually do."

"Don't talk nonsense Lel. If you feel that you should cry than do so. Crying comforts a person even though many associate it with women and children. However, who knows how many men wish to cry to comfort their hearts, but cannot do so. So if you feel like crying, don't hesitate. Crying helps the sick and the sad. It is beneficial both physically and spiritually!"

After a while they stood up and resumed walking. Dun Karm continued speaking as if nothing had happened. He spoke about the war and mentioned a few events he had been through when he was in Belgium.

Slowly they arrived at the 'Tumbata' which as its name implies is the highest side of the 'Blat' area.

When they reached that spot Leli had already regained his senses. Dun Karm's words comforted him as no other words had done before.

The sun was setting and they were enchanted by the splendor of the sky. Those who have never experienced sunset on the horizon cannot appreciate the beauty of nature or imagine the amazing hues of light.

In the distance a number of small clouds could be seen above the horizon like a flight of swallows. They gradually changed colour from snow white to a silvery hue as they approached the sun. Finally as they got closer they took on a golden colour.

At sunset the clouds did not glitter as before but their colour became more astonishingly beautiful. The sea beneath them looked like a golden pond. Such heavenly bliss!

"How beautiful, Lel!" said Dun Karm. Both of them stood

stuck to the ground amazed at the unexplainable beauty surrounding them.

All of a sudden Leli told Dun Karm:

"Why is man so foolish? Why does he seek power and self esteem when he possesses strength and such amazing natural beauty!"

Dun Karm smiled and sweetly replied:

"That's true Lel! As foolish as that person who believes that no one created nature and that it has no other explanation other than, that man is simply physically attracted to it by its beautiful and varied colours!"

XIX

The gardener is pleased when his first blossom opens up. How much more should a mother be pleased when she gives birth to her first child?

This kind of happiness affects everyone. Whoever receives the news rejoices together with the mother.

Everybody rejoiced when Sunta, Lippu ta' Braġ's wife gave birth to their first born.

There was nothing wrong with Sunta except that she was a little bit short in height. Lippu, her husband, although rather dark-skinned was good looking like the rest of his brothers.

Sunta had a baby girl and the child was as sweet as her parents.

Lippu lost his head over the baby and pampered his wife too.

"Sunt, look at those sweet lips! Look, mother, she's opened her eyes! Mother, look at those beautiful eyes! Have you ever seen such beautiful eyes O Lord, how pretty! She almost smiled at me!"

Pawla, Sunta's mother, was proud of her daughter! Who could blame her? Every mother is proud of her daughter following her first successful childbirth.

"God bless her! She looks fine, Marjann, doesn't she?"

Given that Sunta was her son's wife and given that she always wanted to have a baby girl, Marjann heartily replied to Pawla and told her:

"True, God bless her, Pawl! Praise be to God! I feel as if I am finally relieved from a sense of heaviness in my heart."

EPILOGUE

Several years passed since Sunta had her first child. In the years between Sunta and Lippu had lots of other children. Sunta's mother no longer boasted about her daughter's pregnancies in contrast to others who were unable to conceive. Not only that but she would be terrified when her daughter told her: "Mother, we've done it again."

In the past, a lot of events happened in Malta that ought to be recorded.

These were the years when Malta was granted self-government. Years characterized by great social and political upheavals.

These were the years when the word 'politics' was on everybody's lips.

Ħaż-Żgħir, too was influenced by those ideas. The villagers passed through the same experiences that other people in other towns and villages of Malta and Gozo went through. Some argued: "We're lucky to have that man defending us!" Others said: "We would get fed up under their rule " Some young people who returned to Malta from overseas incited the people against the clergy since they argued that they were the cause of what was happening. If it weren't for them everything would be fine. On the other hand, the parish priest warned the villagers to open their eyes and to ignore those people who wanted to destroy their Religion. Those who supported the parish priest repeated what he said to their opponents. They almost attacked them or prevented them from entering church.

When the arguments became very heated, some young people from Ħaż-Żgħir refrained from going to church. In that way their political opponents became more aggressive.

It wasn't the first time that fighting broke out. People were imprisoned, families broke up, men lost their jobs and their Faith because of their political beliefs.

All this is history and in time everybody forgot what had happened and everyone resumed his normal way of life. Most people returned to work, and the Islands enjoyed peace once again as if nothing had ever happened.

❖ ❖ ❖ ❖ ❖

Leli did not take part in any political activities during the twelve years that Malta enjoyed self-government. For him it was as if nothing was happening. He continued living as before, away from people, isolated and disinterested in everything that was happening around him.

Leli's behaviour didn't change a lot during those years. His hair started getting white, his face flabby and wrinkled.

He never recovered from the illness he had contracted in the prime of life.

The memory of what happened to him during the first three or four years of his illness gradually faded away so that he could hardly remember what he had been through. He forgot how people made fun of him, how sorry he had been for the way people treated him, the nights he stayed awake longing to die to escape that miserable life.

Those memories faded away into the past. Although Leli forgot all about them that experience had changed him a lot! From a nice and kind young man, Leli had turned into an angry and sad person. He hated those who turned him down and criticized what others praised. He hated everything and deserved to be hated by everybody else.

Besides his mother and wife there were few people who were prepared to put up with Leli. If his mother had to compare Leli's present character with that of seventeen or eighteen years before she would say that he was a totally different person.

Marjann recalled Leli as an eight or nine year old boy, kind, happy and praying with her in a very adult way. When sometimes he returned home sad, because he would have had a fight with his friends, he would place his head on her lap and cry. He cried until she kissed him and then he would fall asleep kneeling down on the floor resting his head in her lap.

He was still a nice, kind person when he was growing from childhood to youth. He was always sorry for those in need and became worried when his mother was sad!

However, all that was over. His illness, from which he never recovered, changed Leli completely. He became insensitive, his mind obfuscated and he reached a state where he didn't distinguish between good and bad as if they were two branches from the same tree trunk.

When a person perceives life in this manner, he fails to care about anything.

Although, Leli did not participate actively in the political activities taking place in Malta at that time he generally favoured those who argued against the clergy.

When sometimes people praised or criticized someone he would say: "Alas, how foolish you are! Don't you realize that they are working for their own interests: some want to become famous, others to enrich themselves at peoples' expense! Any person who believes them is a fool!"

He passed his time either at work or at home. Sometimes he stayed reading or feeding the chickens and the rabbits, which his wife kept. In winter he would go for a walk while on Sunday he would accompany Vira to Valletta.

He didn't care much about anybody or anything but he still remained attracted to his wife. He showed her compassion and when he happened to be in a good mood he would think of ways to please her to help her forget the past when he had offended her with his behaviour.

If it hadn't been so, it would have been impossible for Vira to continue living with such a man. She had to put up with him or else they would have separated.

❖ ❖ ❖ ❖ ❖

The villagers accepted Leli's absence from church because they believed that he was mad and secondly because of his relationship with Dun Karm.

Leli's lifestyle didn't leave him many friends and several people didn't greet him any more.

Only Ġużepp ta' Snien and Ġanni ta' Kejla remained friends with Leli. They would invite him to accompany them during the hunting season to have some fun as they used to do in the past. He enjoyed that very much.

❖ ❖ ❖ ❖ ❖

One day Leli went out hunting together with Ġużepp. The latter had been insisting with Leli to do so for some time. It was a weekday. As they were eating some bread on a rock ledge they noticed a farmer moving up a cliff-path carrying a sack full of fodder on his back

"Ġużepp, do you see that farmer?" asked Leli.

"Of course, Lel? They have such a tough life."

"True, Ġużepp! But did you know that that person is happier than I am?"

Ġużepp laughed. "Don't talk nonsense, Lel! You have everything you desire? Listen, Lel: forgive me but once you started this discussion let's continue with it. You have some idea in your head, you started reading, you isolated yourself and now you hate meeting people however, if you're determined to recover you can be your old self again. You're not an old man! Why don't you mix with people? And renew your friendship with God! Forgive me Lel for speaking to you this way!"

"No, no Ġuż. Please continue and don't be shy. I'm not going to be angry at what you say! Say what you please as if you're speaking to yourself. Meanwhile I'm listening to you."

Ġużepp plucked up courage and continued with what he had to say.

"I feel sorry Lel when I hear people speaking against you. I almost had a fight recently, because of you with Salvu l- Ħajjat.[52] He was saying, amongst other things that they should have done to you what they did to freemasons and stoned you to death long ago. He also mentioned that Dr. Sulnata is no longer your friend. He said that you're worrying your mother and father to death and was surprised how your wife was still living with you!"

When Ġużepp stopped speaking, Leli said: "This is how much the villagers love me! I deserve more than that!"

Ġużepp looked at him and said: "However, I put the blame on you, Lel! If you want you can change your life and draw peoples' sympathy towards you once again. You're not leading a bad life. What's keeping you from going to Church and taking care of yourself? After all, Lel: you know as much as I do that we only have one soul and if we lose our soul we will be condemned for ever."

When Ġużè had nothing else to add, Leli replied:

"You're right, Ġuż. Given the kind of life you lead, you are far happier and at peace with yourself than me. However, although I'm aware of all this I cannot do what you're saying! I would like to but I cannot! Don't ask me why because if I had to explain to you, you wouldn't understand.

"I have lost something, Ġuż, which, once you lose it, you'll never get back."

Ġużepp who failed to understand Leli's words said in his heart of hearts: "Leli hasn't lost anything! He lost his mind and that's all!"

❖ ❖ ❖ ❖ ❖

Like everybody else who enjoyed reading, Leli loved writing too. He used to keep a diary and spent time jotting down what he had been through or what he would have been thinking about.

He kept to himself whatever he wrote and never published his writings in books or newspapers. He would have liked to do that very much but he believed that he was not up to it.

He kept what he wrote as memories. In time these memories made quite a collection and they would have made a very good book.

Soon after he married, Leli started writing his thoughts and, the events of his life. He ceased recording his ideas at the time he was having an affair with Klara ta' Buqerq but he wrote the happy and sad events of his life since his marriage.

Leli didn't bother what kind of writing he left at home which Vira could find and read especially after what had happened to him because of Klara. He cared even less since his illness.

Vira came across Leli's writings often and she read them carefully. When she came across something that concerned her she would renew the happy or sad memories relating to that event.

If we had to analyze those memories and edit them we would find that they relate to Leli's life since his marriage.

❖ ❖ ❖ ❖ ❖

Although Vira often read those memories she never spoke to Leli about them.

She felt that those writings reflected what he had been through and therefore, she couldn't help reading those memories whenever she came across them.

She felt sorry for what she did but she never revealed to her husband that she read all his writings.

❖ ❖ ❖ ❖ ❖

Amongst these writings there were sections which no matter how many times she read them, she never understood what her husband meant by them. Amongst those writings there was a passage which Vira loved reading even though it seemed confused. She loved reading the following extract from the rest because she felt that when Leli wrote it he was in a deep state of melancholy.

Feast of St. John, 19

"How time flies!

"Eight years have passed since I got ill and what a time this has been for me! Years characterized by pain and ridicule... What's happened to you Lel? What has happened to the dreams you used to cherish?

"Do you remember when a long time ago you used to dream about love and the possession of greater knowledge?

"Do you remember the time when you never imagined that your health could deteriorate? That as time passed people loved you more and more and that your fame would spread in all the towns and villages? That some day you would come to appreciate what others failed to understand and that way you would find the kind of happiness others searched for and never found?

"Now do you realize how wrong you were?

"You not only didn't find what others were looking for but you also lost what you had and now you don't have anything left nothing!

"You were wrong Lel! Very wrong!

"You failed to realize in time that neither knowledge nor freedom from all ties lead to happiness!

"The happiness you searched for was within your reach. It was in your hands before you lost your Faith in exchange for the pursuit of knowledge!

"But, why did this happen to me? Why did I lose all hope and happiness and I have nothing left, nothing except Vira and my mother?

"I could feign but I'm unable to do so! If I can deceive everyone, I can never deceive myself! For this reason I am to blame for whatever happened. I was aware of what I was doing and I could have realized that my behaviour could only have landed me in trouble!

"I am to blame for my failure!

"But, what about tomorrow?

"Who knows whether tomorrow I will retrieve what I lost?

"Who knows?"

❖ ❖ ❖ ❖ ❖

Whoever passes from Midħna street in the afternoon - the cleanest street in Ħaż-Żgħir - one could see an elderly woman in one of the better houses there. Her hair as white as snow, a wrinkled sweet face and a look indicating that she had experienced a lot of trouble during her lifetime.

She would be sewing or holding a half-made sock and two or three children calling her 'grandma' from here and there would surround her.

If one looks closely at her one will know who she is. It's Marjann ta' Braġ surrounded by Lippu's children whom she loves a lot.

God bless her! She's still a hardworking woman as she used to be when she was forty. She passes her time sewing, darning or knitting socks for her son's children.

However, if one goes closer one will notice that besides knitting she is also praying.

Her prayer is the following: "O Lord, before I die I beg of You to help Leli regain his Faith. Please accept my prayer although I'm not worthy and I shall die in peace."

THE END

NOTES

1. Don, Rev., Fr., used for diocesan Catholic priests and followed by the Christian name.
2. Fifteen Wednesdays of prayers and other practices of religious devotion, before August 15, the feast day of the Assumption of Our Lady.
3. Short for *raħal* (village), preceding some village names in Malta but not in Gozo, with final *l* assimilated with the initial consonant when this is one of the Sun Letters (vide: Tagliaferro N.: *Vocabolario Topografico dell'Isola di Malta, 1900-1905*. Ms preserved in the Malta University Library; Wettinger G. : *The Lost Villages and Hamlets of Malta in Medieval Malta* (ed A Luttrell). London, 1975.
4. The seventh letter of the Maltese alphabet, orthographic symbol of the voiced post-alveolar affricative consonantal phoneme in the Maltese phonological system, phonetically equivalent to English *j* (Aquilina J., *Maltese English Dictionary*, 1987: 372)
5. *ta'* + def. art. = *tal-*, of the (the final consonant l of assimilates with the initial sun letter of the words following it giving rise to *tan-nies* = of the people). *Minsi* = forgotten; pp of *nesa*. *Tal-Minsijin* - 'of the forgotten'. Also *Il-Mensija* name of a district and fields near the church called *tal-Minsija* beyond St. Julians on the way to *Tal-Balal*.
6. Meditation on Bach's prelude in C
7. vide fn 5, *Frawla* = strawberry
8. vide fn 5, *Kajla* = Possibly refers to a measure of roasted beans, peanuts. Land measure (18.74sq.m), one sixth of a *siegħ* (ten kejliet). Boissevain J. in his book *A Village in Malta* says: "Each family is a distinct social group and each has its own nickname. Persons may also have individual nicknames. These nicknames are social labels that serve to identify and fix the distinct social personality of the person or group to which they are affixed. The Maltese word for nickname is *laqam* (from graft, *tlaqqam*). A nickname is given to an individual or to a family by the village. The village also changes them.

"In contrast to the surrounding European countries, where the use of nicknames in the rural areas is also widespread, Maltese very often use the nickname as a term of address. In Sicilian the word for nickname is *'nguria*, which means insult, and many of the nicknames are insults. They point to weaknesses of character or body of the persons and families they designate. In Sicily it is a grave offence to use a person's nickname in his presence. The same is true in Spain (Pitt-Rivers J., *People of the Sierra*, 1954: 168). This is not the case in Malta.

"Most nicknames are composed of the noun plus the preposition "of" (*ta'*). These are combined with the Christian name. The person who receives the nickname is referred to by a definite article plus the name...Children usually inherit the nickname of their father's. Though sometimes the village ignores the father's nickname and the children are called by their mother's nickname" (1969: 43-44.)

9. Vide fn 5 & 8, *laħlaħ* = to rinse (clothes)
10. *Seddaq* = (pp : *mseddaq*; II form of the verb *sedaq*) to render just, upright and true.
11. *Saramni* = (of *saram* ż pronoun suffix i; pp : *misrum*) to make a tangle of something; to confuse.
12. *Imqarqaċ* = a perky/saucy person.
13. *Indannat* = a very angry, vexed and disappointed person.

14 Group of priests who volunteer part of their ministerial office to give sermons and hear confessions from time to time in different parishes; the Mission is divided into the great Mission and the small Mission, the difference being that the former has more priests taking part and stays for a longer period in a parish.
15 Notwithstanding the deep religious sentiments, which such a statement implies, it was also a question of political and economic power enjoyed by the Maltese clergy at that time. Carmel Cassar in his essay *Everyday Life in Malta in the Nineteenth and Twentieth Centuries* whilst quoting Sir Harry Luke's remark that 'the Maltese are among the most devoted sons and daughters of the Roman Catholic Church' (*Malta, An Account and Appreciation*, 1960: 221) also notes that 'the islanders, notably country folk, depended directly on the local priests, making the church the centre of village life, and the parish priest its first citizen. The priest combined teaching and several other advisory duties with the spiritual role. He was also the main link with the world outside, with the church acting as a meeting place,' (in V. Mallia Milanes, *The British Colonial Experience*, 1988 : 91) Koster doesn't fail to notice that 'the church owed its dominant position on the islands in part to the British authorities who granted it important privileges in exchange for assurances of loyalty and support.' This had a cyclic effect in that 'what made the Maltese Church into a bastion of power were the protection and massive support of a population which in those days clung to it as the principal symbol of Maltese identity vis-à-vis the colonial power.' (ibid, 79) Herbert Ganado related that when, in the 1920's, he was invited by a friend to the Siġġiewi village feast, his friend's father asked him whether he had first been to the parish priest (*Rajt Malta Tinbidel*, Vol II, 1974-1977: 19).
16 When the British Governor Alexander Ball transferred the Law Courts from Mdina to Valletta, those who were sentenced to death used to be hanged at a place in Floriana known as *It-Tomba* (The Tomb). Others used to refer to that area as *Tat-Tripunti* (three pointed) due to the formation of the three bastions jutting out. The people living in Floriana asked the Governor to transfer the place where executions were held to another area, as people refused to set up house there.
   When the prison was built in Kordin, executions used to be held in the public area in front of the prison. However, executions were held within prison walls as from 1880. The first person to be executed in Kordin was Anġlu Farrugia nicknamed *Il-Krozz*. The most humiliating moment for the sentenced prisoner used to be when he was processionally led from prison to the place of execution through the streets of Valletta. The streets used to be full of people as if it was a feast. The dead body of the sentenced person used to be buried in a hole in the ground. There was no sign where sentenced persons were buried neither was their tomb marked by a cross or epitaph. (my translation. Joseph Galea, *F'Ġieħ il-Ħaqq - Id-delitti Kriminali 1800-1900*, Police Association, 1982: 29).
17 Can. John Azzopardi in his introduction to the book by A.H.J. Prins, *In Peril on the Sea* says that "vows were frequently made by individuals or groups in peril on the sea or ailed by maladies or else faced with mishaps and accidents. Mementos of these vows are the hundreds of charming and sincere little pictures presented in many sanctuaries and rural chapels in Malta and Gozo. These naive paintings, as well as other votive offerings as chains, manicles, vestments, objects in silver and models of galleys, were

accepted by rectors of churches and placed for permanent display within the walls of our sanctuaries, not as objects of cult or works of art but as popular expressions of gratitude for graces received through the intercession of the Blessed Virgin and our patron saints. The records of the Pastoral visits document an abundance of such votive paintings." (1989: IX).

18. C. Tabone in his book *The Secularization of the Family in Changing Malta* indicates that "The Church, considered as a social institution, occupied a predominant position in the Maltese social structure till some time after the Second World War. At this time the Church alone had universal presence, which operated effectively at all levels of the social life through its parishes as formal agencies, and through its priests as its formal agents."(Malta, 1987:151)

    E.L.Zammit in his work *The Behaviour Pattern of Maltese Migrants in London* with Reference to Maltese Social Institutions indicates that some emigrants state that in Malta they used to go to Church to please their parents and to avoid their neighbour's gossip. (Oxford, 1970).

19. E.L. Zammit in his book : *A Colonial Inheritance - Maltese Perceptions of Work, Power and Class Structure* with reference to the Labour Movement, observes that "A less noticeable yet equally deep-rooted response to colonialism is the widespread resort to patronage. This practice colours social interactions at almost every level. In spite of its universal condemnation as a corrupt practice it is reportedly the most effective way of securing scarce resources" (Malta University Press, 1984: 17)

20. The Maltese always loved hunting initially perhaps as a key source to obtain food and later on as a sporting habit. This particular activity of the Maltese can be traced back to the mid-eighteenth century. Carmel Testa in his book *The Life and Times of Grand Master Pinto 1741-1773* indicates that "a few weeks after his election Pinto tried to curb indiscriminate hunting. In February he decreed that anyone caught hunting with guns, nets, dogs or hawks or who kept any hunting equipment without licence from the Falconier, would be punished with three years on the galleys. Hunting for rabbits, hares and partridges was strictly prohibited; any infringement being punished with five years on the galleys. In March the islands of Comino and Cominetto, were declared out of bounds to hunters. Later he also decreed that no hunting firearms were to be carried inside Imdina and the villages of Żurrieq, Qrendi, Siġġiewi, Żebbuġ, Mosta, Naxxar and Għargħur. The hunting season was closed between Christmas and the feast of St. Mary Magdalene (22 July)." (1989; 61)

21. Read Carmel Cassar's interesting study *Fenkata : An Emblem of Maltese Peasant Resistance?* (Ministry for Youth and the Arts, 1994). Cassar states inter alia that "The availability of rabbit meat to all social levels seems to have enabled fenkata (rabbit stew) to become the acceptable meat dish to all Maltese, particularly the rural population. This situation may have prompted a correspondent of the 'The Daily Malta Chronicle' to write in 1930 that 'For very many years the breeding and rearing of rabbits has been regarded as an occupation, bordering on a pastime...the breeding of rabbits for food consumption is common with the peasantry of most countries...' It also explains the relative popularity of rabbit hunting in modern times. A parliamentary question to the Minister of the Interior in May 1994 indicates a total of 294 licences for wild rabbit hunting in Malta and Gozo." (page 21)

22. Gambling is another activity that is very popular among the Maltese. This particular activity can also be traced to the times of Grand Master Pinto.

Testa says that "on 21 January 1754 he prohibited all forms of gambling in an effort to eradicate that vice. If the culprits happened to be members of the Order they were to be expelled and sent to prison for a long spell; Maltese and foreign gamblers were to suffer whipping and exile. (1989; 145)

"Pinto made strenuous efforts to curb gambling. On 15 December 1768 he prohibited all forms of gambling, in public or in private, 'since the vice of gambling is daily increasing.' Those who infringed that order were to be exiled for three years; if the culprits were of the fair sex they were thrown for the same period into one of the local women's conservatories; the stakes were to be forfeited to the Treasury; the judges had the faculty to impose a stiff fine instead of exile; neophytes were punished with three years on the galleys. Those who provided the gambling facilities and those who were present at the gambling tables and did not reveal the culprits to the authorities were treated as accomplices and similarly punished. Informers were rewarded with 25 scudi levied on the property of the offenders. Bets on games of dexterity were permitted, provided such bets did not exceed 2 scudi per person for the whole session." (ibid; 316).

Nowadays Maltese Governments have institutionalized gambling given that its a very good source of revenue while licences are granted to operate Casinos on the Island. However distinction is still made between the legal and illegal type of gambling.

23 "In the early years of British rule, internal transport consisted mainly of *kalessi* - horse-drawn carriages which seated two passengers, increased to four by 1831 The *kaless* (caleche) remained in use up to the 1870's, although by then it had evolved into a slightly-improved and more comfortable model. The *kaless* was an expensive means of transport which only a few could afford.

"The introduction of the horse-drawn omnibus in 1856 was beneficial to most of the population But although it was much cheaper than the kaless the common worker could not afford it still The omnibus company was even entrusted to carry mail from 1859 onwards which marked a general improvement in the postal service

"In the last decade of the nineteenth century, a more popular form of transport came into being. This was the karozzin (cab), a modern version of the kaless, with the coachman having his own seat and not obliged to walk beside his carriage

"The bicycle, at first mostly restricted to British officers, was also introduced around 1870. By 1890 its use had spread and had become common among civilians.

"A novel means of transport was the railway, with fares everybody could afford. [It was] introduced in 1883

"In 1903, the Electric Tram Company was established, which secured a more practical means of transport than the railway

"The tram proved popular, to such an extent that it was strongly opposed by cab drivers whose livelihood depended on the number of passengers they carried

"By the 1930's both tram and railway companies were doing badly and the Government had to close them down. Meanwhile the harbor area had a system of dgħajjes (passage boats) Though the ferry service proved to be of great convenience to the growing urban center around Marsamxett, the need was felt for an even more efficient system of transport. By 1905, this was partly solved with the introduction of the Scheduled Bus Service " (Carmel Cassar, *Everyday Life in Malta*, in *The British Colonial Experience - The*

Impact on Maltese Society, edited by Victor Mallia-Milanes, 1988, 113-115).
24 Ganado in his book *Rajt Malta Tinbidel* states that "[During the early part of this century] the wages were extremely low. Skilled workers received 2s/6d and 2s/ daily. Unskilled workers received 1s/6d and 1s/ daily" (1977; 7, vol 1). Ganado also states that "the scarcity of commodities and the meagre wages couldn't cope with the cost of living. [This led to the] 1917 'strike' at the Dockyard. It was the first 'strike' to take place on the Isand. The workers contended that the 10% wage increase was not enough to meet the increasing cost of living which had doubled." (ibid; 164, vol 1) (my translation)
25 Tarcisio Zarb in his book *Folklore of an Island* - Maltese Threshold Customs says, "Traditionally, in our society courting was restricted to a bare minimum. A girl and a boy running about by themselves were considered to be in danger of losing their chastity, especially the girl. Fear of defying this convention and especially of the dire consequences which may follow resulted in a marked segregation between the two sexes.

"In the old days, especially in villages, marriage was contracted by a broker, a match-maker, *il-huttaba*, who agreed to bring about a matrimonial alliance for a small pittance. This way of contracting marriages sometimes made it somewhat hard for the couple to have frequent meetings between themselves before marriage. Usually such meetings were carried out clandestinely, but even such encounters were difficult to hold, since the solidarity of the community of which they formed part was strong against such meetings: everyone would have been ready to report to the parents of the couple concerned, especially the girl's. In order to avoid such happenings, marriages used to be hurried as much as possible.

"In a closed community like Malta's, talking with your future husband in the streets by yourself with no one as a chaperone elicited unfavorable gossip " (1998; 152-153)
26 *Wahhaxni* = one who inspires fear.
27 Carmel Tabone in his book *The Secularization of the Family in Changing Malta* indicates that "traditionally speaking, children were considered as God's gift, and a large family as having the blessing of heaven. At one time this was expressed by a common saying: *It-tfal barka t'Alla*, meaning literally that children are God's blessing (Such a saying was used when parents who already had quite a large family were expecting another baby. People encouraged them by saying : *tibzax taqtax qalbek, it-tfal barka t'Alla*, meaning: do not lose heart, children are God's blessing. In like circumstances, other sayings were used, always with a religious connotation, as : *la tas-sagrament hallihom ha jigu*, meaning: since they are fruit of the sacrament (of marriage) let them come.). In fact families till not many years ago were really large. The 1948 census reported that a quarter of the completed families still had over ten children. At this time Malta was one of the countries having the largest number of persons under fifteen years of age, or 34.8% of the population " (1987: 87)
28 Carmel Cassar in his article *Everyday Life in Malta* states that "The spread of poverty is best reflected in the hordes of beggars, male and female, roaming the streets of towns, particularly Valletta, where one particular locality was named after them (Nix mangiaris steps outside Victoria Gate, Valletta). Beggars were an unpopular sight with the British authorities and there were various attempts to control them. Commissioners, such as Sir Penrose Julyan in 1880, noted that there was 'too much charity' in Malta. In the 1850s

Valletta was described as 'a nest of beggars'" (R. Grima, *Malta and the Crimean War* in *The British Colonial Experience - The Impact on Maltese Society*, Victor Mallia Milanes, 1988, 104).

29 *Ħatba* = wicked person (fig.)
30 The 24th International Eucharistic Congress, in honour of the Sacrament of Love and Peace was held in Malta in April 1913. Cardinal Dominic Ferrata, Prefect of the Holy Congregation of the Sacraments, Archpriest of the Lateran and previously Nunzio at Paris, was the Papal League. In Malta Mons. Pietro Pace was still Archbishop and in spite of his age – he was 82 at the time – stood the strain of the Congress well. He looked upon it as the crowning point of his life. Five Cardinals and 40 Bishops besides foreign Congresists and other representatives attended the Congress. It was an unprecedented event in the Island's annals. The religious fervor shown during the five days of the Congress (23 - 27 April) was very impressive.
31 *Mitħna* = windmill.
32 *Landier* = tinsmith.
33 *Għaġin* = farinaceous food like macaroni, spaghetti
34 *Skejjen* = pl. of *skuna*, schooners.
35 *Bċieċen* = pl. of *beċċun*, pigeons, young dove that has not started flying yet.
36 *Bukketti* = bunch of flowers or small petards which open out in the form of colourful nosegays (in pyrotechnics).
37 This forms the theme upon which Mintoff's philosophy was based and which Ellul Mercer shared. E.L.Zammit in his work *A Colonial Inheritance* states that "the emphasis on the supremacy of work over all other activities has become one of his (Mintoff's) constant themes. In contrast to his predecessors in office who had a more relaxed attitude, he himself offers a living example of hard work. Malta's new Constitution, passed by Parliament in 1974, proclaims the country to be "a republic based on work"" (1984: 59).
38 *Warrabni* = To move out of the way
39 The Dead Woman's Arm
40 Falzun The Wizard
41 *Għajjur* = a jealous person.
42 *Pecluqa* = indiscreet talker.
43 *Imfattar* = a stout person of awkward figure.
44 *Karrozzin* = a horse-driven cab.
45 *Bdielu* = to change one's opinion.
46 *Ħanut* = shop.
47 *Seksuki* = fond of gossip.
48 *Nofs ras* = an alienated person.
49 *Sittatlieta* = possibly this means three for halfpenny.
50 *Wardija* = name of an area in the neighbourhood of St Paul's Bay.
51 '*Ara - kemm - naf*' = a nickname associated with a person who loves showing off that he/she is better informed than others.
52 *Ħajjat* = tailor.